North Somerset

D1334376

1 2 0361239 5

APPOINTMENT IN VENICE

APPOINTMENT IN VENICE

Sally Stewart

Severn House Large Print
London & New York

This first large print edition published in Great Britain 2004 by
SEVERN HOUSE LARGE PRINT BOOKS LTD of
9-15 High Street, Sutton, Surrey, SM1 1DF.
First world regular print edition published 2003 by
Severn House Publishers, London and New York.
This first large print edition published in the USA 2004 by
SEVERN HOUSE PUBLISHERS INC., of
595 Madison Avenue, New York, NY 10022.

British Library Cataloguing in Publication Data

Stewart, Sally
   Appointment in Venice - Large print ed.
  1. Governesses - Italy - Venice - Fiction
  2. Venice (Italy) - Fiction
  3. Large type books
  I. Title
  823.9'14 [F]

  ISBN 0-7278-7346-6

Printed and bound in Great Britain by
MPG Books Ltd, Bodmin, Cornwall.

One

In a fast-moving world some things remained the same after all: Sarah recognized one of them the moment she walked into the lawyer's office. Cheltenham wasn't renowned for being ahead of fashion, but even so the resistance that Crabtree Winterbottom were still putting up to the winds of change had something heroic about it. She supposed that a minion or two, hidden away in the warren of rooms, kept them more or less in touch with the new century, but Mr Crabtree's desk and the large leather armchair she was escorted to had certainly been there since the reign of Queen Victoria. The chair proved unexpectedly comfortable and she leaned back in it, content to wait while the lawyer concluded the private consultation he seemed to be having with himself. At last he was ready to begin.

'Miss Cavanagh, correct me if I am wrong: you're experienced in teaching young children; you are familiar with Italy and its language; and you would be prepared to live there for two years, subject to a probationary period proving satisfactory.'

Did she hear, in his precisely-phrased last sentence, a hint of astonishment? Not sure enough to risk a smile, Sarah nodded instead and, approving of a candidate who didn't see any need to chatter, Mr Crabtree went on himself.

'I stress the duration of the appointment because Contessa di Brazzano asked me to do so. If it is likely to conflict with some ... ah ... personal commitment of your own, there would be no point in continuing this discussion.'

He regretted the stipulation, thinking that it would probably put off the only promising applicant he'd found. There was nothing startlingly attractive about the woman in front of him, but the intelligence and humour he saw in her face would surely have appealed by now to some man, and he reckoned that his wife – his yardstick where the opposite sex was concerned – would approve of Sarah Cavanagh.

It took a moment for her to reply. 'My only attachment now, Mr Crabtree, is to an older brother and his family. My marriage ended five years ago, by which time my father had left the Cathedral Close at Gloucester and returned to being what he preferred – a rural priest. I went back to live with him at Pendock until he died a month ago. Now, of course, the rectory has been handed over to the new incumbent.'

There was no tremor in her quiet voice, but Mr Crabtree didn't miss the shadow of sadness that briefly touched her face before she smiled at him. 'I'm being told by Matthew and his family to make my home with them at the farm, but it's time I bestirred myself – "got a new life", I believe is the current phrase!'

Mr Crabtree's nod confirmed that even he had heard of it, but his next question took her by surprise. 'May I ask why Italy appeals to you, or how you come to be so familiar with it?'

'It was my ex-husband's favourite place – the other country we're all supposed to have where we feel at home,' she explained slowly. 'He was a history don whom I married the moment I left Oxford. To begin with I thought we'd found the perfect match, but he began to take part in a series of television programmes that unexpectedly made him famous. He became the celebrity he still is and I rather got left behind. I eventually resumed my maiden name, settled for the peaceful obscurity of life at Pendock, and a teaching job in Tewkesbury.'

She looked up to find the lawyer watching her. He didn't seem inclined to comment on what she'd said but she had the feeling that he'd somehow understood what she'd left unsaid – the hurts and humiliations that her brilliant husband had so carelessly inflicted, and then the long, slow road to recovery in the peace of her father's home, until his illness and the desolation of his recent death. Mr Crabtree was a lawyer, of course, and no doubt observed often enough the see-saw of highs and lows on which most of his clients were perched; but she sensed now a change in the tone of the interview. She could even ask a question of her own.

'Are you very well acquainted with the di Brazzano family, Mr Crabtree?'

His thin lips twitched a little. 'You mean that you would have expected a Venetian contessa not to know that Cheltenham exists?' Sarah nodded, and the lawyer removed his half-moon glasses, then leaned back in his chair in order to explain.

'I've known Laura di Brazzano since she was born. One of her forbears was the Winterbottom who began this firm with my great-grandfather. As Laura Kentish she became a rather famous opera singer until she married Fabrizio di Brazzano ten years ago. You know her name, I see.'

Who didn't? Sarah reflected; the English singer had been a superstar. 'I even have some of her recordings,' she commented. 'Her voice was very beautiful, but I remember now reading that she'd given up her career and settled abroad.'

'A reputation for quarrelling with opera house directors didn't help, I believe,' Mr Crabtree commented drily, 'and Laura became a very temperamental diva indeed. But it's true that her voice *was* suited to Italian music – Verdi, Puccini, and the like.'

It made his own vocal preferences clear, Sarah thought, Mozart, of course, and Handel, as light relief from the more austere heights reached by Johann Sebastian's choral works. She was imagining him in thrall to the mathematical perfection of a Bach cantata when his voice brought her back again to the matter in hand.

'Count di Brazzano has three children, two of them by his first marriage. Franco is eighteen, and a law student at Bologna; Beatrice, whose mother died when she was born, is now ten. Emmanuele, aged six, is the only child of the Count's second marriage. He was ill with rheumatic fever as a very small boy and still remains frail.'

For the first time it seemed to Sarah that Mr Crabtree hesitated over what to say next, but he finally made up his mind.

'Your responsibilities would only concern Beatrice and Emmanuele, of course; even so the job is not a sinecure, I'm afraid. Both children are privileged in the accepted sense of the word. In my own view they are also the product of a family that doesn't function very well. While their parents lead too-busy social lives, Beatrice and her half-brother are largely left to the care of servants. I think they're very much in need of someone who will take an intelligent, loving interest in them, but I can't offer you the job without a warning that the personalities involved may make it stressful and perhaps impossible. From the little you have said I feel that your own life has been difficult enough. Perhaps you should refuse what I am offering you.'

It was a novel way of conducting an interview for a job, but even though he must have thought so himself, Sarah could see no amusement in his face; matters were obviously too serious for that, and she found herself liking him very much for his concern for the di Brazzano children.

'It's true that my marriage failure hurt, and I should hate to find myself proved inadequate *again*,' she said at last. 'But I'd like to try, at least for the probationary three months. That ought to be long enough to settle things one way or the other.'

A smile, charming in its unexpectedness, suddenly lit Mr Crabtree's face. 'Then I wish you well in Venice. My secretary will make all the arrangements and inform the countess of the time of your arrival. Shall we say a week from today?'

Blinking a little at the turn of speed Mr

Crabtree could show when he wanted to, Sarah found herself agreeing to the ridiculous idea that she could be ready in seven days' time to abandon what remained of her old life and set her face towards a perilous foreign future. Then, with the courtesy that, like his office furniture, belonged to a bygone age, the lawyer escorted her outside to her car. Bemusedly she remembered to switch on the ignition, and her last glimpse of him was of his little friendly wave as she drove away.

The journey back to Highfold was a thing of blind corners and steeply-climbing narrow lanes. To avoid disaster needed concentration at the best of times; now wasn't the moment to let her mind drift to what she'd just committed herself to. In any case, her most immediate problem was how to break the news to Matthew and Meg that she wasn't going to remain with them at Highfold. Her large, slow-talking brother was occasionally persuaded by his family to go visiting outside Gloucestershire, but he went under duress, and returned home thankfully. He would reckon, even if he managed not to say, that anyone who chose to live in a city so exotic and environmentally unsound as Venice could only be unhinged. Meg, his wife, would try to make allowances for a sister-in-law whose life had been sadly derailed again, but no more than Matthew would she understand the need that Sarah knew was driving her away.

She got back to the farm just as Meg was calling the children indoors for their tea: James, the eldest, so like his father and so simply intent on walking in Matthew's footsteps, that his adult life already seemed writ clear; John, two years younger, the gentle dreamer of the family, reminding Sarah of her dead father; and last but far from least, the daughter of the house, a four-year-old witch called Harriet – Harry to her brothers, whom she'd managed to enslave for life while still in her high chair.

With tea in progress, only one subject of conversation was required. The naming of Harriet's new pony had already occupied them for the past three days, but she now had finally opted for 'George', smiling away her brothers' objections that the pony happened to be a girl.

When the children had been persuaded to go to bed and Matthew was back from his usual nightly check that all was well with his livestock world outside, Sarah knew that the moment of truth was upon her. She was still trying to decide how to begin when Meg suddenly pointed an accusing finger at her across the supper table.

'You've been up to something, Sarah love.

It couldn't have been shopping that took you over to Cheltenham; you didn't do any.'

'I *was* shopping – for a job...' The answer came slowly. 'A job in Venice, as it happens!' She smiled at the consternation in her sister-in-law's face, but grew serious again when she looked at Matthew. 'Let me explain, then you can tell me how mad I'm being! When I was clearing things out at the rectory, I came across an advertisement: "Wanted in Venice, an Italian-speaking governess for two young children". I looked out of the window at the rain flattening the daffodils and thought of sunlight on rose-pink palaces and green canals.'

'It doesn't rain *here* all the time,' Matthew pointed out. He stared at his sister's thin face, and then spoke more vehemently than usual. 'You're exhausted from nursing Father – it's a good, long rest you need, not a job anywhere at all.'

'I need something to do,' Sarah corrected him gently. 'I love Highfold and all it contains, and I can only go away knowing that you'll be here for me to come back to. But I *have* to make a fresh start, and the job I was offered this afternoon at least sounds worth doing. Mr Crabtree, the lawyer employed by Countess di Brazzano, was professionally discreet, but fair-minded enough to warn me that what I was about to join wasn't a rumbustious, warm-hearted Italian house-hold!'

'He meant that the countess is a frightful high-society bitch,' Meg said frankly, 'and her husband will either ignore you or expect to climb into your bed. Matthew, can't you forbid Sarah to go?'

'She'll probably cope with the parents all right,' he told his anxious wife. 'It's the children she has to worry about.'

'Too true,' Sarah acknowledged ruefully. 'Mr Crabtree was worried about them himself – it's what I liked most about him.' She took a sip of the wine Matthew had just poured into her glass, then smiled cheerfully at them. 'Don't fret, my dears; I can surely survive three months' probation. After that, the countess may send me packing anyway. As it happens, though, she was born as English as you or me. Before her marriage she was a famous opera singer, Laura Kentish by name.'

'It gets worse,' Meg said tragically. 'Spoiled-brat children, a temperamental diva, and a flaky Venetian count, not to mention what is probably a waterlogged ruin mouldering into the Grand Canal! We shall certainly expect you home at the end of the three months.'

It seemed so likely that Sarah had to agree, but there the subject was allowed to rest because Meg, with the loving smile her daughter had inherited, announced that it was time for bed.

A week later, faithful to the instructions sent by Mr Crabtree's efficient secretary, Sarah allowed herself to be stowed into Matthew's car and driven to Heathrow. Meg and the children went too, of course, and their company was a distraction she was thankful for. Between reassuring James – who'd been reading about Venice – that it wasn't on the point of sinking beneath its lagoon, and being reassured in turn by Harriet that the pony wouldn't forget her while she was away, there was scarcely any time at all to think about the ordeal ahead.

But once delivered into the brisk, impersonal care of British Airways, there came a moment when she had to watch Matthew shepherd his family away. Half-blinded by sudden tears, she struggled not to be swamped by loneliness. She was a mere thirty-two, she tried to remind herself, sound in wind and limb, and more or less in her right mind. Self-pity was a trap she had no excuse to fall into. It was time to lift her head out of despair and take a fresh look at the world; time, in doing so, to acknowledge the friendly stare of the dark-haired girl sitting opposite her across the aisle. Then she thought of something else that wiped sadness away and made her smile instead.

Mr Crabtree's good wishes received before she left Highfold had been kindly meant. She doubted if he'd *intended* them to sound like his sympathetic farewell to a gladiator being led to the waiting lions!

Two

Half an hour later, installed in one of the aircraft's window seats, Sarah waited for the moment of take-off. Nothing afterwards would equal the excitement of it, in her view, for the remainder of the flight. Once the monstrous bird had hauled itself into its true element above the shifting layers of cloud, there was only unchanging blueness outside her little window; time to get out her book. Reaching down for it in the bag at her feet, she noticed something else – the shaking hands of the passenger in the next seat who was trying to unfasten the tray in front of her. They were a silent cry for help that turned Sarah at last to recognize her companion – the girl who'd watched her in the departure lounge, but now it was fear that filled her dark eyes, not curiosity.

16

'You don't enjoy air travel,' Sarah remarked calmly. 'My own pet aversion is spiders; I've given up pretending that I shall ever grow to love them.' She smiled as she spoke, and the tense face beside her tried to smile back.

'It's the going-up and coming-down,' the girl explained unsteadily. 'I'm all right once we're on the level, especially if my neighbour's kind enough to talk to me! My name's Zoe Hartman, by the way, and you'll have guessed where I hail from.'

It wasn't difficult. Her flat drawl and the casual perfection of her clothes – suede jacket and Prince of Wales check trousers – unmistakably suggested Upper-East Side New York.

Sarah abandoned all thought of her book and introduced herself instead. Keeping Zoe Hartman's mind off the ordeal of air travel was as good a way as any of dealing with the sick anticipation building up inside herself.

'This isn't the time of year when most people take a holiday in Venice,' she suggested, 'but *is* that why you're going?'

'It's more holiday than anything else, but I'm enrolled for a course in Italian at the university. My darling godmother insists on that – she's great on self-improvement, and so's my Pa. Any child of his is expected to be sharper and more successful than he is. I

17

doubt I'll manage it!'

Not sure whether she was expected to sound envious or sympathetic, Sarah offered a cautious enquiry instead. 'Why is your godmother involved – does she live in Venice?'

'Since her husband died, yes, for half the year. Elsa always goes back to New York in the fall, when the opera season starts. Until then she'll be in a palazzo – well, one floor of a palazzo – that she rents every spring and summer.' Zoe's flow of information was halted while lunch trays were delivered by a harassed-looking stewardess.

'Now I want to know about you,' she continued afterwards. 'I'm good at guessing about people as a rule, but I'm not tuned in to *you* at all.' She stared again at her companion then shook her head. 'It comes of being English, I guess. *We*'re an open book, but you'd prefer the rest of us *not* to understand you!'

Sarah examined the neat compartments of food on the tray in front of her, felt her nervous inside rebel at the thought of accepting anything at all, and settled for some bottled water instead. 'There's not a great deal to understand. I'm heading for a palazzo as well, but that sounds grander than it is. I'm going there to work for a family I don't know. The di Brazzanos' two small children are probably plotting even now how to make their new governess's life a misery!'

'A *what*? I don't believe it. Nobody's been a governess since – who was it? – Jane Eyre bumped into Mr Rochester.' The American's bright glance swept over her companion again – the simple tweed suit and neat brogues could be said to match the part all right, but surely a governess was some kind of servant and she couldn't fit this composed woman into that role at all.

'You're *not* serious, are you?' she asked uncertainly.

Sarah's transforming smile appeared, reminding the American girl of an earlier moment in the departure lounge. Something had suddenly lifted the Englishwoman's sadness then, and instead of being offended by a tactless query she was amused again now.

'Yes, I'm serious,' she said. 'I gave up working when my father was ill, but teaching *is* what I do. I rather liked the idea of doing it somewhere more exotic than in a school in Gloucestershire.'

Flying fears now forgotten, Zoe gave an entrancing grin. '*Now* I've got it – no exciting Mr Rochesters any more in rural England! I wish you luck in Venice, Sarah, but be careful – I've been there with Elsa before and I can tell you that charming Italian men need watching. Newcomers are the flavour of the month when they arrive, but their shelf-life is very short as a rule!'

Sarah tried to look grateful for what was so clearly meant to be kind advice. She decided not to point out that she was probably ten years older than her new-found friend, and equipped with some hard-won experience in how to keep charming Italians at bay. She didn't even consider mentioning the rest of the truth – that her return to Venice was not to search for something new but to exorcise what the city stood for in her past.

'I don't think I need be very careful,' she said at last. 'Governesses hover invisibly between the salon and the servants' hall. Even you don't quite believe I'm real!' Seeing that Zoe was looking sorry for her, she shook her head. 'Don't worry, please. Even if I survive three months' probation, the job is only for two years.' She stopped speaking to listen to the captain's announcement that they were nearly there, then glanced out of the window at the island-dotted lagoon beneath them. 'I'm more nervous than a woman of my advanced years has any right to be, but I can't help feeling intrigued as well. My father would have said that it makes a good mixture for the start of a new job!'

Zoe's answering smile this time was full of unexpected sweetness. Sarah had already registered that she was exceptionally pretty, and blessed with the perfect skin, hair and teeth that wealthy young Americans seemed to have as their birthright. But she also had warmth, and probably some of her father's shrewdness to lend a welcome touch of astringency as well.

'We won't lose touch, will we?' she suddenly asked. 'I'll want to know how you get on, and there must be an EU law that says even the Italian nobility can't keep governesses chained to their children *all* the time. Write me your address, and I'll give you mine – Elsa's name is Mrs Vandenburg, by the way.'

Sarah looked at what she was scribbling down. 'We'll be on opposite sides of the Grand Canal – with long enough eyesight you'll be able to see me waving to you across the water.'

'Oh! You know Venice already. I was going to show it to you.' Zoe's vivid face looked disappointed and Sarah quickly shook her head.

'You still can. I came here a long time ago.'

It was as much as she intended to say, and she managed to sound as if her acquaintance with the city was not only ancient but trivial as well. Even so, Zoe might have persisted with another question if the plane hadn't noticeably just begun its slow descent towards Marco Polo airport. She smiled gratefully when Sarah took hold of her hand, and a few minutes later let out a sigh of relief as they taxied along the runway on the rim of the lagoon.

Released quickly by Customs and Immigration officials, Zoe picked out her godmother at once among the waiting crowd, and led her new English friend towards a middle-aged woman expensively swathed in cape, Cossack hat, and high leather boots. Mrs Elsa Vandenburg was living testimony, Sarah reckoned, to the care with which her late husband had provided for her. Perhaps she was a kind and generous godmother but a lightning glance assessed Sarah's likely worth and wealth, and she saw nothing there to linger over. Zoe was detached efficiently from her travelling companion and shepherded outside to Mrs Vandenburg's waiting motor launch and boatman.

Left unclaimed herself, Sarah tried to have faith in Mr Crabtree. He'd promised that she'd be met, but while she waited for someone to arrive she felt desperately alone and nervous. The truth was that on a cold, wet day in March she didn't want to be in Venice at all. Thank God Matthew wasn't there to remind her about sunlight and rose-pink palaces. The Venetian Lagoon under winter rain was just about the most desolate and disturbing spot on earth.

'*Signorina Cavanagh*?' a soft voice enquired behind her.

She turned and smiled at the small, swarthy man who waited for her answer. *'Si, sono io.'*

'Buona sera,' he went on, bowing over the hand she held out. *'Sono Michele, del Palazzo di Brazzano.'* An operatic wave of the hand indicated the *'uscita'*; then he gathered up her luggage and led the way outside. She followed obediently behind, wondering what description Mr Crabtree had passed on that had enabled Michele to identify her so surely.

The journey across the lagoon was choppy and unpleasant – nothing like her earliest memory of it. Then, already dazed with happiness, she'd seen it in shimmering summer beauty. Happiness hadn't lasted, but the Serenissima's magical beauty had, even when everything else had changed. The bleak seascape she was watching now seemed unrecognizable as the same city.

They turned at last into the comparative shelter of the Bacino and the mouth of the Grand Canal, and Michele explained that he was the palazzo's major-domo – butler, boatman, chauffeur, and whatever else the count required. His wife, Claretta, was the di Brazzanos' housekeeper. Sarah studied his face under the cap set at a rakish angle and tried to guess his age. Too young to have known anything of the war, he must nevertheless be reminded of it often enough.

Claretta had been the name of Mussolini's ill-fated mistress who'd redeemed herself by dying bravely with him when he was caught by the *Resistenza*.

'*Ecco il palazzo*,' Michele suddenly said, and Sarah had to put aside the painful past, freshly aware of how little prepared she was to face a very uncertain future. She watched while the boat's engine was cut and they glided neatly to a striped mooring pole in front of a tall, Gothic-windowed house. The water-gate was closed, but a flight of stone steps led up from the landing stage, and she was helped out on to them by Michele, who resumed terra-firma duties by first removing his nautical cap and reefer jacket.

The outer stairs led to a pair of ancient doors, and then a curved and shallow-stepped staircase that wound round the mezzanine floor of the palazzo and brought them to the *piano nobile*. Climbing slowly because she refused to arrive gasping for breath, Sarah saw Michele ahead of her come to a deferential halt. Two men were now making their way down the staircase.

The elder of them glanced at the newcomer with the same assessing stare that she had noticed in Mrs Vandenburg, but his '*Buon giorno, signorina*' was courteous enough. His companion, perhaps a student still but aping sophisticated airs, didn't bother with a greeting. Instead he offered the man beside him a remark about her which Sarah wished she hadn't been able to hear or understand. There was just time to remember what Mr Crabtree had said about the count's elder son before Michele knocked at another set of handsomely carved doors and then ushered her into what, in the dim afternoon light, seemed to be an enormous, cavernous room. Sarah made her way cautiously to where her employers sat waiting for her – perhaps expectant that she'd trip over some tasselled rug or occasional table lost in the gloom.

The count bestirred himself sufficiently to get up from a massive brocade-covered armchair and briefly shake Sarah's hand. Then he introduced his wife, who remained where she was, seated on the other side of a fireplace that could have roasted an ox. There was a polite enquiry as to her journey, a mention of Mr Crabtree, and then the count excused himself from the rest of the interview. He was obliged to hurry away to a meeting, but would look forward to a better acquaintance with Miss Cavanagh in the future. Then, with a formal kiss on his wife's hand, Fabrizio di Brazzano set out on his own long march across the room and, with nothing else to do for the moment, Sarah watched him go. He was a handsome, iron-grey haired man now verging on the portly. He looked quite kind, but he was vain enough to glance in each ornate mirror he passed.

His departure left her alone with the countess – a high-society hostess, ex-operatic star, or was there any remaining trace of the English provincial girl she'd once been? It wouldn't take long to find out, Sarah thought, but meanwhile, several things were obvious already: Laura di Brazzano was years younger than her husband; she was still beautiful in a fine-drawn, haggard way; and she looked merely bored at the interview ahead.

She spoke in English, and admitted briefly to her long acquaintance with Mr Crabtree. Then came a precise recital of the governess's duties: Sarah was to complete the education that Beatrice received, rather unwillingly, at the local convent. Emmanuele – here the countess's voice lost some of its briskness, as if he represented a problem she hadn't been able to solve – needed to be prepared to go away to school in two years' time, but illness had delayed his progress, and he was still frail and underdeveloped for his age. Laura di Brazzano's impersonal voice might have been speaking of a child she scarcely knew. From what Mr Crabtree had said that might even be true, Sarah thought, appalled by the possibility.

Then the countess coolly brought the conversation to an end. The governess would be assisted by Bianca, the nursery maid, and relieved by Signora Vanni, Michele's wife, on her days off. The children would, of course, lunch with their parents whenever other engagements allowed; but in general their place was on the calmer top floor of the palazzo.

There followed a silence that Sarah felt it safer not to break. If she said anything at all, it would only be to point out that this unnatural woman in front of her needed a foster-mother for her children, not a governess. Mr Crabtree had been right – they *were* neglected in the real sense of being desperately short of proper parental love and care. Fuming and sick at heart, she couldn't decide whether to resign without even starting when, as if reading her thoughts, the countess suddenly caught her unawares.

'Hubert Crabtree promised me that he'd found the person we needed, Miss Cavanagh. I'm afraid you won't find us easy, but will you at least try?'

For a moment she was the much simpler English girl she'd been thirty years earlier. Sarah found herself nodding in reply, knowing the moment for one of those times when, even for the right reason, the wrong decision was probably being made.

'Yes, I'll at least try,' she agreed; whereupon the countess tugged at a bell rope and, when Claretta Vanni appeared, asked for the signorina to be shown round the house.

Still uncertain what to do next, but strongly inclined to hand the countess back her job, on the grounds that Mr Crabtree and his candidate had both made a mistake, Sarah became aware of the housekeeper's considering stare. Signora Vanni waited, she suddenly felt sure, for the moment, now or not much later on, when the *Inglese* admitted defeat and took herself back whence she'd come. It was all that was needed to tip the balance in favour of staying, and she smiled cheerfully at the woman before offering her a greeting in Italian. The housekeeper replied without warmth or welcome, and then suggested that a tour of the palazzo might as well begin.

By the end of it, Sarah felt sorry for a woman whose job it was to run a house that must once have kept a small army of servants busy. Now, she and Michele, a couple of maids, and an odd-job man, between them did everything that was required. The tour finished on the top floor, where the children's quarters were. They included, Sarah was thankful to see, a small kitchen, where Bianca prepared the children's breakfast and tea. Her own bed-sitting room was modest compared with the grandeur downstairs, but it was comfortable, and its windows looked across the Grand Canal to the splendid statue-fringed skyline of Longhena's masterpiece, Santa Maria della Salute. Sarah pointed to it with pleasure, but the housekeeper looked very unimpressed.

'Bigger than most, but it's just another church,' she calmly pointed out. 'Venice has too many of them in my view.'

It was an unusual view for an Italian woman, but Sarah realized that Signora Vanni seemed not to resemble her more effervescent compatriots in other ways as well.

'Thank you for showing me the house,' Sarah said next. 'There wasn't any sign of the children. Are they out?'

'Bianca is fetching Beatrice from a dancing lesson. Emmanuele's gone with her. They'll be back soon.'

Determined to get *something* out of this oddly unresponsive woman, Sarah tried asking for her help. 'You must know the children very well. Tell me about them, please, before I meet them.' It was a question that she should have put to the countess, she realized, but perhaps Signora Vanni understood why that had seemed so difficult.

'They're very different – had different mothers, of course,' the housekeeper finally admitted, 'but Beatrice takes after her father; Emmanuele doesn't. You won't find either of them easy. The last girl who was here soon gave up.'

That seemed to be all the housekeeper was prepared to say, but Sarah tried again. 'On the way into the palazzo, I saw two people going out; was the younger of them Beatrice's elder brother, Franco?'

The signora nodded. 'He's home from Bologna at the moment. You'll not get any help from him with Emmanuele; he gets on better with his sister.'

Sarah thought despondently of the sneering youth on the stairs, and hoped he didn't spend much time at the palazzo. Governesses were required to know their place in the scheme of things, but Franco could easily provoke her into forgetting hers, and if nothing else did, that would end her stay in Venice soon enough. Unaware of being stared at by the housekeeper, she was surprised by what Signora Vanni said next.

'You look tired. The English like tea, I believe. All you need for it is in the kitchen, and Bianca and the children won't be back just yet.'

It wasn't much of an overture, but it was something, and Sarah's warm smile thanked her for it. 'I don't know what *you* fall back on in times of stress, but a cup of tea certainly works wonders for us. Will you join me in the kitchen?'

The housekeeper shook her head. 'I've

work to do downstairs, and tea doesn't agree with me in any case.'

The slight mellowing hadn't lasted long; still, Sarah tried to be encouraged by it as she brewed her tea and carried it into her room. From there she could watch the comings and goings on the canal, and look across to the splendour of the Salute whenever she needed to lift her heart. Venice had almost defeated her the last time she was here; she couldn't let it happen again.

Three

She was on her knees, unpacking, when she saw reflected in the mirror in front of her a small boy who stood watching in the doorway. Before she could even get to her feet, he was gone – someone else at the palazzo who wasn't minded to make her feel welcome, it seemed.

After a moment's hesitation she went in search of him, knowing that she must start as she meant to go on. He was in the day nursery-cum-school room, hunched up on a window seat that she guessed was his chosen private territory. If he heard her come in he wasn't going to look round.

'Hello,' she said quietly. 'I think you must be Emmanuele.' There was no reply, and she decided to ignore for the moment the countess's request that English should be spoken. In his own language she explained that they must introduce themselves properly – it was what people did when they met for the first time. At last he did turn to look at her and she saw the faint flush of colour in his cheeks, as if he'd felt reprimanded.

'*Scusami, signorina. Sono Emmanuele di Brazzano.*'

He even remembered that he must bow over the hand she held out, an imitation of his father's stately gesture that she found touching. But it was no attractive waif who stood looking at her; his sallow face refused to smile and his small body was skeletally thin. She'd never seen a child who so completely lacked the roundness and vitality of extreme youth. His dark eyes watched her warily, as if he'd learned to expect very little from contact with the adult race. Mr Crabtree had been right; instead of love and laughter the di Brazzanos had merely offered their son the complicated ritual of the dining room when they had nothing more exciting to do. Sarah wondered how long it would be before she told them what was expected of more normal parents.

She was about to ask Emmanuele where his sister was when a small commotion sounded in the corridor, and a moment later Beatrice danced into the room, followed by a smiling girl of about eighteen, presumably Bianca, the nursery maid. The child still wore her practice dress of leotard and tights, and her long, dark hair was drawn back tightly as befitted a budding ballerina. She was pretty and plump and full of the confidence that Emmanuele so obviously lacked, perhaps because her father was amused by her grown-up ways and spoiled her when he remembered she was there.

Bianca bobbed a little curtsey but shyly waited for the *Inglese* to open the conversation, and it was Beatrice who got in first, with a bold glance that seemed too clearly borrowed from her elder brother.

'I'm Beatrice, and this is Bianca who looks after us. I think you're the English signorina Mamma told us to expect.'

Sarah, smiling, agreed, but Beatrice hadn't finished yet. 'Our last governess didn't stay ... well, they never do. *She* was very stupid, poor thing, and Emmanuele wouldn't talk to her. He doesn't talk much at all.'

That at least, Sarah reflected, was likely to be true. He'd now abandoned a conversation that didn't interest him and retired to

33

the lonely isolation of the window seat. She felt lonely herself, and made helpless by her lack of knowledge of this strange family. But some authority had to be exercised here and now if she wasn't to be beaten before she'd even begun.

She ignored Beatrice and spoke to the maid instead. 'Bianca, you know the children's routine and I don't at the moment, so will you look after them this evening? We can have a talk later on when they're in bed, and I've finished unpacking.'

'Beatrice has her bath now after her dancing lesson,' Bianca explained. 'Signora Vanni will send supper up – Donna Laura is entertaining guests this evening.'

For the benefit of the watching newcomer, Beatrice went pirouetting out of the room. She'd been expecting the new governess to ask *her*, not Bianca, what ought to be done with them and the showy exit was to insist that Beatrice di Brazzano, at least on the top floor of the palazzo, was accustomed to taking centre stage.

Sarah watched her go, wishing that she wasn't reminded quite so forcibly of Franco. Now, left alone with Emmanuele, the only one of the three children who probably wouldn't deliberately set out to be difficult, she thought he was the one most likely to break her heart. Expensive toys littered the room, but he ignored them, apparently engrossed in watching the raindrops that played a game of tag down the windowpane. She crossed the room to stand by him, wondering why and how long ago the barrier he hid behind had been erected. His cap of dark hair was as smooth as a seal's head, but she knew better than to touch it. At not yet seven, he was a more private person than most adults she knew.

'The rain reminds me of my home,' she said quietly. 'It's often wet there.'

'I know,' he answered after a long pause. 'Bianca told me. Her grandfather went to *Inghilterra* a long time ago.'

He picked up a book lying on the seat beside him; they'd conversed enough, the gesture seemed to suggest, and the governess was now dismissed.

Well, at least he'd said *something*, Sarah told herself wryly, and she couldn't wring more words out of him.

'I'm going to finish unpacking,' she commented. 'There are some books to bring in here, but perhaps you don't feel like helping.'

'No, thank you,' he answered politely. 'I prefer to stay here.

'Just like my nephews at home,' Sarah pointed out. '*They* always know what they'd rather be doing, too! *Ciao*, Emmanuele.'

Then she walked out of the room, hoping that she'd managed not to leave behind the faint whiff of defeat. The small boy might look frail but he was a di Brazzano, and she felt sure that any sign of weakness would be spotted and despised.

She made no attempt to intrude for the rest of the evening. Tomorrow would be time enough to begin showing them that she wasn't another stupid 'poor thing' who needed to be got rid of easily. But depression had settled on her nevertheless; no one had yet made her feel welcome, and she was not only tired but hungry as well. Her in-flight lunch had been left untouched, and breakfast at Highfold seemed a lifetime ago. It was better not to think of them at the farm at all – Meg supervising the children's bedtime rituals, and Matthew sipping the evening glass of whisky that he enjoyed.

She was about to take her mind off hunger and homesickness by writing to them, when a knock sounded at her half-open door. An older woman than Bianca stood there holding a tray.

'*La cena, signorina – fegato alla veneziana, una nostra specialità.*' Then, as she put down the tray and turned to leave again, natural courtesy got the better of whatever resentment she felt at having to wait on the new-comer. '*Buon appetito!*'

Sarah thanked her with a friendly smile, grateful to see that along with the dish of delicious-smelling liver, there were cheese, luscious purple grapes, and a small carafe of wine. Now she could add a postscript to her letter to Meg that at least she was going to be adequately fed.

The good food made her feel better, and she went along the corridor afterwards to make herself some coffee. Bianca was in the kitchen, laying the table for breakfast.

'Is all well with the children?' Sarah asked. 'I didn't offer to help – I wanted them to get used to the idea that I'm here!'

The maid's face broke into a pretty grin, 'Everything's well ... in fact, hunky-dory, signorina!' She brought out the absurd English expression with an air of triumph, and giggled at the astonishment in Sarah's face. 'It's what my grandfather says – he taught me all the funny words he could remember.'

'Emmanuele mentioned that he'd been to England,' Sarah remembered. 'How did that come about – was he working there?'

Bianca nodded. 'On a farm, it was. Nonno was captured in the war and sent to your country. He was very pleased – food to eat, no more fighting, and he even fell in love there! Afterwards he went back and married his English girl, and they're still together, still very happy.'

'Here in Venice? I'd love to meet your English grandmother.'

'No, signorina; they live at Castelfranco,

over on the mainland. Nonno's retired now but he worked for Signor Leopardi, the count's cousin. I was brought up there, of course.'

'But you like being in Venice?' Sarah asked, wondering if she imagined a certain wistfulness in the girl's voice.

Bianca's shoulders lifted in a little shrug, the inevitable Italian gesture that said life must be accepted as it was. 'I like to take care of the children even though they ... well, they are difficult sometimes. But Venice isn't my home; I'd rather stay at Castelfranco.' Now the yearning in her voice was unmistakable – Italians called it *campanilismo* – the thing that never ceased to link them to the place where they belonged.

'Tell me about the family here,' Sarah suggested next. 'I'm groping in the dark at the moment.'

Bianca considered this idea, expressed for her in Italian, and nodded as if she understood the newcomer's problems. 'I didn't know the count's first wife,' she began slowly. 'That contessa died when Beatrice was born. Donna Laura is Emmanuele's mother. She's English like you and my granny, but she's not the same at all. Perhaps it comes from being famous – she even sang at La Scala in Milan, you know.'

It was Sarah's turn to nod. She was

anxious to keep Bianca talking, without making her nervous as to what should or should not be said about the people she worked for. 'I know that Emmanuele was once very ill. He still looks frail, but he also seems to be living in a private little world of his own. I realize that the count and countess are often out, or engaged with other people here, but don't his brother and sister take any notice of him?'

'Beatrice sometimes – when she's in a good mood,' the maid admitted. 'Franco is mostly away, but Emmanuele doesn't mind that; his brother makes fun of him.' This time it was Bianca's expression that gave her away, but Sarah tried to give Franco the benefit of what doubt she could.

'Elder brothers aren't always helpful. There's a big age gap between him and Emmanuele, but that will matter less as they get older.'

The mulish set of her mouth suggested that this suggestion cut no ice with Bianca. *'Franco non mi piace,'* she said flatly, and that was that.

About to abandon the di Brazzanos, Sarah remembered one last question. 'I think I saw Franco leaving the palazzo with another man – much taller and older, but there was a family likeness between them.'

'Signor Leopardi's son, Giulio,' Bianco confirmed. 'He runs the estate at Castel-

39

franco. His father reads books all the time since the signora was killed in an accident.' She considered what else she might safely say. 'My grandfather loves Signor Leopardi, but he says that Belmonte was almost ruined by the time Signor Giulio was old enough to take over. Things are better now, of course, because a strong man is in charge, Nonno says.'

Sarah was left with the impression that Giulio Leopardi didn't please Bianca any more than Franco did, but it seemed unfair to indulge idle curiosity about a man who was of no concern to her. Instead, she merely asked for the children's daily routines to be explained, and finally wished Bianca a thankful goodnight. The endless day was over, and she longed to fall into bed and sleep; but her tired mind lingered on too many images – Zoe Hartman's sick anxiety in the plane, the unhomely grandeur of the palazzo's rooms downstairs that seemed to echo the lifestyle of their owners and, most vividly of all, Emmanuele's bony shoulder blades poking through his sweater as he stared out of the window at the rain-swept canal.

The night seemed short but she was up early enough the next morning to share breakfast with Bianca and the children. Beyond a mumbled *'Buon giorno, signorina'*,

Emmanuele ignored her, making a long drawn-out business of pretending to eat the warmed-up rusks that Italians call toast. Sarah sympathized with him, finding them equally unappealing herself, and decided that the housekeeper would have to be tactfully sounded out on the possibilities of producing something else. Beatrice, on the other hand, tucked in with gusto, and between mouthfuls of lavishly-buttered rusk kindly explained that the walk Sarah proposed wasn't how they normally started the day. In fact, apart from *her* dancing lessons and visits to the *sorelle* at the convent, and Emmanuele's weekly call on Padre Ambrosio, they weren't expected to walk anywhere at all.

'Well, you are now,' Sarah informed her with a friendly smile. 'I need you to show me round the neighbourhood, which presumably you know; after that we can explore Venice together.'

Furious dark eyes glared at her across the breakfast table. 'Ordinary people walk,' announced the daughter of the house. '*We* don't; Michele takes us in the *motoscàfo* when we go out.' She thought of an additional objection and pointed at her brother. 'Emmanuele's not *robusto* like me; you'll make him ill again.'

Sarah smiled now at the small, silent boy who'd given up on breakfast but was certainly aware of the battle of wills around the table. 'It will only be a little walk to begin with, because I don't feel very *robusta* either!'

She could see anxiety in Bianca's expressive face and knew that she'd boxed herself into a corner. If a self-willed, well-built child of ten refused to cooperate, she could scarcely be hauled bodily out of the palazzo doors. She cast round desperately in her mind for some inducement that Beatrice would find it hard to resist – a trip to the top of the campanile, perhaps? Elevenses at Florian's? – but was still trying to decide, when Emmanuele's gruff little voice suddenly made itself heard.

'Michele says there's a great English warship in the Bacino. It's fastened to the Molo, and people are allowed to visit it.'

'*Your* choice tomorrow then,' Sarah said quickly to Beatrice. 'We'll do what Emmanuele wants this morning. You must dress up for it, of course; the captain will expect you to.'

That just saved the day. No tantrum was possible while Beatrice was considering the possibilities of her wardrobe and making a choice that the English captain would approve of. They set off only an hour later, after she'd changed her mind three times, and Sarah had agreed that a scarlet anorak, navy-blue skirt, and red and blue striped tights would be appropriate for the call they were about to make on the Royal Navy.

Alas, when they'd crossed the piazza and walked out on to the Molo nothing was fastened to it at all except the usual fringe of gondolas waiting for the tourists brave enough to visit Venice in late March. A loitering boatman confirmed that the warship *had* been there, but had slipped its moorings early that morning. Sarah waited for the scene that Beatrice would now enact, but – probably not for the last time, she realized – the count's daughter suddenly took her by surprise. Beatrice looked at her brother's white, bleak face and managed to forget her own disappointment.

'Never mind, Emmanuele. The warship will come back, we'll see it another day.'

'And meantime it's as cold as charity standing here,' said Sarah. 'What we need is hot chocolate at Florian's. Which of you knows the way?'

'*Stupido*, it's only just around the corner,' Beatrice pointed out more or less correctly. But she was happy to take the lead, while Emmanuele limped along beside Sarah, silent and with his usual air of detachment from the rest of them.

The lit windows of the café, a fixture on the Venetian scene since the early eighteenth century, beckoned them across St Mark's Square, promising warmth and some redemption of the morning's failure so far. But in the doorway Emmanuele came to an abrupt halt.

'I don't want hot chocolate. I should like to go home.'

Sarah answered at once, before Beatrice could gather herself to rend her brother. 'You needn't order anything at all, but your sister and I *would* like a hot drink. I'm afraid you must come in with us while we have it.'

He gave a little shrug, a gesture copied from the adults whose behaviour he observed so carefully, and followed Beatrice inside. The day so far had been a fiasco, Sarah realized. Even the delicious chocolate put in front of her by a friendly waiter tasted bitter in her mouth. Since breakfast she'd merely managed to enrage Beatrice and alienate Emmanuele still further. It only needed the cold, damp excursion to give him a chill for her cup of failure to overflow.

Four

With the help of Bianca's information, Sarah worked out a programme that she hoped would bring some needed regularity to the children's lives. It would have been natural for their parents to show some interest in it too, but as yet she hadn't seen them on the top floor at all. Then, on her third morning there, the housekeeper appeared with a message from the countess: children and governess were to lunch downstairs.

Beatrice, of course, found it necessary to change her clothes, announcing that jeans and a T-shirt weren't quite approved of in the dining room. Emmanuele seemed to take no notice of the invitation and went on reading until he was told that it was time to put his book away. But his shuttered face was paler than usual as they went downstairs, and Sarah realized with a stab of anger against his parents that he was dreading the elaborate ritual ahead.

He kissed his parents politely on both cheeks as a small son should, but when they were seated at the table his fingers trembled over the array of cutlery beside his plate. Then he saw what the *Inglese*, sitting next to him, picked up and quickly followed suit.

But it was Beatrice who came to actual grief. She helped herself neatly enough from the dish of asparagus that the maid offered her, but couldn't manage the scissor-like contraption with which Italians choose to eat the vegetable. A fat, white spear, like a wax candle, Sarah thought, slid out of the child's grip on the scissors and skidded over the polished table. The countess asked Agnese in a pained voice to clear the mess away and, very close to tears, Beatrice looked imploringly at her father. But the count was busy sipping wine, and it was left to Sarah to try to come to the rescue.

'We tackle this differently in England,' she told the children. 'Just in our fingers, and the melted butter running down our chins is reckoned to add to the fun!' Then she looked-ed across the table. 'I expect you remember, Donna Laura.'

'I'm afraid I don't,' came the cold reply. 'In any case, the children live in Italy, not England.'

What now? Accept the snub or risk a fight that would gain nothing for the children and earn herself the sack? Sarah bit back the words on her tongue, but laid down the damned scissors; even the sight of the asparagus sickened her now. Then something unexpected happened. She saw Emmanuele – silent, aloof Emmanuele – wink at his tearful sister! An extraordinary glint of mischief in his face, not glimpsed before, said that together they could laugh at what all the stupid fuss was about. Beatrice managed a watery smile in return, the next course appeared, and the count exerted himself to make some conversation.

At last the ordeal was over. The fond father got up to go, and the children were allowed to escape upstairs; but the countess invited Sarah to remain behind and share coffee with her. While they waited for Agnese to serve it and leave the room, Sarah had time to stare at her hostess's fine-drawn, haggard face. Not a happy woman; that was clear enough. Did she regret a career given up too soon for a marriage that hadn't proved worth the sacrifice? Could she really be as dissatisfied as she looked with a life that to most women would have resembled Shangri-La?

'I'm afraid you're not happy here, Miss Cavanagh,' Sarah suddenly heard her say. 'You'd like to tell me that I'm a disgrace to English motherhood!'

It was another astonishment to find that

the countess could smile, but Sarah was still too angry to be disarmed, and she answered truthfully.

'A disgrace to *Italian* motherhood, perhaps; unlike us, they tend to kill their children with kindness. I may as well be hung for a sheep as a lamb and ask why you don't even seem interested in your own son, much less in Beatrice?'

There was a little silence in the room broken only by the chiming of a clock on the marble mantelpiece. Sarah listened to it, waiting to be told that her probation period was already over, but Laura di Brazzano had a weapon of her own to fire first.

'You've been here long enough to have settled in. Have you failed – like several women before you, I must admit – to get two rather difficult children to accept you?'

The question was acute and painful, but it had to be answered honestly.

'I'm not accepted yet, merely put up with because I'm here. Perhaps that's how it would be however long I stayed, although I hope not.' Sarah waited, got no reply, and had to go on. 'Beatrice seems confident and very self-willed, but she longs for her parents' reassurance that she's as pretty and clever as she wants to think she is. Emmanuele is more difficult because he's more complicated. He pretends to prefer his own lonely little world, but it's more probably true that no one here has bothered to try to winkle him out of it.'

The countess stared at Sarah, comparing her with the treasure that Hubert Crabtree had promised he was sending them: a serene-looking young woman, he'd said, intelligent, but gentle and unlikely to cause the least disturbance. So much for a lawyer's judgement of women! But perhaps he hadn't seen Sarah Cavanagh as she was now, with the flush of anger in her thin face, and grey eyes full of accusation.

'Mr Crabtree painted a misleading picture of you,' Laura said abruptly. 'He quite forgot to mention that you can't have been a private governess before – your career would never have lasted this long.'

'I imagine it's not about to last any longer,' Sarah suggested. 'I'll only say how very sorry I am that I've failed with the children.'

The countess's voice sounded fretful now. 'That's another thing you're *not* supposed to do – put words into your employer's mouth! I want you to stay, please, at least for the three months we agreed. After *that* we can decide.' She sipped her coffee and then put the delicate cup down as if its slight weight was too much for her. 'You'll have gathered that I'm not very maternal. I was ill when Emmanuele was born; after that I couldn't have any more children, and didn't want them. But I'd given up the only thing that I *could* do.'

'Which was to sing – most beautifully,' Sarah suggested quietly.

'So people said,' the countess agreed. 'I haven't performed in public since I retired, but I'm about to now, much against my better judgement.'

'Your voice will have been rested,' Sarah pointed out.

'It will also be rusty as hell!' Laura di Brazzano gave a little shrug. 'I'm committed now, in any case – my husband is the chief organizer of a great charity gala at La Pietà just after Easter, and the singer he wanted couldn't come. It involves a huge amount of work, but helping to preserve Venice has become Fabrizio's personal crusade. He's rather good at *that*, as it happens.'

She said it with only the faintest emphasis, to leave on the air a hint of his failure in all other ways. Fabrizio di Brazzano hadn't, Sarah realized with an unexpected twinge of sympathy for them both, been able to make up for the life Laura Kentish had given up.

'I'll stay, of course, for the three months we agreed,' she confirmed, 'and I should like to attend your concert, if I may.'

'An olive-branch I can't resist,' the countess pointed out wryly, getting up to indicate that the interview was at an end. Sarah wasn't sorry to take the hint; it had been a taxing half-hour. But she slowly climbed the stairs to the top floor thinking how strange it would be if she ended up learning to pity as well a woman that she deeply disapproved of.

Nothing more was said about the contretemps at lunch. United for once, the children had dealt with it in their own way, and probably preferred it so.

Sarah went on with what she hoped they needed – more systematic teaching than they offered much sign of having received so far, and a daily outing to give them exercise and fresh air. Emmanuele quickly showed benefit from the new régime; with an intelligence sharper than his sister's, he absorbed lessons so readily that Sarah realized how bored he'd been before. Better still, there was now some colour in his face, and he could manage their walks without lagging behind on the way home.

Once they'd begun to move outside the immediate neighbourhood of the palazzo, even Beatrice began to take an interest in the lagoon-encircled city of her birth, and she no longer despised the public *vaporetto* for the return journey from some of their longer outings, when they were getting tired.

Looking out of her bedroom window each morning for the pleasure of saluting the Salute, Sarah was often reminded of Zoe

Hartman and wondered how the American girl was getting on. Venice wasn't crowded so early in the year, and even its outer districts weren't a day's march from its heart, but they'd never bumped into Zoe on their travels, and Sarah had no expectation now of hearing from her. Mrs Vandenburg had given the impression that there'd be no moment to spare in their non-stop social life.

But one morning Signora Vanni appeared upstairs with a note for Sarah – brought by a liveried boatman, she said, sounding rather impressed. Zoe suggested a meeting that she would turn up for unless Sarah telephoned, and the assignation was inevitably for Harry's Bar, of course – no mere café for Miss Hartman.

With Bianca left in charge, Sarah set out for the rendezvous with a sudden feeling of release – it was the first time she'd escaped from the di Brazzanos for an hour or two since the moment she'd arrived. It was no distance to the Calle Valloresso, but Zoe was there ahead of her, waving from the table upstairs that Sarah was shown to.

'Oh, it's great to see you,' she stated with a bright grin. 'The evening's on me, need I say, and we start with Bellinis; they're obligatory at Harry's Bar, but they're delicious anyway – a mixture of prosecco and peach juice.' She ordered the drinks and, with the air of an old Venetian hand that Sarah found amusing, suggested that *bigoli in salsa* would be the dish to enjoy. Then, when the entranced waiter had walked away, she stared intently at her guest.

'You look tired, and I'm *not* surprised.'

'I'm tired but still here,' Sarah pointed out with a smile. 'It's more than seemed likely a week ago.'

Zoe nodded sympathetically. 'Elsa knows the di Brazzanos and, now, so do I – they came to dinner with us. My guess is that dear Fabrizio – whose forbears are founder members of the Golden Book – wouldn't normally hob-nob with the likes of my godmother, but money talks, *non è vero?*'

'Your Italian's coming on apace, but you're too young to be cynical,' Sarah suggested firmly. 'If the count *is* influenced by Mrs Vandenburg's wealth, it's not on his own account. For this glorious place to survive people like him must pay attention to people like her.'

'I know,' Zoe agreed quickly, 'but it's nice of you to stick up for them. Elsa says that her ladyship is a bitch!'

'Not entirely ... perhaps not at all; but I'll admit she's not the easiest woman in the world to get on good terms with.' Sarah sipped what the waiter had put in front of her. 'Delicious and new since I was here before!'

But Zoe wasn't to be put off the scent. 'I expect the children are a pain – well, children mostly are.'

'Not entirely,' Sarah said again, 'but *I* haven't been a great success so far. I'm still the bossy *Inglese* who insists on telling them what to do, which they're not used to. But they badly need someone who'll take an interest in them.' She waved the problem away and smiled at her companion. 'Tell me about you. How's the course going?'

'All right, I guess, but I'm too old to be attending school. Italian's what people speak here, naturally, but I think it's a bit *passé*, don't you? The smart ones among us are learning Russian and Chinese.'

She was more shrewd than cynical, Sarah thought – a chip off the old Jewish block that was Pappa Hartman. There was silence for a moment as food was put in front of them – the *bigoli* turning out to be spaghetti deliciously dressed with butter, onions and anchovies; then Zoe turned the conversation back to the di Brazzanos.

'Franco came with his parents to dinner – a seriously awful piece of work, don't you agree?'

'Yes, from the little I've seen of him,' Sarah had to admit. 'We pass on the stairs sometimes but Emmanuele, aged six, already has better manners than his half-brother.'

Zoe nodded, then suddenly her expression

changed, as if the moment she'd been waiting for had at last arrived. 'Now we come to the good news. Franco has a cousin called Giulio Leopardi. I sat next to him at dinner and, Sarah, *he*'s divine – a dish, a dream, a total delight!'

'Who inspires you almost to poetry! But the message is clear that you're rather taken with Signor Leopardi! I got a glimpse of him at the palazzo one day, and Bianca, the children's nursemaid, has mentioned him. She was brought up on the Leopardi estate at Castelfranco.'

'Running that is *his* job now, after his father almost allowed it to go to ruin. He slaves away at it and doesn't come here nearly enough. It's a big responsibility, I think – when he forgets to smile his face looks rather stern. But when he *does* smile...!'

Her voice faded into silence and Sarah hesitated to disturb an enchanted daydream. But a prosaic word of caution was needed, and it surely ought to come from a governess if from no one else.

'Zoe dear, you spent one evening in his company. I grant you that he looks all right, and I'll take your word for it that he smiles very nicely, but remember there's a lot you don't know about him. He might have women galore on the mainland, providing he has a moment to spare for them!'

The American's vivid face was suddenly tragic. 'You can't *laugh* me out of being knocked over by him, but Elsa had something to say as well. She's very clever at sussing people out and she's sure there's something going on between Giulio and Laura di Brazzano. The poor woman must be years older than he is, but she's still beautiful in her own way. I don't blame her for wanting a lover – *I* would with boring old Fabrizio for a husband – but she can't have Giulio Leopardi. I need him myself.'

It *wasn't* a laughing matter, Sarah realized. Zoe had just spoken the sober truth, at least about herself if not about Laura di Brazzano.

'Zoe, listen please. Venice is a small, enclosed place where gossip spreads as easily as the plague did once upon a time. Your godmother might well suspect the countess of being a rather unhappy woman – I think she *is* – but what she yearns for isn't a hard-working relative by marriage years younger than herself. She misses the career she gave up to marry the count. Attend the concert she's going to take part in soon and you'll realize that I'm right. She had, probably still has, a glorious voice. If you renounce a gift like that how can you hope to be happy?'

'I know about the concert,' Zoe admitted. 'Elsa's involved, of course, and she's taking a huge party of guests. But maybe she doesn't understand about Laura – she's a businesswoman who likes to meddle in things artistic! Her cronies wouldn't be generous either – there's no fun in that! Laura *might* want Giulio *and* her career back, of course; we shall have to see.'

'By all means; but meanwhile it's time I left. Can you find your own way home on foot like the rest of us, or do you summon a water-taxi in a lordly American fashion?'

She asked the question with a smile, but Zoe's face was grave. 'The taxi, of course. Sarah, stay in touch, please. Elsa doesn't have your kind of approach, and we take our silly little lives too seriously.'

Sarah promised to do her best, and they parted company outside a moment later. The night was cold but fine after all the recent rain, and walking through a moonlit, lamplit Venice was a pleasure she remembered from long ago. A companion was needed, of course, to share the dramatic contrasts of light and shadow, but life's perfect moments never repeated themselves. She thrust the thought aside, and tried to concentrate instead on the fervour in Zoe's voice when she spoke of Giulio Leopardi. Venice was a place where people felt almost obliged to fall in love, but the American girl was sharp and sensible, not a weak-minded adolescent. The divine Giulio had much better return very soon to the mainland, taking his unpleasant young cousin with him.

Back at the palazzo, she let herself in with the antique key provided by Michele and climbed the beautiful, curving stairs, with the pleasure they always gave her, to the faintly-lit, wide landing on the top floor. She had it in mind to look in quickly on the children to make sure that all was well, but at the top of the stairs she was brought to a sudden halt. The corridor wasn't empty, and in the far doorway of Bianca's room the little maid was locked in a silent struggle with Franco di Brazzano. She was distressed, dishevelled, and in tears, but making no noise for fear of waking the children. Sarah took a deep breath, then started at a run towards them.

Five

She caught up with them just as Franco pushed Bianca into her room and tried to close the door.

'Let go of her at once, and then get out of this room. Better still, don't come up here again if your only intention is to pester Bianca.' Sarah's voice was held low, but it lacked nothing in angry contempt.

With self-esteem already pricked by one unwilling servant, Franco now found himself being mauled by another; but remaining drunkenness helped him achieve a show of bravado. 'Britannia on the warpath! Hasn't anyone told you, *cara*, that the poor old lady doesn't rule the rest of us any more? I don't need an English spinster to say whether I can amuse myself with a mere nursery maid or not.'

The sneer at Bianca was one too many, and Sarah's hand swept up to land on his face with a hard and satisfying slap. 'Go *now*, before I fetch your father.'

She thought it took what remaining self-control he possessed not to strike back. Instead, he stood glaring at her, white-faced and enraged, but sufficiently sobered now to understand her threat. She and all her family were briefly consigned to hell in gutter language that a canal boatman wouldn't have used to a woman, and then he flung himself out of the room and down to the floor below.

In the silence left behind, Sarah was aware that she was trembling, and that Bianca, who'd retreated to the far corner of the room, was silently, desperately, engaged in weeping.

'It's all right,' she said unsteadily, walking towards the girl. 'The English that Franco despises so much always pull themselves together with "a nice cup of tea", and it's exactly what we're both going to have now.' She took the little maid's hand and led her along to the kitchen. Still talking gently, she made mugs of tea and put them on the table.

'It *isn't* all right, as you said,' Bianca suddenly murmured. Her tear-filled eyes stared tragically at Sarah. 'Franco will say I invited him into my room ... and, signorina, you *hit* him.'

The note of stunned astonishment in the girl's voice at the enormity of what had

happened made Sarah grin despite the
agitation of the moment.

'So I did,' she remembered with pleasure.
'It's not something I make a habit of doing,
but I rather enjoyed it!'

Bianca was beyond seeing any humour in
the situation at all, and it wasn't difficult to
know what was troubling her now.

'You're really anxious, I'm afraid,' Sarah
said, serious now, 'but there's no need to be.
Franco won't trouble you again, and he
can't do anything to damage you with
Donna Laura – it's *he* who is in the wrong,
and he knows it, despite the brave show of
defiance.'

'But what about *you*, signorina? I think he
will hurt you if he can.'

Sarah shook her head. 'Don't fret, as we
say at home. It's a little storm that will soon
blow over.'

More or less comforted, Bianca was sent
off to bed, but back in her own room Sarah
felt less confident than she'd sounded. The
one certain thing was that she'd made an
enemy of Franco; male vanity and pride had
been stung in a way he wouldn't forgive.
What he could achieve was hard to see, but
his obvious move would be to enrol the
children, who were far from being disposed
to see her as anything but a nuisance in their
lives.

It was an unpleasant thought to try to go

to sleep on, but something else was troubling her as well from earlier in the evening – the memory of her conversation with Zoe Hartman. She'd denied it, but suppose Mrs Vandenburg *was* right about the countess after all, and what Laura di Brazzano hankered for was not her old life back again, but a different one altogether with her husband's cousin? If so, the possibilities for storms ahead seemed almost endless, and what hope was there of protecting two already insecure children from the emotional fallout?

She fell asleep at last but woke again early, recognizing what had driven her awake. The thudding pain in her head was familiar, and so were the distorted vision and flashing lights when she opened her eyes. Sudden nausea sent her staggering to the bathroom for an exhausting bout of retching, and she was shakily heading back to her room when Signora Vanni, who liked to start the day before anyone else was stirring, suddenly appeared in the corridor. Her expression, usually one of calm indifference to the only servant she didn't control, changed at the sight of Sarah's sheet-white face.

'The signorina is ill?' she asked, almost with concern.

'The signorina has a headache!' Sarah admitted, with an unsuccessful attempt at a smile. 'To make matters worse, this is

Bianca's day off. I hate to spoil it but...'
She stopped, obliged to fight rising sickness
again, and the housekeeper suddenly took
charge.

'You must go and lie down at once, I
think. Bianca needn't stay – I'll send Agnese
up to look after the children.'

'Thank you, signora ... thank you very
much.' Dimly aware of unlooked-for kindness in Michele's wife, Sarah went thankfully back to her own room, swallowed more
pills to replace the ones she'd just retched
up, and lay waiting for the migraine to pass.

Two hours later the worst was over; she
could see clearly again and the hammer
blows in her head had faded to a dull ache.
When Agnese thoughtfully appeared with a
tray of tea, she could smile and insist that
she was almost back to normal.

'The children are being very good,' she
added as the maid turned to leave the room.
'I haven't heard a sound from them all the
morning.'

'The signora told them they'd probably
worried you to death,' Agnese reported.
'That gave them something to think about!'

She smiled encouragingly at Sarah, and
went away thinking it no wonder that the
poor thing looked washed out. In Agnese's
experienced opinion, the count's children
were enough to wear down even a good,
strong Italian woman; so what chance did a

frail-looking *Inglese* have? Beatrice was bad enough with her high and mighty ways and sudden tantrums, but Emmanuele was a good deal worse. He wasn't like a normal child at all ... look at him now, silent as usual, and still as a statue, staring out of the school-room window.

He was still there half an hour later when Sarah walked into the room. She saw him turn round, but the sight of her sent him charging out into the corridor, suddenly released from whatever paralysis had kept him there. For once he was even making a noise.

'Beatrice ... *la signorina non é morta,*' he shouted as he went in search of his sister. '*Ella vive ancora.*'

But at the lunch table a little later on he was silent again, and even Beatrice was less talkative than usual. Both children watched Sarah carefully instead – in case of a sudden relapse, she supposed. Afterwards, when she suggested a walk, Beatrice agreed unenthusiastically, but Emmanuele said nothing at all. It was his way of expressing disapproval, Sarah thought. She knew now that he liked their days to be ordered and familiar. This morning she had disturbed the usual pattern by being unwell.

Outside the palazzo, Beatrice, at least, began to look more cheerful. She always enjoyed their outings in fact, and particularly liked what they were going to do now – take the *traghetto* across the canal to the Salute, and walk back over the Accademia bridge. After all the recent rain, the afternoon had turned fine and suddenly the city was coming to life again. No longer sodden-looking and grey, the palaces that lined the canal were umber and rose-pink, and the waters in the canal danced and sparkled in the sunlight.

They said goodbye to the two boatmen who had rowed them across, stopped for a moment to admire the great church that always seemed to float protectively at the entrance to the city, and then slowly made their way home.

Beatrice chattered as usual but Emmanuele trudged beside her, stoically or stubbornly silent. Watching him, Sarah felt close to despair. He was refusing, with a single-mindedness she'd never met in any other child, to share any of their pleasure in the sunlit afternoon. Locked in some world of his own, he didn't even seem to mind his isolation any longer. Being alone was exactly what he was used to. Sarah thought of her brother's children at Highfold ... shy John, exactly Emmanuele's age, wasn't the sturdy farmer-in-the-making that his elder brother was, certainly wasn't a beguiling chatterbox like Harriet; but he belonged equally with them in the heart of a loving family. This small, self-contained scrap who plodded by her side might never learn that he was expected to share his life with the people around him. Unaware of the joys of love and friendship, how could he not grow up selfish as well as lonely unless she, or his mother, or his priest, or *someone*, could dismantle the barrier he'd got accustomed to hiding behind.

Their circular route back to the palazzo through the Campo San Stefano took them past a flower stall heaped – with an artist's eye – into a heavenly cornucopia of spring. Massed tulips, white, gold, pink, and flame, jonquils and freesias to send out shafts of perfume on the air, and great bowls of violets and primroses. Everything was there, and everything was beautiful, especially the primroses that spoke to Sarah of an English spring. She halted the children while she made her choice, and then handed Beatrice the nosegay to carry home.

'Mamma always has flowers – lots of them – downstairs,' the child pointed out. 'Are these for us?'

'No, they're to give to Agnese,' Sarah answered. 'She has her own work to do, but she was kind enough to look after you and Emmanuele this morning. These are for you to say thank you with.'

Beatrice was strongly tempted to say that Agnese was a servant who naturally looked after them when she was needed to. The words were on her lips, but something in the *Inglese*'s face told her that this wouldn't be a good idea; they had crossed swords on enough occasions already for her to know that, in some way she couldn't understand, the outcome of their battles usually seemed to be in this quiet woman's favour. She looked at her brother, hoping that his quicker brain would suggest something helpful, but he was staring at the flowers as if he hadn't noticed such things before and, now that he had, they needed all his concentration.

'Very well,' said Miss di Brazzano grandly. 'Of course I shall give them to Agnese. But she'll be very surprised, because we don't normally say thank you.'

It was the moment, Sarah realized afterwards, when she either had to find humour in her situation, or admit that it was more than she could bear. For now, she would somehow not weep over a ten-year-old who revealed unthinkingly the strange precepts on which she'd been brought up.

'By all means let us surprise Agnese,' she said calmly, and then walked on, leaving the children to follow or not, as they felt inclined.

But the day had one other surprise in store apart from Agnese's astonishment – Beatrice had been quite right about *that*. With

Bianca not yet returned, Sarah herself supervised the evening routines of bath and bedtime. She said goodnight to the children and retired to her own room to read, the usual ending of a day at the palazzo. But on the spur of the moment, before getting into bed, she peeped first into Beatrice's room, where a shaded night light showed the child to be already deeply asleep. No arrogant, unlikable termagant now; she was simply a pretty child, half-smiling at some dream that obviously pleased her. Sarah blew out the light and moved quietly into the room next door. Here the night light showed her someone who was still awake, and Emmanuele's dark eyes stared at her as she went to stand beside his bed.

'Shall we bring *you* flowers tomorrow, because Bianca wasn't here to look after us?'

It was a serious question, she realized; Emmanuele was always intent on knowing exactly where he stood.

'No flowers are needed,' she answered firmly. 'It's what I'm here for – to look after you.' She thought it was the end of the conversation, that he'd only remained awake while he tried to work out the answer for himself. 'Shall I blow out the light now? It's time you were asleep.'

He answered with another question. 'Will you be here tomorrow – for certain, I

68

mean?'

She looked at his tense, pale face and finally understood. Fear, not sullen resentment, had driven him into silence all day long, and it was fear that had kept him awake now.

'I promise I'll be here. Now, will you go to sleep?'

A faint sweet smile lifted the corners of his mouth and then a little nod agreed that, yes, he would. She smiled back, blew out the light, and returned to her own room. The extraordinary day, begun in pain, had ended in contentment, because she'd surely glimpsed just now the first tiny shoot of acceptance that Emmanuele had ever offered her. The barricade was still in place, but it wasn't impregnable, and bit by bit she might gradually be able to dismantle it.

Six

It was almost the end of Lent; soon would come not only the great celebrations of Eastertide but the equally important return of spring. Wandering about the city with the children, Sarah registered its changing tempo and a different air about its citizens. God be praised, they seemed to be saying; we've survived another winter. No more duckboards over flooded squares, sunlight now instead of rain, and the delightful certainty of another profitable season about to start. She sympathized with the Venetians but couldn't help preferring the city quiet, and the lagoon in its misty, winter-time beauty.

She said as much to Zoe Hartman over coffee at Florian's and got laughed at by a girl who insisted that the Serenissima *needed* her summer crowds. 'It's eerie otherwise, too full of ghosts – lost hopes and past glories!'

'There speaks the difference between your

youth and my crabbed age!' Sarah pointed out. '*You* look confidently towards the future, while I suspect it won't begin to match what was achieved in the past.'

'We walk on the moon if we want to ... send information by satellite around the world ... even manage to stamp out a killing disease or two!'

Sarah held up her hands in a gesture of defeat. 'You win that argument, of course; but we can't produce another Will Shakespeare or Titian, and I doubt if we'll ever build anything like St Mark's again.'

Zoe smiled at her warmly. 'You aren't crabbed with age, just tired of being a governess ... though now that I look at you properly you don't seem tired at all. In fact, I'd say you're quite getting the hang of things at the palazzo!'

'Not that perhaps, but I'm making a little progress; Beatrice no longer has to be dragged towards her desk, and Emmanuele forgot himself enough to smile at me this morning!'

'You'll grow too fond of them in the end. More likely, they'll grow too fond of *you*. What happens then?'

'I'm only on probation till the middle of June; if I'm asked to leave – which I think is very probable – the children will have forgotten in a week that I was ever there.' Afraid of having sounded forlorn, Sarah spoke more briskly of something else. 'There's a lot of excitement in the house at the moment – some of it is even seeping up to the top floor! Donna Laura's old singing teacher has been invited to help her rehearse, and the count is always just on his way out or in with a retinue of slaves and assistants.'

'Do either of them ever remember that they have children upstairs? Probably not, I guess.' Zoe's dry question suggested that she might have been just such a forgotten child herself; she'd spoken with a kind of wry affection about her father, but hadn't mentioned her mother at all.

Sarah noted the fact but didn't comment on it in case it was something that Zoe still found painful.

'I've reminded the di Brazzanos that *they'll* be expected to take the children to San Marco on Sunday,' she said instead. 'I usually go with them to Mass, but on Easter Day I'm determined to be at St George's on your side of the canal. I'll sing the Easter hymns *there* as a good Anglican should!'

It was Zoe's turn to avoid a delicate subject. Sarah's father had been a clergyman, she knew; better not to mention that a half-Jewish atheist like herself never reckoned to attend a church at all, of any description.

'What about the concert at La Pietà?' she asked next. 'Will you come with us? Elsa's giving a party afterwards for everybody who matters in Venice, including Laura and Fabrizio!'

Unable to believe that Mrs Vandenburg would put her in that category, Sarah shook her head. 'Thank you for the thought, but no. I've explained to the children why their parents are more invisible than usual at the moment, and it seems only right to take *them* to the concert. Emmanuele will listen to the music. Beatrice will point out to me all the people she recognizes, and make a note of what every woman is wearing!'

Zoe smiled at the idea, but Sarah could see that her mind was elsewhere. She was at the stage of infatuation where only she and the inhabitor of her dreams, waking and sleeping, counted for anything at all; the rest of the human race had become dispensable. Then, sure enough, she began to talk about Leopardi.

'Giulio is coming to Elsa's party, of course, but he's staying on your side of the canal, with dear Laura. Godmother doesn't put it into words, but she doesn't have to; I know what she's thinking. How convenient to have one's lover under the same roof for a change!'

'She has a low opinion of them both, it seems,' Sarah pointed out.

'Not low; realistic, she'd say, based on more experience than a vicarage-reared governess is likely to have had!'

Sarah let the slur pass and tried for humour instead, because her companion sounded upset. 'Should I prowl along the palazzo corridors all night, just to prove your godmother wrong?'

Zoe's tragic expression relaxed at last. 'I'll report the offer – at least it might change Elsa's view of governesses!'

'You mentioned Giulio Leopardi's father the last time we met,' Sarah remembered. 'Bianca speaks of him with great affection – the *padrone*, she still calls him.'

'Which just goes to show the unfairness of things; he's been a lousy *padrone*, by all accounts, and avoids other human beings like the plague. I find that very strange, and so does Elsa – she's a social animal!'

'Are you happy with her?' Sarah was suddenly curious enough to ask, recalling the elegant, hard-faced socialite she'd glimpsed at the airport.

'You mean, wouldn't I be better off in some less cynical, more loving, not to say honest-to-God *Anglican* household?' Zoe suggested with a grin. 'Dear Sarah, the answer is probably yes, but Elsa and I rub along very well, and in her own way she's a good, kind friend to me.' Then, with a glance at her watch, the American girl got up to leave. 'Which reminds me – I love talking to you, but I promised I'd be back

74

for dinner. Elsa's found some new celebs to entertain – from London, I think she said. *Ciao, cara*; see you soon.'

She blew a farewell kiss and walked away, watched – Sarah noticed with interest – by the women as well as the men at the surrounding tables. It was time to settle the small bill – her treat this time – and leave herself, and remember as she threaded her way through the linings of the city – as the Venetians liked to put it – that it was after her last rendezvous with Zoe that she'd interrupted Franco's manhandling of Bianca. She knew that he was still in Venice while the Easter vacation lasted, because she occasionally passed him in the palazzo and he stepped aside for her with a mock deferential air that made her long to box his ears again. But tonight, at least, all seemed peaceful when she reached the top floor.

She could hear the television set in Bianca's room but then came something unexpected as well – the tinkle of piano keys being played in a one-fingered assault on what sounded like 'The Bluebells of Scotland'; every English child's first attempt at a 'piece'.

But it wasn't a child who sat at the old upright instrument in the school room. The countess was there, picking out notes with the desperate intensity of a child blocking out something else she couldn't bear to think about. She swung round and her white despairing face was shocking. 'I've been waiting and waiting for you to come in.'

'Well, I'm here now,' Sarah pointed out quietly. 'What can I do for you, Donna Laura? Are you unwell?'

The countess's thin hands flicked the suggestion away impatiently. 'I'm not unwell, but I can't *sing* – I can't sing at Fabrizio's ridiculous concert, but he wouldn't believe me when I tried to tell him. I should have known, of course,' she went on feverishly. 'He understands nothing about me at all.' Tears, that Sarah suspected were quite foreign to a woman whose crises were usually dealt with in a different way, now trickled down her cheeks. 'I can't tell you how dreadful it is to be married to a stupid man. I need ... I need...' But who or what it was that she longed for so desperately she managed, with a last grab at self-control, not to confess to.

Uncertain, now, whether she was being made privvy to a prima donna's pre-concert nerves or the breakdown of the di Brazzanos' marriage, Sarah picked her way cautiously towards the truth.

'Tell me about the singing. You *said* you'd be rusty, but there's still time to practice.'

'How can I?' the distraught creature facing her demanded. 'My singing teacher won't come – we had too many bloody fights in the past, and she'd enjoy knowing that I'd been booed off the platform. This isn't England, Sarah – no kindly quarter given here to a singer who should have stayed retired.'

'There must be someone in Venice who could help you. If not, practice by yourself. You can't have forgotten what exercises are needed.'

'Of course I haven't forgotten. But I need an accompanist. The one I advertised for I sent packing this morning – a ghastly, posturing creature who seemed to think he was an undiscovered Paderewski waiting for his big chance!'

There was a long pause before Sarah spoke again. 'I don't know what you've chosen to sing. If the accompaniments aren't too demanding I could play them for you to rehearse with – well enough, at least, for you to judge whether or not you *can* go on with the concert. Would that help?'

The countess smeared away her tears with a simple gesture surely not used since she'd been a schoolgirl. 'Of course it would help,' she said more quietly. 'When can we start?'

'After breakfast tomorrow, if Bianca takes Beatrice to her class at the convent. Emmanuele won't mind listening to you – he loves music already.' She stated it as a fact; it wasn't a point to be scored off a mother who needed to be taught about her own child. Laura di Brazzano's nod admitted nevertheless that there *was* something to be learned, but she said merely that one rehearsal would be enough to settle whether she went on with the concert or not. Then she wished Sarah an abrupt goodnight and walked out into the corridor.

The following morning, after a scene with Beatrice who expected the singing rehearsal to await her own return, Sarah went downstairs with Emmanuele. A harassed-looking count met them at the door of a room she'd seen only during her first brief tour of the house with Signora Vanni. Surprisingly, his concern seemed to be for an unprofessional accompanist who was almost certain to be savaged by his neurotic wife. Even more unsuspected was the glimmer of despairing humour in his face.

'You were not engaged to be shouted at, signorina, but I fear you will be! My wife is very grateful to you, and she will try to be calm; but where performing is concerned she cannot be calm for long.'

He meant well, Sarah realized, but the countess was right, he didn't understand. The nervous dread of trying and failing to reach the standard she required of herself seemed to him merely excessive and even nonsensical.

'Donna Laura wants to do her best for

you,' she suggested. 'Emmanuele and I won't mind if she shouts a little.'

The count looked down at his small son, surprised to find that Emmanuele's usually solemn face was smiling at the governess. *They* seemed, he thought with a faint sense of regret, to understand one another; the only one not included was himself. He did all that he could do by opening the door, and left them to walk into what was part-library, part-music room.

The countess was already there, leafing through the piles of sheet music strewn over the top of the grand piano.

'I thought French music to start with,' she announced, too intent to even smile or say hello. 'Charpentier's "Depuis le Jour", and then some Fauré. His "Les Roses d'Ispahan" is lovely, but maybe the "Chansons de Venise" would be more appropriate.'

She gave Sarah just time to settle herself at the piano, and then rushed on. 'I've been doing scales and breathing exercises, so we can make a start. Don't worry if your part's a mess – so will mine be.'

At the end of half an hour it was obvious that she needed more rehearsal, but it was already not a mess. Her voice was still intact, and still beautiful – even a little deeper and richer than it had been ten years earlier.

Smiling unsteadily because of memories

the songs had evoked, Sarah pointed to Emmanuele. 'Your son is entranced, quite rightly. Of course you can sing at the concert, but you know that already yourself.'

'I can if you'll play for me,' Laura di Brazzano said. 'Where did you learn to accompany like that? It's harder than the singing, I used to be told.'

'There was always music at home when I was a child, and both my brother and I went to the Choir School at Gloucester Cathedral. But Matthew became a farmer, and I knew I wasn't good enough to be a professional musician. I don't regret that – music is still a joy, not an occupation.'

'Will you play for me at the concert?' the countess asked, then suddenly corrected herself. '*Please* will you, if I promise to behave myself?'

'I still think you should try to find a professional you can work with,' Sarah insisted, 'but if you can't, then I'll do my best.'

She saw the countess's face relax into the smile that she had passed on to her son. Neither of them used it very often, but it was worth the wait when it came. 'I'm supposed to make two appearances. Something Italian for the second half of the programme?'

'Why not something English? There'll be lots of Anglo-Saxons in the audience. Would you sneer if I suggested a simple, exquisite folksong like "The Green Hills of Somerset", or Haydn Wood's "A Brown Bird Singing"?' A glimmer of amusement lit her eyes for a moment. 'I could certainly play those if I had to!'

The countess sifted through the music again, and pulled out the first song Sarah had suggested. 'Play the damn thing now then.'

At the end of the last lovely note she unexpectedly turned towards her son. 'What do *you* think, Emmanuele?'

'*Bellissima*,' he said, with such conviction in his gruff little voice that even Laura smiled.

'Regard it as settled then,' she agreed wryly. 'I shouldn't have asked. Another rehearsal tomorrow morning?'

Sarah shook her head. 'On Monday, I think – you're taking the children to St Mark's tomorrow; it's Easter Sunday.'

'Oh God, so it is, and you aren't coming with us – they won't like that. Change your mind – it *is* something to see and hear even for a shaky believer like myself.' She stared at Sarah for a moment as a thought occurred to her. 'You're staying away because you reckon that the di Brazzanos should trudge over to the Basilica looking like a family for once; well, Franco is almost certainly a nonstarter, I can tell you.'

Sarah privately agreed, but didn't say so.

'It will be his loss then; but maybe he'll surprise you. When the children are in bed may I use this piano to practise on? The one upstairs is painfully out of tune.'

'There's no reason why not – my husband doesn't like this room.'

Emmanuele tugged at Sarah's hand, and she smiled down at him. 'I'm being reminded that it's time we went. Beatrice doesn't like to be kept waiting!'

They were almost out of the room when Laura di Brazzano spoke again, for once without her usual briskness.

'Miss Cavanagh ... Sarah ... I was upset last night, talking too much and probably not making much sense.'

'Then I needn't try to recall the conversation. *Arrivederci*, Donna Laura.'

The door closed behind them but the countess stayed where she was. She pretended to be looking at the sheet of music in her hands, but she wasn't registering the printed notes at all. Instead, she was seeing her son put his hand in Sarah Cavanagh's, as though that was where it confidently belonged.

It was a memory that prevented her making any complaint when they set out for St Mark's the following morning. The day was fine, and all the bells of Venice seemed to be ringing. The joy in the air should have been catching, probably was for the people all around them who were also answering the campanile's insistent summons to the celebration. The children walked between herself and Fabrizio, Beatrice convinced as usual of her leading role in the procession and happy to talk whether her father seemed to be listening or not. Emmanuele walked beside his mother but found nothing to say, and she was too honest to pretend to herself that it was the child's fault. Sarah Cavanagh might be having a damned good try, but she couldn't work miracles; the di Brazzano household would stumble on in its usual dislocated, unhappy way however many bells rang out the message that Christ was risen.

Seven

The service at the English church was satisfying enough, but Sarah walked away from it knowing that she was homesick for Pendock. Easter had been the high, glorious moment of the Christian year for her father, much as he'd loved the Nativity as well, and her mind was full of memories of him and the family at Highfold.

Crossing Accademia bridge on the way back to the palazzo, she stopped in the middle of it to lean against the wooden railing. Time to remind herself to be grateful, not to weep for all things dear and lost; she was looking at one of the world's great views – painted by a thousand artists from the brilliantly good to the downright bad – its colours changing as the Venetian light itself constantly changed.

Lost in thought, she wasn't aware of someone coming to stand beside her until he suddenly spoke her name.

'Miss Cavanagh? My name is Giulio Leopardi. We haven't been introduced, but I was with Franco di Brazzano the day you arrived at the palazzo.'

'I remember,' she confirmed, turning to look at him. 'I'm afraid Franco didn't realize then that I understand Italian.' If her intention had been to embarrass this self-possessed man she realized that she hadn't succeeded. Instead of blushing to recall Franco's comment at the time, he was examining her now with the Italian male's confident stare, although its interest was too clinical to be pleasurable.

'I gather from my young cousin that you and he don't...' He lingered over the right choice of word. 'Appreciate one another.'

'For the moment that sums it up very

nicely,' Sarah agreed. 'Perhaps we shall both improve on acquaintance.'

Giulio Leopardi considered the woman in front of him and acknowledged to himself that, at least in one important respect, Franco had got things wrong. The *Inglese* wasn't a woman to be laughed at even though she lacked the obvious, luscious charms that he and his friends thought added up to female beauty. Without the vivid colouring of Italian women, she didn't insist on being noticed; but her fairish hair had the texture of fine-spun silk, and her grey eyes were both unusual and beautiful. Franco had insisted that she was a typical governess, soured and spiteful, but perhaps that wasn't true either.

'You misunderstood my cousin's behaviour the other night. He'd been encouraged, and reacted as most young men would,' Leopardi suggested.

'There was no encouragement,' Sarah answered steadily. 'Franco was simply pestering a girl who has the disadvantage of being a servant in his father's house.'

If she wasn't sour, she was certainly stubborn, but he could see that she might need to be to survive in the di Brazzano household. Aware now of being on shaky ground, he tried another tack.

'Donna Laura tells me that you're going to perform with her at the Pietà concert – you

85

have unsuspected talents, it seems.'

Sarah suspected that a hidden sneer was intended, but decided to ignore it. 'I hoped she'd find a professional pianist, but I'm afraid she thinks the English devil she knows is better than an Italian one she doesn't. Fortunately I shall be invisible at the back of the platform while I try not to hit too many wrong notes.'

She hoped they'd now talked for as long as politeness required, and cast around in her mind for a casual, cheerful farewell, but before she could decide on her exit line he reverted suddenly to the beginning of the conversation.

'Remember something about Franco, please. He resented his father's remarriage, having been very attached to his mother, as most Italians are. Family life at the palazzo since then hasn't done much to reconcile him to the change.'

'Sons *do* love their mothers as a rule, but ten years should have been time enough for Franco to grow up,' Sarah pointed out. 'Perhaps *you* could help him – older cousins are sometimes looked up to as role models, I believe.'

'And there speaks the governess, I'm afraid, always ready to show the rest of us the path of duty!'

It was said with a faint smile that irritated her even more than the comment did. But she was tired of fencing with him, and aware that there were limits to what her position among them entitled her to say.

'Thank you for the reminder that my own path of duty lies across the bridge,' she answered politely instead. *'Arrivederci, signore.'*

But she walked away depressed by the encounter. Giulio Leopardi *looked* what he obviously was not – a man intelligent, interesting and attractive enough to enthral Zoe Hartman and, if gossip was true, his cousin's wife as well. The deception was part of the usual Venetian form, of course; here was the city of illusion par excellence, where nothing was quite what it seemed, and optical effects were dazzling until you learned how the tricks were worked.

Watching her move away, Giulio Leopardi registered the free stride that was different from the way Italian women walked, but she was a different, alien creature altogether. Perhaps that was why he'd stopped to talk to her. She'd been staring at the view and he could easily have passed by without her noticing him. But there'd been an air of sadness about her that had made him use the excuse of talking about Franco. He'd got a lecture for his pains, and been provoked into sneering at her. Laura had already complained to him that her lawyer's description of the governess he'd picked out had been less that accurate, but it was Giulio's considered view that Sarah Cavanagh as yet had scarcely begun the work of turning palazzo life upside down; she'd probably complete it before she left.

In honour of the day, lunch was downstairs. For once, Franco was present as well, and obliged to offer Sarah a just sufficiently courteous bow. There was also a stranger in the dining room, whom Beatrice happily pounced on as someone she was pleased to see. The count introduced him to Sarah as his nephew, Lucchino Vittoria, come from his home in Rome to stay in Venice for a while. She had to survive the usual appraising stare – it seemed to run in the family – but in Lucchino's case it became an appreciative and very pleasant smile. She thought he was exactly what the awkward lunch party needed – someone lively enough to jolly the conversation along, and kind enough to see that even Emmanuele wasn't left out.

The subject of the concert inevitably cropped up. After Count Fabrizio had listed the chief supporters expected to be present, starting with the patriarch himself, it was Beatrice's turn to seek for more important information.

'Mamma, everyone in Venice will be staring at you ... you'll have to look especially beautiful. What will you wear?'

But for the first time in his life Emmanuele felt ready to put a mere sister in her place. '*Stupido* ... people will be coming to *listen*; the music will be beautiful.'

Watching his eyes fixed on his mother's face, Sarah sent up a little prayer that she wouldn't decide to wither both children. The countess was outwardly calm, restored to some not very convincing equilibrium. There was no knowing what would destroy it again and drag them all into the eye of another emotional storm. For the moment, though, there was no storm; she was even smiling.

'You're both right. Of course I shall look beautiful – in crimson silk, Beatrice; I hope you approve! But, as Emmanuele says, the music *will* be more important than the way we look.' She shot a glance at Sarah. 'Still, I hope my accompanist won't be wearing anything that clashes with crimson?'

'No, sober grey,' Sarah confirmed. 'My ambition is not to be noticed at all.'

'Unlikely, I think, signorina.' Smiling at her, Lucchino didn't notice Donna Laura's frown of displeasure, but Emmanuele misread his mother's expression and, normal shyness forgotten, marched into battle again.

'There's no need to worry, Mamma. We are going to clap *very* loudly.' His earnest face promised her that all would be well, and it seemed to Sarah that, perhaps for the first time in his life, Laura di Brazzano was seeing him as he really was: a lovable, intelligent, small boy. It was by no means sure whether the count's gala evening would turn out to be a triumphant success or a failure best forgotten; but it seemed certain to mark some defining moment in their lives, after which nothing would be quite the same again.

When lunch was over, Lucchino suggested an outing on the lagoon. He looked hopefully at Sarah but she shook her head.

'I expect the children would love to go, Signor Vittoria; but I shall stay wedded to Donna Laura's piano for the next hour or two.'

It was left to Franco to inject a note of smiling malice into the conversation. 'I'll keep you company, Luc, in that case; not quite the same as the indispensable Miss Cavanagh, but better than nothing, I hope.' The words themselves weren't necessarily offensive but the intention behind them was, and confirmed when Franco's glance met hers with the steely hiss of sword blades saluting.

'Not the same thing at all,' Lucchino agreed, ignoring the tension in the air. 'I shall make *you* work; it will be your job to steer the boat.'

He was kind as well as adroit, Sarah realized, but she was thankful to leave the room.
Giulio Leopardi had been right about the
stresses and strains of life at the palazzo.
Italians were theatrical people who thrived
on drama, but it made them wearing to live
among.

She spent most of the following two days
rehearsing with the countess, while Lucchino cheerfully kept the children entertained and ran errands for the count, whose
organization of the gala seemed to be the
subject of frantic, frequent change. During a
break in rehearsals, Donna Laura announced the arrangements for the coming evening: Michele, having delivered her husband
and Franco early to La Pietà, would return
for Lucchino, Sarah and the children.

'That leaves you undelivered,' Sarah
pointed out.

The countess frowned at the comment.
'Not at all,' she said coolly. 'My husband's
cousin will look after me. After the concert
we must all attend a party given by Mrs
Vandenburg, but Michele will drop you and
the children here on the way back.' She
spoke in the condescending tones of their
first meeting. There were to be no grounds
for imagining that the governess's position
in the house had changed. Her own distraught outburst in the school room one
evening hadn't ever happened either.

The woman was under a great deal of strain, Sarah tried to tell herself – she must perform in front of several hundred very important people, who would also be highly critical, and they probably wouldn't spare her if her comeback proved a disastrous mistake. Even so, her manner was an affront now, and Sarah didn't in the least mind pointing out that Cinderella was invited, if not to the prince's ball, at least to Mrs Vandenburg's party.

'You *know* Elsa Vandenburg?' Laura enquired, sounding genuinely surprised.

'Not at all, but I met her god-daughter on the flight out from London. It's Zoe Hartman who has sent me the invitation. I can find my own way there, though, if I decide to go.' Two could play the *hauteur* card, after all. But, not for the first time, she was disconcerted by the countess's sudden change of mood.

'You can do anything you set your mind to, I feel sure, but wouldn't it be stupid to refuse the offer of a lift?'

'Yes, it would,' Sarah agreed honestly, 'and I hope I grew out of cutting off my nose to spite my face years ago!'

They were suddenly smiling at each other, aware that mutual understanding was vital if they were to be able to perform together.

Two evenings later, feeling sick with nerves,

Sarah went downstairs to find Lucchino and the children waiting for her in the hall.

'Our English heroine who has ridden to Donna Laura's rescue!' he announced, smiling at her kindly.

'Put another way, our English amateur pianist, who may prove the countess's downfall,' Sarah amended, feeling too overwrought now to cope with a charming compliment she would otherwise have enjoyed.

'Time to go,' Lucchino pointed out gently, 'but there will be no downfall, Sarah. Now, *en bateau, mes enfants*. It's a fine evening and we shall have a lovely ride to La Pietà.'

He was quite right; even Sarah sat entranced as usual by the spectacle of Venice at night, especially when Emmanuele's hand stole into hers, offering the comfort he thought she needed. All the same, the journey was too short; she wasn't calm enough when it was time to be handed out of the boat and confront the white marble faade of Santa Maria della Visitazione, otherwise known as La Pietà. Inside, unlike many Venetian churches that are permanently plunged into near-darkness, all was light and grace, with Tiepolo's huge *Triumph of Faith* painting blazing across the ceiling. They were early, and the rest of the audience was only just beginning to arrive – elegant enough in conventional evening dress but not to be compared with the splendours of the past.

'Imagine what it was like when Vivaldi was music master here, and his orphan virtuosi sang and played themselves into Venetian history,' Sarah said regretfully.

'I would have been wearing scarlet velvet or brocade,' Lucchino agreed, 'instead of a boring black dinner jacket; come to think of it, I should undoubtedly have been the *Doge!*'

They were smiling at the idea when Count Fabrizio bustled towards them, looking happy and relaxed now that his great enterprise was finally under way.

'My dear Miss Cavanagh – welcome,' he said, kissing her hand as if she were one of the duchesses and countesses it would soon be his duty to greet. Amused by the gesture, she found it touching as well; in some unexpected way it had given her confidence a welcome little boost. She was led away to join the other performers gathering in a side room, and found there an ashen-faced Laura with Giulio Leopardi. Her eyes glanced at Sarah without seeing her.

'I can't do this,' she muttered. 'I was mad to think I could. Giulio, you should have stopped me making such a fool of myself. Oh God, why *didn't* you?'

She was only just under control; could as easily walk out, Sarah realized, as go through with the concert. If the man holding her hands couldn't provide the reassurance she needed, the count would have two gaping holes in his programme and a lot of angry customers outside.

'*Amore*, listen to me, please,' he said in a low, gentle voice. 'The signorina is safely here – she hasn't run away or fallen into a canal, so that's your worst anxiety over! This waiting is very bad, but you've survived it a thousand times before, and the moment you begin to sing you'll be happy again – happier than you've been for years; *non è vero?*' His smile for her was full of such tenderness that Sarah felt it was something an onlooker shouldn't have seen. Whatever was between these two – and Elsa Vandenburg was surely right in believing it to be a love affair – it wasn't something to be dissected by malicious Venetian gossips while they sipped prosecco and nibbled the little sweet biscuits they loved.

Sarah turned away, but suddenly the countess spoke to *her*, sounding calmer now. 'What do *you* say, Sarah Cavanagh?'

It was time to muster every ounce of courage she could, and at least *sound* confident. 'Let's cry "God for Harry, England, and St George!" Signor Leopardi, Lucchino, and the children are outside ... waiting for you to trample over the competition.'

'Then we'll have to, won't we?' Laura slowly agreed. 'But it's *us*, you know; not just me.'

Sarah nodded, thinking that it was now time Giulio Leopardi went away. As if he read her mind, he gave her a little bow, kissed Laura's cheeks, and promised to be waiting for her in the interval. Then he walked away, and when Sarah hurriedly asked about the other performers in the room, Laura quietly described them – a solo pianist, a very prestigious string quartet and, as a bow to Vivaldi's own era, the choir of female voices that had the daunting task of opening the concert.

Giulio Leopardi was proved right half an hour later. There was the dreadful moment of walking out on to the platform when Laura's turn came, and the agonizing business for Sarah of adjusting a too-high stool. Then they nodded at each other, the opening bars of the first song rippled under the pianist's cold fingers, and they were off. Laura began with a tremor of nervousness but, looking out on to the hushed darkness in front of her, sureness and joy returned – this *was* what she could do, she would weave around all these bemused and faceless people in front of her the spell of Fauré's enchanted music.

Her three French pieces brought the first half of the programme to an end, and the audience was already in no doubt of the artistry that had been silent for far too long.

At the conclusion of the English songs, as the last exquisite note of 'The Green Hills of Somerset' floated towards heaven and died away, there was a moment of total silence, followed by a storm of applause. The Laura Kentish of old had been reborn in this beautiful creature, clad in crimson, who was now clutching the hand of a slender woman dressed in grey – English too, the programme said. Who would have believed, the Venetians told each other afterwards, that unromantic Anglo-Saxons could produce that kind of music?

Eight

It was over at last – the terror only just controlled, the unlooked-for triumph, and all the fuss and clamour that followed. Huddled in the stern of the boat afterwards, Sarah felt tired to the marrow of her bones. More than anything else in life, a quiet journey home to bed seemed desirable. Instead, she was on her way to a party, given by a woman she didn't even know. There would be still more fuss, and much more noise, because hundreds of Italians, released from the need to sit and listen, would all be talking again.

Mrs Vandenburg's palazzo was *en fête* – flambeaux lighting the exuberant stonework of the façade, music drifting out of open windows. Inside the house there was warmth, and the overpowering fragrance of white lilac and out-of-season lilies. Liveried servants ushered guests upstairs to the *piano nobile* where, resplendent in black velvet and a few flawless diamonds, Mrs Vandenburg waited to receive them.

Count Fabrizio advanced to bow over her hand, she kissed and congratulated Laura, then it was Sarah's turn. Remembered from her arrival with Zoe at the airport, the governess now merited a closer look. The choice of dress was clever, Elsa thought – distinctive among so much Italian flamboyance – it suited her unusual colouring. More important, though, her escort tonight was the Marchese Vittoria's son, Lucchino. Mrs Vandenburg was never at fault in matters concerning the social register.

'Miss Cavanagh, my god-daughter reckons you've been holding out on her! She expected to see you in the audience this evening.'

'I expected that myself until a week ago,' Sarah explained. 'When I can spot Zoe I'll make my peace with her.' Then she moved aside to make way for the next guest, and Lucchino shepherded her towards the comparative freshness of a window embrasure.

'You don't like crowds, even when you're not exhausted,' he suggested gently, 'and you're wondering why you came! A glass of wine and some food will make you feel better, but we can leave whenever you say the word.'

She obediently sipped the glass of wine he summoned from a hovering waiter, then smiled at him. 'Better already, thank you. But you're far too kind and I shan't dream of dragging you away. I expect you know most of the people here, and you must stay and talk to them. There's no problem about strolling home on my own – Venice is a very unviolent city.'

'Why *did* you accept Mrs Vandenburg's invitation?' Lucchino asked, watching her glance round the crowded room.

'Curiosity, mainly – I may not get another chance to attend such a high-class Venetian revel!' Her smile faded into gravity for a moment. 'Apart from anything else, I'm still on probation.'

'When the time comes, Laura will implore you to stay,' Lucchino predicted. 'She hasn't the reputation of getting on with people, especially with other women; but it's clear that she's decided she can trust you.'

Sarah's glance followed his to where the

countess, flanked still by Giulio Leopardi, was holding court. As usual, her husband was some distance away, listening courteously to an elderly marchesa. The evening's success had been his as well as the prima donna's, but Sarah couldn't help thinking that he'd been excluded from it now. She found herself wanting him to claim back Laura and remind his cousin's son, and everyone else, that it was for *him* to stand beside his wife.

But a moment later the small group of people around her was disturbed by someone else. A girl in a cloud of rose-pink organza broke in to take hold of Giulio's hand and, with a brilliant smile at the countess, lead him towards the ballroom next door, where couples had begun to dance. It was a bare-faced piece of poaching, Sarah reckoned, but Zoe had the tactical advantage of being on her home ground. No guest in her godmother's house could have refused her, even supposing that Giulio was blind to her ravishing prettiness in the pink dress, or to the fact that she was twenty years younger than the woman he'd just left.

Sarah's sympathy, directed at the count a moment ago, now veered round to Laura. The evening had held too much emotion already. Zoe's challenge – and Laura would certainly recognize it as such – had come at a bad moment. Her stricken face gave too

100

much away, and tiredness and strain, not visible until now, added to the sudden disintegration. She was adrift again, and helpless to hide the fact from anyone who looked at her. Sarah's small anxious murmur had scarcely left her throat before the scene changed again, because what she had longed for five minutes ago was now happening. Count Fabrizio had abandoned his elderly friend and was stationing himself beside his wife. He tucked her hand inside his arm, but kept his own fingers clasping it. Her ravaged face turned towards him, and Sarah saw his answering smile as he lifted her hand to his mouth and kissed it.

'Another outcome of this extraordinary evening,' Sarah muttered unsteadily. 'I've just seen Count Fabrizio clearly for the first time.'

Lucchino gave a little smile. 'You thought my uncle didn't care about his difficult wife? Quite wrong, Sarah; he adores her. Now, you must have some food; I think you're faint with hunger.'

She was settled at a small table and told not to move while he went foraging at the huge buffet arranged along one side of the room. Sarah did as she was told, wondering about the scene they'd just watched. Had they seen the abrupt ending of whatever had held Giulio Leopardi linked to Laura, or would Zoe find that even her youth and boldness and sheer desire weren't enough when matched against ingrained habit, long association, or just the older woman's refusal to let go.

Sarah watched Lucchino being intercepted as he threaded his way through the crowd. It was no surprise to see that everyone seemed to like him. Sophisticated but not world-weary, experienced but not cynical, he was above all a very kind man.

'You must have been hiding,' a blithe voice suddenly spoke beside her. 'I've been looking for you all over.'

'Until you decided to shanghai Giulio Leopardi and disappear next door,' Sarah pointed out, after a glance at Zoe Hartman's smiling face.

She was stared at in turn, but now Zoe's smile was fading. 'You sound stern, *amica*, as if I'd done something wrong.'

'Who am I to judge what's right or wrong?' Sarah asked tiredly. 'It *was* cruel, I think, but perhaps you'll tell me that you were being cruel only to be kind!' Then she shook her head at what she'd just said. 'Don't tell me anything at all; it's nothing to do with me.'

'I'll spell it out anyway, I think,' Zoe insisted. 'It was time Laura di Brazzano faced the truth. For years she's managed to make Giulio feel responsible for her – she could only feel secure and more or less content as long as he was there to dance attendance on her.'

'All right, but did you need to make her face the truth quite so publicly?'

Zoe gave a little shrug. 'OK, I chose the wrong moment for *her*. But I'm not sorry, Sarah. At least I've danced with Giulio. He won't be able to forget me now because I know he felt the same electric tingle that I did when he touched me.' Her mouth smiled again at the wonder of it, but she tucked it away in her memory to be lingered over later on. 'Why are you sitting here alone? You should be sharing the limelight with dear Laura.'

'Lucchino is at the buffet, getting food. He'll be back in a moment.' She looked across the room just as the eddying groups of people reformed to show her someone she hadn't seen earlier. Her sharp intake of breath sounded to Zoe so like a gasp of sudden shock that she stared anxiously at Sarah.

'Honey, something's wrong; you've gone all faint-looking. Are you feeling unwell?'

'I'm all right, thanks,' Sarah managed to murmur. 'I thought I recognized someone I knew. It can't be him – he must have a doppelgänger.' But she still stared in the same direction, at a tall, bearded man whose charming way of meeting a new acquaintance – head slightly inclined towards them

– was painfully familiar.

Intrigued as well as concerned, Zoe had the kindness not to pry. 'If you're looking at that tall man with the air of a Viking sea king, I can tell you who he is – Elsa's latest catch, a very fashionable academic called Professor Steven Harding, from London.'

'From Oxford,' Sarah corrected her quietly. 'When I knew him there only his students lost their hearts to him. He looked different then – no beard, and no aura of success!'

The crowd eddied again, and the man she could see now was Lucchino, steering his way towards them with a plate of food in each hand. He smiled wistfully at Zoe.

'This was meant for two of your godmother's famished guests, but courtesy compels me to offer *you* my lobster salad.'

'You're safe, *amigo*, lobster doesn't agree with me! In any case, I'm supposed to be looking after people, not enjoying myself with friends. *Buon appetito!*'

She moved away to smile at someone whose badge of office proclaimed his importance – the Mayor of Venice – who bowed over the hand she held out.

'Zoe's a heartbreaker tonight in that gorgeous dress,' Sarah said without envy. 'She's alight with happiness – the result of one dance with Giulio Leopardi.'

Lucchino shook his head at the dry note in her voice. 'You're more generous to her than to him. Will it make any difference if I tell you that he's my good friend? When his mother was killed, he was twelve years old. At the time of the accident his father was driving the car. From then on Luigi just retired from the world. The estate was left in the hands of a manager who robbed and nearly ruined it. As soon as he was old enough Giulio had the job of getting Belmonte back on its feet again. He's done it, but it hasn't made him an easy man to know or like.'

'Zoe hasn't found it a problem,' Sarah pointed out. 'She's enchanted with him, and it *isn't* just a passing fancy for a man who seems to belong to someone else. Will he understand or care?'

'There's been a long ... connection with Laura di Brazzano,' Lucchino admitted. 'I expect that worries you. But Giulio will hurt neither of them if he can help it.'

Sarah nodded and let the subject drop. She took another sip of wine from the glass a waiter had just refilled, and managed to smile when she saw that Lucchino was staring at her untouched plate and then at her.

'You've eaten almost nothing, and you look transparent with tiredness, *cara*. We can thank Elsa for a splendid party, and tell Fabrizio that we're going home. Does that sound right?'

'It sounds perfect to me,' she confessed. 'The truth is that I should have known better than to come in the first place.' Her voice trembled a little and he suspected that, for a reason he didn't know, she was close to tears. In a minute or two, with Roman finesse, he'd extricated them from the palazzo with all the proper things said, and led her out into the fresh night air, beneath a star-scattered sky.

'A water-taxi?' he suggested, 'or a slower gondola ride?'

'Neither if you don't mind, I'd rather walk back. I'm sure Mrs Vandenburg's party will be described in tomorrow's papers as a "glittering" affair, but I ought to know by now that too much glitter doesn't agree with me!'

It was all that she could say, because too many memories had her by the throat and conversation seemed impossible. Lucchino glanced down at her withdrawn, moonlit face and wondered with a touch of rueful amusement whether she would even notice if he stepped quietly into the canal beside them. She was the most honest woman he'd ever met, but also the most private; a combination he found hard to deal with. The setting, the lovely calm night in which they seemed to be the only people about, was romantic enough, but he knew that she was completely unaware of him. Male vanity was piqued, but it was the reason for her withdrawal now that mostly troubled him.

They walked as far as the bridge, then stopped halfway across, as everybody did, to look down at the dark waters of the Grand Canal, flowing out into St Mark's Basin, the Lagoon, and the Adriatic Sea.

At last Sarah spoke again, as if aware that a companion could expect her to.

'Zoe said once that Venice is haunted by ghosts. At night I have to agree that she's right. So many great houses shuttered and dark ... such complete quietness ... at a moment like this I can't help feeling that the city *is* dying. We shall be left with only the lovely shell of something that was once vibrant and real, not just a beautiful fantasy.'

'It seems to me,' Lucchino commented quietly beside her, 'that you know this place very well. You're sad because it's fragile and very vulnerable, but there's some other problem as well – a personal grief that's upsetting you.'

He saw her nod and because he didn't ask to know what it was, she found she wanted to explain.

'I came here first on my honeymoon ten years ago – the perfect setting, it seemed then, for my own particular fairy tale. Each time we came back afterwards, Venice was still beautiful, but our marriage became more and more unreal. The man I married had left me behind. By then my respected Oxford academic had turned into a famous television celebrity; but *I* was still the same old me, hating the glittering – that word again! – extravaganza that our life had become.'

'Are you still married to him?' Lucchino asked quietly.

'We got a divorce five years ago. I hadn't seen Steven Harding since – until this evening! He's the latest fish to swim into Mrs Vandenburg's net. Presumably he was with her at La Pietà, so he would have seen my name on the programme.'

'And he came and spoke to you, of course. Is that what has upset you?'

Sarah shook her head. 'He didn't come; the divorce was my idea, not his. He truly couldn't understand why I preferred to be a provincial schoolteacher rather than his convenient excuse for not getting embroiled with any of the adoring women who bored him. There were some, of course, who didn't bore him!' She lifted her hands in a little gesture that put the past aside. 'Sorry; I've talked too much about myself. I'll blame it on this very strange evening! To-morrow, back in my governess role, I shall be myself again.'

'Your temporary role, I think,' Lucchino corrected gently. 'You do it beautifully, and

Beatrice and Emmanuele are more fortunate than they realize. But you can't convince me that being a surrogate mother to another woman's children is what you're going to be doing for the rest of your life. I don't believe it, Sarah.'

She stared at him, disconcerted by the gravity of his face. Lucchino took most conversations lightly, but it seemed now that he meant what he said.

'I didn't claim governessing as my life's work,' she pointed out, 'but I'd like to be here for a year or two. Beatrice shows signs of becoming a likeable, interesting child, and Emmanuele is definitely considering throwing in his lot with the rest of us after all!' Her moonlit smile was suddenly beautiful. 'I could stay here talking about them all night, but there's no reason why you should find them as fascinating as I do! Tell me why *you*'re here, instead of doing whatever it is you do in Rome.'

'I don't do anything very much,' he said honestly, then smiled at her expression. 'You're the very picture of a Puritan maid brought up to believe that work is holy! I, on the other hand, believe it's wrong to take a job that I don't need and someone else does.'

'Praiseworthy, in its way,' she agreed, 'but don't you ever get bored?'

'Certainly not – my work is to enjoy life,

and to share my pleasure with others!'

'It is *exactly* what you do,' she had to admit, smiling at him, 'so how lucky we are to know you.'

His hand touched her cheek for a moment, but he only said they must move on because she was getting cold.

He took her hand to guide her down the wooden steps, and didn't release it when they reached terra firma, but she found herself grateful for the warm feel of his fingers; a Venetian night walk seemed to demand the contact. A lover's touch was what was really needed; but she could make do with a friend's hand if she had to.

They walked the rest of the way in silence, both aware that for the moment enough had been said. Back at the palazzo, Signora Vanni came out of her sitting room on the mezzanine floor.

'We walked, Claretta,' Lucchino explained. 'Michele will bring the count and countess soon.'

The housekeeper's face relaxed into a rare smile. 'Signori, the concert went well, I'm told. The children couldn't stop talking about it – even Emmanuele was chattering like a bird. Imagine it!'

She said goodnight, and returned to her own room, leaving them to go on climbing the stairs.

'The evening's discoveries aren't over yet,'

Sarah remarked, almost to herself. 'Signora Vanni cares about Emmanuele. I must have been blind not to have seen that before.' She halted on the landing. 'I belong on the next floor, but this is where you live; so I shall say goodnight and thank you for looking after me so beautifully.'

'I was taught to see a lady to her door,' Lucchino answered solemnly. 'It means climbing yet another flight of stairs, *cara*, but I don't begrudge the effort.'

On the floor above, when she turned to smile at him, he wondered what manner of fool the clever Professor Harding was that he'd had such a treasure in his hand and let it go. His own fingers gently framed her face and then he leaned forward and left a soft, lingering kiss on her mouth.

'Wrong man, I know,' he said a little unevenly when he lifted his head, 'but I'm the one who's here! Sleep well, dear Sarah, the triumph was really much more yours this evening than Laura's; I hope she acknowledges that.'

Then he turned and ran down the stairs, leaving her with the evening's final surprise – the rediscovered sweetness of a man's lips on hers.

Nine

She was prodded awake early the next morning. Beatrice, still in pyjamas and dressing gown, was perched on the bed, ready to pick a bone with her otherwise rather satisfactory signorina. She and Emmanuele had been bundled off home too soon the previous evening and missed some of the excitement; worse still, Sarah hadn't come back with them to discuss the finer points of their first evening engagement. They'd had to make do with Signora Vanni and Bianca, and even Pietro, the odd-job man.

Sarah apologized humbly and, while Beatrice next amused herself by trying on her own bare feet the silver sandals lying on the floor, looked out of the window above the child's head. The domes of the Salute across the canal were silhouetted against a pink-flushed sky; it was going to be a fine day.

'Shall we forget about lessons today – take

a picnic out instead?' She expected to see Beatrice smile, but only got a blank stare. 'What's the matter – don't you like the idea?'

'We don't have picnics. Eating food out of paper bags in the street is what common people do. It's what the *stranieri* do, Papa says, when they come to Venice.'

'Perhaps because they can't afford to buy meals in restaurants,' Sarah pointed out, resisting the temptation to add that the Venetian genius for milking visitors had been at work for centuries. She returned instead to the matter in hand. 'If I promise not to ask you to chew a pizza sitting on the ground in St Mark's Square will you join me on a picnic? We could take the *vaporetto* out to one of the other islands, where no one will know that Signorina di Brazzano is eating out-of-doors.'

Beatrice was familiar now with the *Inglese*'s strange habit of speaking solemnly when her eyes were smiling. She held out for a moment longer, then grinned hugely herself. 'I'll go and tell Emmanuele – no lessons today *and* a picnic!'

She danced out of the room, leaving Sarah to watch the colours deepening in the sky outside, and to reflect on the changes within the palazzo. A few weeks ago Beatrice had struck her as an overweight, self-important, and rather unlikeable child. She was still a little too plump, and a little too certain that in an unevenly divided world she was on the side that mattered. But already she was easily bearable, and would grow nicer with time. Emmanuele wasn't yet the confident, laughing, sometimes naughty creature he ought to be, but it was seldom now that he retreated to the sanctuary of the schoolroom window seat to watch a world he wanted to avoid.

The picnic outing was to give both of them a treat, but Sarah acknowledged to herself another motive as well. Today seemed to be a good day not to be inside the palazzo. There was no telling whether Laura would stay hidden away while she worked out how to deal with Zoe Hartman, or whether she had already prepared the next act of the drama her life seemed to require. Whichever it was, Sarah wanted the children not to sense tensions they couldn't understand. On her own account there were other things to avoid: memories of Elsa Vandenburg's party must fade a little before she could face Count Fabrizio or Giulio Leopardi again, and much more disturbing still was the possibility of bumping into Steven Harding. It was a cruel twist of fate to confront her with him again – an unfair test of recovered peace of mind. Cowardly or not, she'd hide with the children in the lagoon.

Consulted after breakfast, the house-keeper was inclined to think that Donna Laura wouldn't approve of the picnic excursion.

'The children don't normally mix on the *vaporetti* with ... with...'

'Ordinary people,' Sarah finished for her cheerfully. 'I know – Beatrice keeps me informed of all the things they don't normally do! But we're only going as far as Burano or Torcello, not putting out on a sea voyage.'

'Emmanuele is still not strong,' Signora Vanni insisted, 'and he and Beatrice can't swim.'

'Then they should certainly be taught,' Sarah pointed out. 'They're more likely to drown by falling into a canal than have the *vaporetto* sink beneath them.'

Claretta's shoulders lifted in the usual Venetian shrug; it conceded loss of argument but no change of heart, and her expression as she walked away to prepare the picnic said that it was a well-known English madness: a love of the sea, and boats, and driving unfortunate small children out-of-doors. Her revenge was to produce a wicker basket that felt as if it was filled with stones. Sarah accepted it as gratefully as she could and both of them shared an unexpected smile when Beatrice appeared in what she considered suitable nautical rig – jeans, striped jersey, and a bandana round her hair, like the ladies from the Gritti Palace wore when they set out for a day at the Lido.

Their own cruise started from the Fondamenta Nuove, and they disembarked from the *vaporetto* at Burano in time to see the fishing boats come in. It was excitement enough, but Beatrice lingered next over the *punta di aria* on display at the Scuola dei Merletti – lace so exquisitely fine that a breath was enough to lift it from their hands. For Emmanuele, it was the marvellously painted houses lining the canals that made him stare and then laugh out loud. Ochre, magenta, and Prussian blue, as far removed from tasteful pastels as the Burinese could find, were the colours reflected in the water outside their doors.

With the picnic basket beginning to weigh heavily, Sarah was glad to shepherd the children back on to the next boat to arrive, for the five-minute journey to Torcello.

There, on the grassy *piazza* in front of the cathedral, they unpacked Signora Vanni's lunch and fell upon her chicken patties with a gusto that Emmanuele, especially, never showed at home. Sarah was tactful enough not to remind Beatrice that she was doing what common people did, and foresaw from her pleasure in the alfresco meal no difficulty about suggesting picnics in the future.

Afterwards there was the lovely church of

Santa Fosca to visit, and then the ancient cathedral itself. They climbed to the top of the bell tower for a wondrous view to the far reaches of the lagoon, and even Beatrice listened carefully when Sarah described how Torcello first, and then Venice, came to be born.

Back at ground-level again, both children stood staring at the tremendous Virgin and Child mosaic that loomed over them from the ceiling of the apse – the Madonna black-robed and sombre against a golden background.

'The poor lady looks very sad,' said Emmanuele after a while. 'She's weeping, Sarah.'

'Of course she is, *stupido*.' This was Beatrice, taking advantage of some convent teaching to put Emmanuele in his place. 'She knows that baby Jesus is going to be killed.'

His small face, turned towards Sarah, was crinkled in a frown of anxiety. 'Didn't she know he wasn't going to *stay* killed?'

'Perhaps not then; afterwards she did.' She glanced at her watch, mindful of the walk back to the jetty. 'Time we left, I'm afraid. We can always come back another day.'

Emmanuele nodded, reluctant to leave the lady above his head to grieve unnecessarily. 'Yes, I should like to come back,' he said quietly, as he followed Sarah out of the church.

They didn't dawdle on the way, but Sarah saw no need to urge them to hurry; they had even a little time to spare. She was still thinking so when they turned the last bend leading to the jetty and saw the *vaporetto* already out in mid-stream, turning to head back to Venice. An old man watching the boat's departure ambled across to point out the obvious.

'You've missed it; boat's gone.'

'It's gone *early*,' Sarah insisted resentfully.

'Six minutes late,' their Job's comforter answered with a nearly toothless grin. 'Should have left at four o'clock. Next one's at six. You'll be on time for that!'

For once her sense of humour failed. This *wasn't* the moment for a watch-battery to have died on her unexpectedly. The two-hour wait in front of them would be very tedious, but that wasn't the worst of it. The day had been fine but it was still early in the year and the evening would be cool when the sun went down. Signora Vanni would be convinced that she had been right about the expedition; and if Elsa Vandenburg's party the night before had left Laura in one of her more intractable moods she could easily decide that the governess was incompetent and should be fired.

The children had followed the old man's thick Venetian dialect more easily than she had herself and already Beatrice's pout was expressing her displeasure. She wasn't, if she knew it, going to stand there for the next two hours without complaint. Although the afternoon was still warm, she managed a little shiver.

'It's very boring here, and Emmanuele will catch a chill, I expect,' she announced, sounding more pleased than anxious.

'No he won't because we'll go and wait at the Locanda Cipriani,' Sarah corrected her. 'I can also telephone from there and warn Signora Vanni that we shall be home late. Say goodbye to our friend here.'

With this done, she picked up the basket she was beginning to hate – whichever way she carried it, the damned thing *would* bang against her – then, with a cheerful smile for Emmanuele who was looking anxious, she led them back along the path. It wasn't a long walk to the Locanda but they'd already covered a lot of ground in the course of the day. Beatrice was now genuinely flagging, and the limp that Emmanuele had almost lost in the past week or two was noticeable again. By the time they straggled into the hotel, Sarah herself was tired, and also conscious that, after a day out-of-doors, all three of them looked much too grubby for the simple elegance that was the Cipriani's keynote.

She was explaining their arrival to the

receptionist in the hall when the door to an inner office opened and two men emerged to turn along a corridor. Sarah recognized one of them in the same moment that Beatrice did, too late to prevent a hail from the count's daughter that would have done credit to a Venetian fishwife.

'Giulio ... *guardi ... eccoci!*'

'Look at us by all means,' Sarah thought with dismay – a trio of refugees whom the impeccably-suited Signor Leopardi wouldn't even want to acknowledge. But perhaps fearing the same thing, Beatrice scurried towards him.

'We missed the boat, Giulio. Now we can't get home and *povero* Emmanuele is very tired.'

Short of shouting at them from where she stood, Sarah could only advance as well, doing her level best to sound calm and unconcerned. 'We *can*, of course, get home, but we have to wait for the six o'clock boat. When I've telephoned the palazzo and we've tidied ourselves up a little, we shall ask for some tea.'

His glance swept over her, registering – she felt sure – her sun-reddened, shiny face and untidy hair. She couldn't interpret his expression but guessed at a mixture of derision and enjoyment of the governess's discomfiture. So much for always being certain that she could tell other people what

120

to do.

'Your timing *here* was better than in the matter of the boat,' he pointed out. 'The Cipriani only functions in the summer season; yesterday you'd have found it still closed.'

With any other man she'd have admitted to not knowing, but it couldn't be done with this one. 'My watch-battery was what failed us, not my timing.'

His face remained unreadable and she realized she would always be at a disadvantage with him, not knowing what he was thinking; perhaps it was why she couldn't find anything to like in him, despite what Lucchino had told her of his life.

'I'm sorry I haven't time to offer you tea, but I can give you a ride back to Venice if you don't mind leaving straight away.' He said it with such casual, indifferent civility that she was tempted to insist that they would make their own way home ... stay at the hotel all night if they had to.

But Emmanuele was looking at her, aware, as usual, of any hostility in the air; and Beatrice was already smiling at their reluctant rescuer, pleasantly certain that *she*'d been instrumental in making it clear to him that they were there.

'Thank you,' Sarah said stiffly. 'The *children* would be glad of a lift.' Whereas she, given the choice, her emphasis suggested, would prefer to swim back to Venice rather than set foot on his boat.

He accepted this with a brief nod, shook hands with the man he'd been visiting, and led the way outside – a man of few words but no lack of understanding, she realized. He'd assessed her state of mind very accurately and no doubt reckoned that she'd got her just desserts.

Installed in the motor launch a few minutes later, she recognized the boatman as a friend of Michele's; by nightfall, therefore, the entire neighbourhood would have been informed that the palazzo children and the *Inglese*, who was supposed to be in charge of them, had had to be rescued. Beyond fishing out jerseys for both of them to put on, she left the children with their cousin. Beatrice kindly entertained him with whatever regurgitated facts she could remember about Torcello, while her brother shyly asked the boatman about the *bricole* that marked the navigation channels in the lagoon. Sitting in the stern of the boat, Sarah tried to lecture herself on the combined sins of false pride and ingratitude. It didn't matter that, having got off on the wrong foot with Giulio Leopardi, she would probably always be out of step with him; they didn't have to know or like each other. But he was listening with unexpected patience to Beatrice telling him what he no doubt already knew, so there was kindness in him for a child at least.

Without the stops that the *vaporetto* had to make it was a quick journey back across the lagoon. All too soon for Emmanuele, who loved all their water journeys, they had chugged out of the *Basino* for the Grand Canal and were nosing towards the steps beside the palazzo's water-gate. The boat-man kept the engine idling while Giulio Leopardi jumped out and handed his passengers on to terra firma.

'Excuse me for not seeing you upstairs,' he said politely to Sarah. 'I still have one more call to make.'

'Thank you for the ride – I hope we haven't brought you out of your way,' she replied, determined not to be outdone in couresy. 'You saved an inefficient gover-ness's bacon – if that ridiculous expression means anything at all to you translated into Italian!'

'I understand it well enough in English,' he said. 'I spent a year at Cambridge in my youth!' A faint smile touched his mouth, but she saw no amusement in it, only his enjoy-ment of putting her in her place again. She knew too little about these people she'd come among not to make mistakes, but it seemed that she could only learn by wrong assumptions.

He bent down to say goodbye to the

children, then added a parting shot for Sarah. 'Don't miss any more boats in the lagoon, signorina – I have to return to the mainland tomorrow!'

Before she could find a suitable reply, he'd jumped down into the boat again and there was nothing to do but follow the children, already running up the outer staircase. No doubt Zoe would bewail his departure; her own view was that the sooner he left the palazzo the better. On the *piano nobile* a surprise awaited them. The countess, not normally visible at this pre-*aperitivo* time of the day, was standing out in the wide hall that ran from front to back, dividing the house in two. Emmanuele smiled at her, ready for once to launch into an account of the day even before Beatrice could talk first. He wasn't allowed to start but, watching from behind the children, it seemed to Sarah that Laura di Brazzano made *some* attempt to hide whatever rage or anguish now possessed her.

'I'll hear about it later,' she said quickly. 'Go upstairs, please, both of you – Bianca's waiting and you look very grubby! I need to talk to Miss Cavanagh.'

They looked reluctant to go, but when her arm swept an unmistakable gesture towards the stairs, Emmanuele grabbed his sister by the hand and dragged her away. There was a short silence that Sarah decided not to be the one to break. The countess stared at her, biting her lip. At last she began with a complaint that didn't really interest her.

'Claretta said you insisted on taking the children on an outing against her advice.'

'She wasn't so against it that she refused to prepare a very nice picnic lunch for us,' Sarah pointed out with a reasonableness that she thought would inflame the woman in front of her still more.

'You said you were taking the *vaporetto*. You came back with Giulio Leopardi – I saw you. Did you spend the day with him?'

'No, we met accidentally this afternoon at Torcello; we were stranded there because my watch was telling me the wrong time. I took the children to the Locanda so that I could telephone Signora Vanni and say that we must wait for the next boat. Beatrice happened to spot Signor Leopardi leaving the hotel, and he offered us a lift home. If I should have asked permission before taking the children out, I apologize; but I thought you'd be tired this morning and sleeping late.'

She spoke formally, as she would have done at the beginning of their acquaintance. The hours they'd spent rehearsing together as equals were forgotten now. This was Contessa di Brazzano in front of her, and there was nothing equal about their relative positions. To be berated like an erring housemaid by a jealous, neurotic employer set a seal on the ruination of the day, but she suddenly felt too tired and too sad to argue with an unhappy woman driven by demons that she couldn't control.

'I should go and see to the children,' she suggested quietly.

'When I've finished talking to you, Miss Cavanagh. You mustn't imagine that being useful to *me* last night will endear you to Giulio Leopardi.'

'I don't imagine it, and have no interest in him whatsoever.' That, at least, had the ring of truth about it.

Laura's eyes sparkled with sudden malice. 'You nourish hopes of Lucchino Vittoria instead. Does he know that you were married to the man Elsa Vandenburg's besotted with at the moment? Professor Harding was indiscreet enough to mention it! Not, of course, that you should take Lucchino's attentions seriously; in Venice it amuses him to play the *homme galant* to you, but his life is in Rome and so are the various women that his name's been linked with.'

'All I nourish,' Sarah said, stung at last to sharpness, 'is the conviction that he's a kind and charming friend. As for my marriage, over a long time ago, he does know about it, and so did Mr Crabtree. If *he* didn't mention it to you, it was because he judged it wasn't relevant. I didn't expect to see Steven

Harding in Venice; perhaps because he was equally surprised, he was jolted into mentioning our marriage. For as long as I'm here I shall *not* be neglecting the children to amuse myself with him, Lucchino or any other man you care to think of. That made clear, I'll say goodnight and go upstairs.'

She turned the corner to the next flight, waiting to hear behind her the shrill instruction to pack her bags and leave. But it didn't come, and she reached the top floor surprised to find herself still a part of the palazzo establishment.

In bed at last, after toying with a supper she had no appetite for, she chose one of Henry James' most impenetrable stories to coerce her into sleep. But her dreams, though lurid and chaotic, held images that she could all too easily recognize: Steven was the erl-king himself, with Viking helmet and cruel smile; Laura was a Wagnerian tragic heroine, Isolde perhaps, weeping over Giulio Leopardi, got up to resemble an improbable Arthurian knight. Elsa Vandenburg was Princess Eboli, one-eyed and sinister, and Zoe a young seductive Carmen throwing out lures that Tristan, suddenly become a Spanish torero, was unable to resist. In this mad, operatic mish-mash, Sarah searched for a character who might be herself. But she wasn't there, and when she woke, drenched with perspiration from what had turned into a nightmare, that seemed the most disturbing thing of all.

Ten

It was Emmanuele that she found in her room next morning but, unlike his sister, he was content to watch the sunrise until she woke up. In his favourite place by the window, he sat with his chin resting on his hands, absorbed by the changing colours of the sky. She lay awake waiting for *him* now, thinking how strange it was that she hadn't known of his existence a month and a half ago, and how unbearable it would be if she wasn't always to know him in the future. At last he turned round and saw her smile at him.

'*Buon giorno*, Sarah ... where do we go today?'

'Into the school room, I'm afraid; we can't go on adventures every day. In any case, you must visit Father Ambrosio this afternoon, and Beatrice has a dancing lesson, *non è vero?*'

He nodded, accustomed by now to the mixture of English and Italian they spoke together. It might not have been what the countess intended, but Sarah reckoned that it made them feel at home in both languages.

'Father Ambrosio will know the sad painted lady we saw at Torcello?' Emmanuele asked next.

'I'm sure he will. You can talk to him about her.'

The smooth, dark head nodded again, but she had the feeling that Emmanuele's real reason for calling on her so early in the day hadn't yet been disclosed. It came after a moment's hesitation.

'Mamma didn't want to hear about our picnic. Why was she cross when we came home?'

Sarah had to hesitate in her turn. 'I think she was anxious, perhaps. Grown-ups seem cross when they are worried.'

His faint frown agreed that this was so, and she decided it was time to change the subject.

'Do you remember me telling you that I have nephews at home about the same size as you and Beatrice? Well, they'd like to hear from you. They don't know what it's like to live with a river outside their front door and go everywhere by boat when they can't walk.'

'So how *do* they go, Sarah?'

'By riding when they can, or by bicycle. They have a sister called Harriet who is too young to write, but she won't want to be left out. She'll draw pictures for you of her pony, I expect.'

Emmanuele's gap-toothed grin at last appeared. 'I shall send Harriet a drawing of a gondolier wearing his straw hat. Will she like that?'

'Love it, I should think; but John will be your real pen-friend.'

'Who can Beatrice write to?'

'John's elder brother, James; who is going to be a farmer when he grows up, exactly like his father.'

'And like Cousin Giulio also?'

Sarah tried and failed to imagine the elegant figure of Giulio Leopardi in the same company as the large, untidy countryman who was her brother. 'Well, something like,' she agreed cautiously. 'Now, scoot while I get showered and dressed.'

'I'll start on the drawing,' Emmanuele said. 'It will take time, Sarah.' Then he bounded out of the room, his mother's moods forgotten for the moment.

But they were harder for Sarah to dismiss. The moment would surely come when jealousy and pain would combine in an explosion that finally wrecked the household's fragile stability. And even if it didn't, how

130

much longer would Fabrizio di Brazzano tolerate a wife who demanded of him the love and loyalty she never offered in return?

But at least the school room was a cheerful place after breakfast, while Emmanuele painted a canal-side row of houses in colours the Buranese would have approved of, and Beatrice wrestled with the English words that would tell a boy called James Cavanagh how beautiful Venice was.

With both children delivered to their appointed places after lunch, Sarah had another reason for remembering Highfold – a birthday present for Meg was needed, and she knew exactly what it was to be; one of the lovely silk scarves to be found in the Mercerie. With the purchase quickly made, she walked back under the clock tower to fill in time – as all good Venetians did – by drinking an espresso at Florian's. A table sheltered from the afternoon breeze was empty under the roofed arcade, and she was sitting there watching the growing stream of spring visitors when Zoe Hartman's voice spoke behind her.

'Sarah! Just the governess I needed to bump into! But I can only stay a few minutes – an appointment with Elsa's wonderful but temperamental coiffeur calls! If I'm a minute late he'll refuse to see me.'

'Why bother?' Sarah asked. 'Your hair looks gorgeous as it is.'

'I'll come to that. First off, am I still in disgrace? You left Elsa's party so suddenly that I thought you'd had enough of me *and* my godmother.'

'It had nothing to do with either of you,' Sarah said firmly. 'I was tired, that's all, and Lucchino goes to so many parties that he didn't mind missing most of Mrs Vandenburg's.'

Zoe stared at her for a moment, unsure what to say next. This English friend was noticeably gentle in her ways but they didn't, Zoe thought, include tolerance of anyone who pried into her private life.

'One of Elsa's guests was someone you used to know...' she began gingerly. 'Professor Steven Harding. He was the celebrity I told you about.'

'And *you* now know that I was briefly married to him – the countess told me he'd mentioned it. This is where we agree, I think, that it's a very small world!'

Zoe's dark eyes examined her again, half-certain that they were missing something. 'You *sound* calm and unconcerned but you can't really be. Steven Harding's a *dish*, Sarah – every thinking woman's dream, except for me! If being without him doesn't break you up, it *ought* to, that's all I can say.'

Sarah looked at her own fingers; they were clenched round her coffee cup tightly enough to reveal how much self-control was needed not to shout an answer.

'We had a lovely marriage that didn't last,' she explained slowly. 'But it was the marriage itself that nearly destroyed me; that's why I manage much better now *without* Steven. End of story, Zoe.' She smiled at the other girl's expression. 'You're still at enchantment's earliest stage; why should my experience seem understandable to you?'

'It's understandable all right – I'm twenty-two, not seventeen! But this time it's different. That's why I can't let Laura win; it's for Giulio's sake as well as my own.'

Remembering what his farewell comment had been, Sarah looked doubtful. 'He said he was going back to the mainland today; you won't be seeing him now.'

Zoe's radiant smile reappeared. '*I* shall see him; Laura won't. Some friends of Elsa's hire a villa on the Brenta canal, and we're going to stay with them. They're neighbours of Giulio's.'

And almost certainly, Sarah thought, the tortured woman at the palazzo the night before had known about Elsa's friends at the villa.

'Oh God, I can see what you're thinking – I'm being unfair again. Is it some ridiculous English thing that says you can only fight with one hand tied behind your back? If so, I'll tell you that it sounds crazy to the rest of us.' Zoe's face said even more clearly that it wasn't a philosophy for any true-born American to subscribe to.

'We're not very whole-hearted about some battles,' Sarah agreed ruefully, 'probably the ones we don't really want to win! Fight for Giulio Leopardi whichever way you please, but remember that if Laura ever was your average English woman, she isn't that now; she's become thoroughly operatic.'

'I'll remember, but I won't feel sorry for her. Why should I? She's the Countess di Brazzano, for God's sake, not some poor helpless creature from a back slum.'

'She's not poor or helpless,' Sarah agreed, 'but try to feel sorry for her, please. It's been her habit for a long time to rely on Giulio Leopardi. I think she understands now that she can't do so any longer, because *you* are in the way.'

Zoe nodded, no longer defiant, but blushing with pleasure at what Sarah had just said. 'Yes, I do think I am – in fact I know I am; I couldn't feel like this about a man who didn't feel the same about me. It's the most perfect thing I've ever known.' She smiled shyly at the dazzling thought, then got up to go. 'I must run – the magnificent hairdresser will be waiting.' She leaned over to kiss Sarah's cheek. 'See you when we get back, *amica!*'

In a moment or two she was out of sight among the passers-by, whom Sarah now stared at without noticing. It was occurring to her for the first time that although Zoe and Laura were convinced of what *they* needed for security, contentment, or delight, the man himself might be harder to define. The American girl surely had marriage in her sights but perhaps he didn't wish for a wife? Perhaps he had a lover on the mainland with a husband she couldn't leave? Perhaps ... but before she could devise any more alternatives she was interrupted again – this time by the large figure of her own former husband taking the chair that Zoe had just vacated.

'I didn't ask if I could join you,' he remarked; 'you'd have probably refused. I saw how you abandoned Elsa's party the moment you spotted me.'

'I went because I was tired – which is something I seem to have to *keep* saying. Before long I'll have to leave again, and it will be to fetch the children, not to avoid you!' The smile that he remembered lifted the corners of her mouth ... He remembered her mouth too, of course.

'You're looking very well, Steven. The beard suits you.'

She could have added that he'd also put on weight, but even that seemed an advantage, too; he cut an impressive figure altogether. Something *hadn't* changed. His eyes – the beautiful light-blue of aquamarines, she'd thought long ago – still examined her critically.

'You've changed, Sarah – grown elegant and serene.'

It could have been a compliment sincerely meant; she suspected instead a reminder that was typical of him. He hadn't always described her in those terms. Appearances had been important to him, even when she'd been an untidy young graduate student and he'd been very much in love. Even then he'd wanted to make her over, make her into someone she knew she wasn't.

'Zoe told me what your job is here,' he said next. 'How did that happen?'

'I became a teacher, and went to live with my father at Pendock. He died three months ago and I had to move out of the rectory. I could have kicked my heels at Highfold, but I needed something worth doing while I decided where to go next.'

'I'm sorry about your father, Sarah.'

That, at least, she could take at its face value; he'd known how deeply she loved James Cavanagh. 'Enough of me. What brings *you* to Venice? Just inclination, or have you come to work here?'

'Work mainly – a course of lectures at the Cini Foundation over on San Giorgio Maggiore; but I want to rough out a book as well – the history of the Venetian Empire. It's been on my mind for years.'

'So you're here for some time – as Mrs Vandenburg's guest?'

'God forbid,' Steven said frankly. 'She's splendid company, and a splendid, generous friend altogether, but distinctly overpowering at close range! I've rented a couple of rooms at the Pensione Accademia for three months. It's just as pleasant as it always was, by the way ... or are our visits now expunged from memory?'

The quizzical air, the smile, the sharp, attractive persona of the man, were still as potent as they'd ever been, but she was familiar with them now. A successful magician needed to conceal the mechanism of his tricks – perhaps magicians did better not to marry? The odd thought made her smile, but it wasn't the response he was expecting. She *should* have been able to remember, to miss what they'd shared – dammit, to wish that she had it still instead of being a governess!

'I haven't forgotten the pensione,' she agreed, aware of not having answered his question. 'I haunt the paintings in the Accademia, so I often walk that way when I'm off duty.' His frowning expression made her change tack, to a subject he would prefer. 'The book idea sounds perfect – lucky you if it means wandering about the Aegean, looking for Venetian outposts of Empire!'

'It certainly means that, but most of the time I'll be working in the libraries here.' The topic she'd offered him was dealt with and put aside. 'Sarah, this governess business is nonsense, you know. Apart from the lack of ... well, status, which must be unpleasant enough in itself, there's the sheer waste of *you*. A student of the first class, which you *were*, doesn't end up teaching infants!'

She was suddenly reminded of what Laura had once said: 'I can't tell you how dreadful it is to be married to a stupid man.' It hadn't been fair to Fabrizio then, and no one could dispute the intellect of the man sitting opposite her now. Perhaps it was what Zoe would call a 'man thing' – the different cell-grouping that enabled them to contemplate the mysteries of the universe but miss what most women found obvious.

'This isn't where I shall "end up",' she pointed out calmly, 'because Emmanuele will go away to school within the next two years. Until then I'm content to stay here, teaching him and Beatrice, and coming to terms with myself – something I've dodged doing for too long!' She stared at him for a moment, no longer as sure as she'd once been of knowing what he was thinking. 'It's a pity that you mentioned me to Mrs Vandenburg – no one here need ever have known that the di Brazzano governess was

138

once your wife. I don't do you sufficient credit, I'm afraid!'

His blue gaze was fastened on her again, angrily now. 'It amuses you to think that, but you're wrong. However hard you find it to believe, my concern is not myself; I'm thinking of you.'

'Then I apologize,' she said quickly. 'But there's no need to worry about me. I would have taken up governessing years ago if I'd known how interesting it was going to be!' She looked at her watch and then got to her feet. 'Time to go, I'm afraid – the children will be waiting. Good luck with the lectures, Steven, and with the book.' She sketched a little farewell salute but didn't hold out her hand, and in a moment or two all he could see of her was a slender woman in a jade-green jacket and skirt threading her way through the afternoon crowd in the piazzetta. But when even that glimpse of her was lost, he could still see her in his mind's eye – thinner than he remembered, but perhaps that had something to do with the way her fair hair was drawn back now, revealing the delicate bones of her face. He'd never met a woman since who had candid grey eyes like Sarah's; never known anyone who'd given him the joy that she had done.

They'd come to Venice for the first time in high summer, seen the lagoon in the opalescent colours of dawn and the flaming splendour of sunset; they'd left the crowds behind and wandered through the nearly-deserted nooks and crannies of the city, lost in the enchantment of being in love in a setting for a fairy tale. He'd blamed her when the love story began to go wrong, and refused to give her the child that *would* have kept her with him. Now she tended another woman's children, and other men were free to see how beautiful she was. She *should* have stayed his wife. He was still angry with her; but, dear God, how sad he was as well.

Eleven

With Giulio Leopardi back on the main-land, and Franco and his noisy friends cor-ralled in Bologna again for the new term, the palazzo became strangely quiet. Not so much quiet as apprehensive, Sarah thought. Its remaining inmates seemed to walk about on tiptoe, afraid of disturbing a tranquillity that was entirely artificial. A communal anxiety hung over them, stifling normal chatter and laughter.

The children weren't invited to eat downstairs, and even Lucchino's visits to the school room had ceased. Sarah regretted this for their sake, even more than for her own. He did nothing for her pupils' concentration on the lessons she'd carefully prepared, but at least he made them feel they were part of their parents' life, instead of nuisances to be shunted to the top of the house and forgotten. There'd been no mention of him returning to Rome, and Sarah felt sure that he wouldn't have gone without saying goodbye; but *something* had interrupted his morning visits upstairs.

She was on the point of imagining that perhaps she, the children and the servants *were* alone in the great house when Signora Vanni appeared in the school room with a summons: the signorina, not the children, was required downstairs.

Her first sight of Laura di Brazzano was a shock; less than a week after the concert at La Pietà the woman had become an unhappy wreck. No longer young enough for beauty to survive without effort, she seemed to have simply given up. Illness would have justified her unbrushed hair, nightgown and négligée at nearly lunch time but, as far as Sarah knew, she *wasn't* ill, only submerged in misery.

'I haven't been well,' she muttered nevertheless. 'Bad headaches.' Then, with her compatriot's level glance at her, she suddenly spoke the truth. 'Too much wine and not enough food! I'll say it before you do.'

Torn between irritation and pity, Sarah went to sit beside her. Above the sofa, narrow beautiful windows overlooked the same view as her own, but at a lower level.

'Do you do the same as me every morning – look across at the Salute?' she asked. 'The light and the colours change each day, but it's always beautiful.'

There was no response from the woman beside her, and finally she answered her own question. 'All right, nothing seems beautiful at the moment. You hate Venice, and even your own family aren't worth making an effort for.'

'I ask Hubert Crabtree for a pleasant, ordinary governess and he sends me *you*,' Laura said bitterly. 'And you're wrong, as it happens. It's myself I hate, though there are plenty of people here that I dislike. They'd say it's my fault that I don't have friends ... "That cow Laura Kentish can't get on with anybody": I've heard *that* said often enough. But my standards were too high for them; that was the trouble.'

She was suddenly lost in the past, present misery put aside for a moment while she considered old injustices. Not sure that it was the right thing to do, Sarah brought her back to where the diatribe had begun.

'Why hate yourself? My father, who admittedly was a clergyman, was convinced of the redeeming power of love; hatred achieved nothing, he said.'

Laura's mouth twisted in a sneer. 'Spare me the theories of a saintly priest; I have to live in the real world.'

'So did my father, until he died three months ago.' Sarah gave her no time to try to apologize, but simply repeated the question in a different form. 'You're unhappy, but that isn't reason enough to hate yourself.'

'I'm a fool!' Laura suddenly shouted. 'That's what's the matter. I hate being had for a fool.' She got herself under control again and managed to speak more quietly. 'For years I believed in something that didn't exist; everyone else knew the truth, I expect. They must have enjoyed laughing at me – Zoe Hartman especially.'

Sarah hesitated for a moment, then plunged into the heart of the matter. 'If we're talking about Giulio Leopardi, as I suppose we are, I believe his affection for you did, still does, exist. Zoe believes it, too – that's why she sees you as a threat to what she wants very much herself.'

Laura's sunken eyes stared at Sarah. If it was true, then it offered a grain of comfort when she was rubbed raw with self-disgust. 'Zoe will get what she wants,' she said with certainty. 'I've accepted that now, but it's been very hard. People are full of malice, whatever you say, so it will go on being hard until they find someone else's stupidity to gloat over.'

There was a short silence in the room until Sarah spoke again. 'Then you must defeat them by making it *look* easy. Your husband will help you, and so would the children if you'd let them.'

Laura managed a sort of smile. 'Fabrizio is not only helping – he's in charge! That's really what I wanted to see you about. His sister and brother-in-law always cruise in their yacht at this time of the year; we're about to join them. It's not really my thing at all, but at least it will get us out of Venice for a while.'

'A regular postcard from ports of call would help our geography lessons,' Sarah suggested, 'and it would also enable the children to think their parents hadn't for-gotten them.' She said it lightly, but Laura's pale face showed a sudden tinge of colour when she spoke again.

'The other thing to say is that you won't be here.'

It was as unexpected as a blow over the heart, and yet it shouldn't have been, Sarah thought. She'd spoken what was on her mind once too often for the tense, neurotic woman who employed her. 'You don't want me to stay. I'm sorry ... it will mean yet another fresh start for the children.' She tried to speak calmly, then wondered whether she should have shouted her despair out loud. Would Laura di Brazzano, wrapped up in her own bitter disappointment, have heard *that* any more clearly?'

But the countess's face now was expressing something much simpler – sheer exasperation.

'Of course you have to stay ... but not *here*. The servants can take their holiday while we're away, and the palazzo will be shut down. The children would normally go to my sister-in-law in Rome, but they can't go to an empty house there, either.'

Having only made sense of the first sentence, Sarah felt suddenly light-headed with relief. There seemed to be a little problem still, but nothing that needed worrying about as long as she and the children were going to remain together.

'If we can't stay here on our own, I could take them to a quiet resort along the coast – it's high time they learned to swim,' she suggested.

'There are *no* quiet resorts,' the countess said with annihilating certainty. 'In any case, it's all arranged. Lucchino has been over to Belmonte to talk Giulio into ... I mean, to ... to settle it with Giulio and and his father.'

'They don't want us there?' Sarah asked bluntly.

Laura gave the little shrug learned from the Venetians. 'Luigi is a recluse who sees no one; Giulio has a huge estate to run – well, when he's not dancing attendance on Zoe Hartman. I don't suppose either of them *want* you there, but you won't fall over each other at Belmonte; there's plenty of room for all of you.'

It seemed a cavalier way of disposing of someone else's home, but Sarah could see a perverse kind of pleasure in the countess's face at the thought of it. She sensed that her troublesome governess didn't want to go to Belmonte – so all the more reason for her to put up with it. The Leopardis would be very reluctant hosts – all the more reason for them to be lumbered with a woman and children they didn't want. Laura didn't at the moment mind the whole lot of them suffering a little on her account.

Sarah swallowed the words on her tongue because even death seemed preferable to giving this unnatural woman the extra satisfaction of knowing how little she wanted to be at Belmonte on sufferance. Lucchino had done his best for Laura's peace of mind, but nothing for her own.

'When do we go?' she asked, in a voice that barely trembled.

'Michele will take you the day after

tomorrow. Pack for a month, please; I'm not sure how long we shall be away.'

It seemed to conclude the interview. Her responsibilities dumped on someone else, the countess could now bring herself to face the ordeal of a month's cruise on the Marchese Vittoria's no doubt sumptuous yacht. But as she stood up to go, Sarah felt anger draining away. This haggard woman had lost what she seemed to value most, and with it apparently had gone hope and self-respect as well. The Rev James Cavanagh would have been right to say that she was pitiable, not someone to hate.

'Try to enjoy the cruise,' Sarah suggested gently; 'give it a fair chance, and then come back and make a fresh start. Keep on singing now that you've begun again. It's such a terrible waste not to.'

'Waste or not, I shan't perform again, ever! La Pietà was my final public appearance, thank God.'

Sarah could only nod, aware of the reason. Laura remembered it not as a triumphant comeback, but the night when Giulio Leopardi had deserted her for Zoe.

On the way upstairs she glanced at her watch, suspecting that it must be failing her again. A mere fifteen minutes couldn't have been sufficient for the conversation she'd just had. Swung from pity to anger, to relief, and back again to pity, she must now stop thinking about Laura di Brazzano. If the wretched woman could no longer count on Giulio Leopardi as friend, lover, or whatever else he'd been, she had a more devoted husband than she deserved to help her back to stability.

There wasn't time to thank the gods above that the children weren't to be unsettled again; a task more immediately ahead needed attending to, and she hadn't got inside the school room before Beatrice fired the first question.

'Why couldn't *we* see Mamma, too?'

'Because she hasn't been well. Her headaches are *getting* better but she needs to rest in some good sea air. You father is taking her to join a cruise on the Marchese Vittoria's yacht.'

'Then we shall go to Rome instead of being here. That's what we do when Papa and Mamma are away.'

'Zio Guido will also be on the yacht,' Emmanuele pointed out correctly. 'How else does the boat sail?'

Beatrice's shrug dismissed the question. 'He has men to ... to work it, *non è vero*? There is nothing odd about that.' But her eyes were on Sarah's face, and because she was very alive to anything that concerned her own welfare she guessed the truth. 'We *aren't* going to Rome. Are we going to stay here?' It seemed flagrantly unfair, and already she was getting ready to protest.

'We don't stay here, because the servants must have their holiday, and the palazzo will be shut down.' Sarah anticipated Beatrice's roar and went quickly on. 'We're invited' – it stretched the truth a little – 'to visit Signor Leopardi's home at Belmonte. Michele is to drive us there the day after tomorrow.'

Emmanuele, at least, seemed pleased. 'A farm like James and John live on?'

'Not quite, but more like Highfold than Venice is,' Sarah agreed, registering the fact that a visit to Castelfranco hadn't so far been included in the children's education. Luigi Leopardi was clearly a man who could do very well without company.

She resumed the lesson but knew that the perfect construction of an Italian sentence was not receiving its due attention. Emmanuele, usually so eager to learn, was considering what livestock there would be at Belmonte that he could write to Highfold about. Beatrice was mentally reviewing her wardrobe; there would be other children on the estate who had no way of knowing what was reckoned *'le dernier cri'* in Venice. It would be up to her to bring them up to date with fashion's latest trends.

'Jeans or shorts and shirts,' Sarah suggested, able to read her mind accurately by now, 'and a cotton frock for when we go to Mass. We aren't likely to be mixing in high society!' Then she remembered something and smiled. 'But I hope we *shall* get to meet Bianca's English grandmother.'

For the rest of the day there was a pretence of following their normal quiet routine, but excitement was in the air and steadily rising. It was later than usual when they agreed to settle down in bed, and only when she went in to say goodnight to Emmanuele did the question she'd been expecting finally come.

'Sarah, why is Mamma not well?'

'A bad headache, I think, *tesoro*. It's nothing for you to worry about; by the time we come back she will be home again.' And Sarah said it confidently enough for him to give the little nod that said he was reassured.

But tidying up the school room afterwards she felt sad and apprehensive. It was the count's worry whether or not he could bring his wife back cured; her own concern had to be the children. For a month, at least, they'd be obliged to stay with someone who'd been talked into putting up with them. To keep them interested, entertained, and out of range of a reluctant host seemed to be one of the lesser-known labours of Hercules. Books and toys would help, but how many of those could she cram into a car filled with passengers and luggage?

She was, nevertheless, piling things

together – books, drawing things, and board games – when Count Fabrizio unexpectedly appeared in the doorway.

'Miss Cavanagh, you're getting ready to leave for Belmonte, I see. I'm sorry ... it's a disturbance for *you*, I'm afraid, as well as for my cousins. But what else can we do? My wife is ... well, you'll have seen how she is ... a change of scene is very necessary...'

So flustered and unlike himself did he sound that she felt obliged to reassure him as firmly as she had done his son.

'Conte, you need only think of Donna Laura. My own small worry is how much luggage we can take! The children must do *some* school work while we're away.'

His anxious frown lifted a little. 'Take whatever you like. It can travel with Pietro the day after you leave. Bianca will go then too, to spend a little holiday at Castelfranco, but also to help you.'

'Then we shall manage very well,' Sarah confirmed, smiling at him warmly. 'I hope Signor Leopardi won't even know we're in his house!'

'If so, he will miss a pleasure,' said the count unexpectedly, and a wistful note in his voice even suggested that he was aware himself of pleasures missed through always being busy elsewhere.

She supposed that the visit was over, but suddenly he began again, as if recent events

151

had shattered his normal, slightly pompous composure.

'I'm always busy you know – I have property to manage and many committees to sit on. Our efforts are very necessary if this beautiful but ailing city is to survive. I've felt privileged to help, and rather pleased with myself for doing so! But the truth is that I've been greatly at fault as well. My wife and children have had far less of my time than Venice has. Perhaps *you* think that, too?'

The simple question required an answer, not a polite evasion of the truth. She thought she could safely ignore protocol and be honest with him.

'Yes, I do think that,' she agreed quietly. 'It may not be the whole cause of Donna Laura's unhappiness, but it's certainly part of it. Beatrice and Emmanuele don't see many other children, but enough to know that their own family life doesn't much resemble anyone else's. It would be nice if Venice could manage with a *little* less of your time in future!'

Instead of taking offence at her bluntness he suddenly smiled, and she was reminded of the moment at Elsa Vandenburg's party when he had gone to stand beside his wife. It was *his* smile that Emmanuele had inherited.

'I suppose you've been wanting to point that out almost from the moment you arrived here,' he suggested. His fingers fidgeted with the crayons she'd heaped together on the table while he framed the rest of what he intended to say. 'When I married Laura she seemed ready to give up her career for a different one here, but it didn't work out, I'm afraid. She couldn't get on with Franco at all, and Beatrice was difficult. Children of her own would help, I thought. But Emmanuele was sickly from the beginning, and after him there were no more babies. Laura felt a failure, and eventually I gave up trying to convince her that we could be happy as we were. I shouldn't have done, of course – she was left lonely and ... vulnerable.'

'Emmanuele isn't sickly now – he's a child to be proud of. Between us we ought to be able to convince her of *that*,' Sarah pointed out.

'I think so, too,' the count agreed. He said it with a kind of pleased astonishment in his face, as if he himself was seeing Emmanuele clearly for the first time. Then he offered his shy smile again. 'I must allow you to get on with your own work, Sarah. I think you will enjoy Belmonte – it's very beautiful.' Then with the little bow that his son had also copied, he turned towards the door and went away.

Left alone again, she didn't immediately go on with her work. It had been a conver-

153

sation that needed thinking about, and it ended the strange day more hopefully than she'd expected. The di Brazzano marriage had seemed even more precarious than Venice itself, but if Laura had also made the mistake of seriously underrating a man who'd just shown himself to be dignified in near-defeat and unflinchingly honest, then surely there was some hope for both of them? It would be a comforting thought to take with her to Belmonte, and she would try to remember it whenever Giulio Leopardi tried her patience and her temper too far.

Twelve

The following day flew past, and all too soon it was time for them to be waved off from the palace landing-steps. After her monumental hangover the countess still looked pale, but at least she was there, beside her husband. She even smiled when Emmanuele promised to look at his atlas every day and imagine how far the marchese's yacht had travelled.

'We shall think of *you* at Belmonte,' his mother managed to say without flinching. Her voice sounded uneven but, watching her, Sarah decided that it wasn't because she thought of Giulio Leopardi entertaining Zoe there; the poor woman was suddenly realizing that the children could have gone with her, instead of being dumped on the man she must do without in future. But it was too late now: Pietro was already steering the boat out into the main stream, while the children kept on waving to the two diminishing figures on the steps who suddenly looked lonely.

They made the crossing to the mainland by boat because Count Fabrizio refused to garage his car at the Piazzale Roma, the Inferno-esque car park where all the road traffic into Venice was obliged to stop. On terra firma they said goodbye to Pietro and continued the journey by road.

The beginning of it was through the industrial dreariness of Mestre, which Michele denounced, with a lagoon islander's certainty, as being unfit for human habitation. Sarah agreed and didn't point out that many of his fellow Venetians nevertheless chose to live there and commute daily into Venice. But they emerged from the ugly urban sprawl at last into the green landscape of the Veneto.

The children enjoyed the drive for a while,

155

but the day had turned very warm and before long both of them were ominously quiet. Treviso, with its canals and hump-backed bridges, added to their misery by reminding them of Venice, and Castelfranco – charming walled town that it looked to be – made matters worse by not resembling the city they were used to at all.

They were still travelling northwards when Michele announced that they were now on Belmonte land; the gentle slopes on each side of the road were garlanded with vines belonging to their father's cousin, Zio Luigi Leopardi. The news awoke a flicker of interest that revived them long enough to finish the journey. Beautiful wrought-iron gates led to a tree-lined drive, and a moment or two later the house itself came into view.

Count Fabrizio had said that it was lovely, but he hadn't told her the half of it, Sarah thought. Apricot-coloured stucco steeped in centuries of sunlight and rain, shutters weathered to silver-grey, and tall, graceful windows, reflected themselves in a small lake. Peace and silence were almost tan-gible, as if house and lake were under some enchanted spell. Only one sound disturbed the stillness; a small bronze Pan piped his music – a tinkling cascade of water drops – in the middle of the lake.

Sarah followed the children out of the car,

inclined just to stand and stare at what they'd come to; but the tall figure of a man was descending the shallow, curving steps that led down from the front door and with a sudden spurt of relief she saw that it was Lucchino coming towards them.

'I was supposed to have left by now,' he said, smiling at Sarah, 'but I told my hosts they'd have to put up with me for a bit longer; I wasn't going to miss seeing you here!'

More truthfully, she thought, he wasn't going to miss making them more welcome than the Leopardis would. Watching him greet the children, and then Michele as well, she realized again what a kind and charming man he was.

'The longer you stay, I'm sure the happier we shall be,' she admitted frankly. 'Even Beatrice and Emmanuele are strangers in this lovely place; we can do with a friend who knows his way around, so that we needn't be a trouble to our hosts.'

Lucchino, ever tactful, refused to agree that this mattered in the slightest. He was about to try and suggest that the Leopardis, father and son, liked nothing better than to be hospitable, when Giulio himself came through a different doorway at the side of the house. Dressed, as Lucchino was, in faded jeans and a open-necked shirt, he wasn't the elegant sophisticate encountered

157

in Venice. But his frowning expression *was* the same, and Sarah reckoned that his friend had to be blind or insanely optimistic to suggest that she and the children were wanted at Belmonte.

He held out his hand in the briefest of greetings. 'I expected you later, Miss Cavanagh,' he said coolly. 'You must have made good time.'

'Michele did, knowing that the children were anxious for the journey to end – they're not accustomed to road-travel.'

Beatrice, no longer carsick and miserable, stepped forward to kiss her cousin, followed by Emmanuele. Sarah half-expected her host to then walk away, the reception formalities completed, but he went to speak to Michele, now busy unloading the car. Lucchino invited the children to inspect the ornamental fish in the lake, and Sarah waited to be told what to do next. The month-long visit, suggested so carelessly by the countess, already seemed impossible. She doubted whether they would even be able to survive a week unscathed. It seemed a pity when Belmonte *was* so beautiful, but once Lucchino went away there would be no one to even smile at them.

A moment later Giulio Leopardi spoke again beside her. 'Perhaps you should say goodbye to Michele – he's anxious to get on the road again.'

She called the children, wishing with all her heart that they could get back in the car and go with him. But a moment later they watched him drive away.

'Excuse me for not showing you round myself,' their host said next. 'Lucchino can take you on a tour of the estate tomorrow, and Domenica will look after you indoors. She's waiting to meet you.'

He led them up the steps into a wide, stone-flagged hall where a small woman, in the black dress of an upper servant, came towards them. Then, with the necessary introductions made, Giulio Leopardi reminded Lucchino of some work they were doing outside together and they walked out into the sunlight.

Memories of her first encounter with Claretta Vanni were vivid enough for Sarah to expect another frigid tour of inspection. But the first difference was that Domenica was smiling. The next was that she seemed genuinely pleased to show them the layout of the lovely house: salon, dining room, and morning room where breakfast and lunch were taken when it wasn't warm enough to eat out on the terrace. One door she pointed to but didn't open – the library was the *padrone*'s special room, and people only went there by invitation.

'*Molto gentile, il Signor Padrone,*' Domenica explained almost reverently, '*ma un po' triste*

159

ancora.'

Upstairs she led them to their rooms at the rear of the house. Now, instead of the Grand Canal and the Salute domes to look out upon, their view was a wide stretch of lawn, then orchards, and vine-covered hillsides. On the far horizon the great, snow-crested barrier of the Dolomites reared up between them and Austria.

Sarah turned to smile at the little housekeeper. 'The rooms are lovely, thank you. In fact, Belmonte is beautiful altogether.'

Looking pleased, Domenica agreed that it was so. 'Thanks to Signor Giulio,' she said earnestly. 'Much hard work is still needed but, God be praised, he is young and strong.'

Her devotion to the family she served said something about the Leopardis, Sarah realized, and there was also Lucchino's affection for them to take into account. It seemed unlikely, but perhaps there *was* a side to Giulio that he successfully kept hidden from the world at large; she hoped so if Laura di Brazzano was right in saying that Zoe would get what she wanted.

'Now, I'll leave you to unpack,' Domenica said next. 'The children's supper will be ready downstairs at six o'clock, signorina. Your own dinner is at eight o'clock with the family.'

It took a moment for the meaning of that

to sink in; when it did, Sarah shook her head. 'There's some mistake, I think. I can eat with the children if you like, or by myself as I do at the palazzo.'

'Not at Belmonte, signorina,' the housekeeper said cheerfully. 'Signor Giulio's instructions are that you join them downstairs. We always do what *he* says, you know.'

'I'm sure you do,' Sarah agreed, with a rigid smile, no longer surprised that the man had become the arrogant, autocratic creature he was. Pray God that Zoe changed her mind about him – she wouldn't always be as infatuated and malleable as she was now, and then the chances were that *their* marriage would become another divorce statistic.

A couple of hours later, with the children settled in their new rooms and tired enough after the long day to be ready for bed, she was steeling herself to go downstairs. She'd forgotten to ask Domenica how formal the evening meal was, but it scarcely mattered in any case. A simple tunic of jade-green linen would have to do; the clothes she'd brought with her included nothing more elaborate.

Ready too soon, but aware of feeling more nervous the longer she stayed in her room, she went downstairs into a lamplit but empty salon. A piano in one corner of the room beckoned, and she lifted the lid to run her fingers over the keys. The instrument looked unplayed, but someone had troubled enough about it to keep it tuned, and its tone was mellow and sweet. Unable to resist temptation, she sat down on the stool, and began to play Debussy's 'Clair de Lune'. Then, as the last note died into silence, a quiet voice spoke behind her.

'No one has used that piano since my mother died.'

Sarah swung round to see Giulio Leopardi standing by one of the long windows that led out to the terrace. The window was open because the night was mild, and the scent of an early climbing rose on the wall outside drifted in. She knew she would always remember its fragrance because of a moment when she'd been made to feel a trespasser on sacred ground.

'I'm very sorry ... I won't touch it again,' she said with difficulty.

His hands sketched an impatient gesture. 'Of *course* play it, whenever you like,' he insisted harshly. 'It isn't meant to be silent.'

She hesitated for a moment then spoke again. 'I've only come down now because Domenica said it was your instruction, but I don't dine with the di Brazzanos in Venice and don't expect to dine with you here.'

'What happens in Venice needn't concern us,' he answered in a quieter voice. 'At

Belmonte you're a guest.'

Sarah shook her head. 'I'm afraid that's not true – the children and I are a nuisance that you haven't been able to avoid. I know that your father prefers not to be sociable, and if he seems unhappy about my being down here, I shall ignore your instruction in future.'

His long straight mouth twitched and for a moment she had the strange idea that he was amused, but his voice sounded as calmly opinionated as usual. 'Then I must remind you that a governess isn't allowed to ignore instructions. Your duties *here* include sharing our meal at night.'

He was as smooth as a chunk of Carrara marble, she thought – nothing to get a grip on anywhere. Perhaps a sudden change of subject would disconcert him. 'Have you seen much of Zoe Hartman? She told me that she was going to be staying near Castelfranco.'

'We see her quite often. She'll be over again soon because she knows that you are here. Now, come outside and meet my father; it's warm enough for a drink on the terrace, but not to dine out there yet.'

He stood aside for her and caught the perfume that she used – more delicate than the 'Etoile de Hollande' clambering up the wall beside him. Her soft green dress suited the setting, where brighter colours wouldn't have done, and he could see easily enough why Lucchino had insisted on not leaving. This quiet, stubborn *Inglese*, so entirely different from the women his friend was in the habit of escorting around, was like her choice of clothes – unemphatic but effective.

Lucchino was sitting at the terrace table with a white-haired, frail-looking man who nevertheless got to his feet as Sarah approached. His thin hand felt cold as she put her own into it, but the shy, sweet smile he also offered suggested a more gentle disposition than his son's. He spoke in English, very correctly but slowly, and Lucchino pointed out that their guest could manage Italian rather more fluently.

'The signorina will bear with me, I'm sure,' the *padrone* said simply. 'Perhaps she is tired of hearing only our language spoken.'

Sarah's lovely smile acknowledged the courtesy, and then she thanked him for letting them come to Belmonte. 'I hope the children won't be too noisy, signore. I'll do my best to keep them out of range of the library windows!'

Suspecting that innate politeness would prompt the reply that no amount of noise mattered in the least, Giulio stepped in to forestall it.

'My father is hard at work in the library –

although *he* won't say so – on a comparison of your Elizabethan and our contemporary poetry.'

'An old man's way of pretending to be busy,' Luigi said wryly.

'Or a scholar's labour of love,' Sarah suggested instead. 'My own father had one as well. He was an Anglican priest whose dearest ambition was to persuade Christians and Muslims that they *could* join forces easily enough if they'd put prejudice and hatred aside.'

'A fairly hopeless ambition, I'm afraid, in today's world,' Lucchino put in.

'I think so,' Sarah admitted ruefully. Then amusement glimmered in her face. 'His sermons on the subject were a source of baffled pride to our dear parishioners!'

The *padrone* was still chuckling over this when Domenica arrived to say that dinner was ready indoors.

The meal was simple but delicious: risotto, as much the staple antipasto for north Italians as pasta was for the south, then veal with salad, cheese and fruit. The wine, like most of the food they ate, came from the estate. Enjoying it all, and the conversation that went with it – inspired, mainly, by Lucchino – Sarah tried to remember how much she'd dreaded coming downstairs. But still mindful of what Steven would no doubt have described as her 'status' there, she didn't linger when the leisurely meal was over, but stood up and said goodnight. There was a little silence when she'd left the room, and Giulio had returned to the table after opening the door for her.

'Extraordinary!' said Luigi Leopardi at last. 'I mean that Signorina Cavanagh should be a governess.'

'Well, yes,' his son agreed. 'But remember that she's a very extraordinary governess! Three months ago Beatrice was a too plump, too self-aware brat, and Emmanuele was an inarticulate, pale ghost who limped about the palazzo as if he didn't belong there. The children she will keep away from your windows tomorrow aren't recognizable as those little misfits at all.'

'Then I shall insist on meeting them,' Luigi said, getting up to leave. 'If Miss Cavanagh has made such a difference at the palazzo, I suppose we should consider what she might do here! *Buona notte*, my dears.'

It was Giulio who spoke first after he'd gone.

'Our *Inglese* has made a difference already, wouldn't you say? My father enjoyed himself this evening; he wasn't merely being courteous to the stranger that *you*, my friend, had wished on him. I can't remember the last time I heard him laugh out loud, and I doubt if you can either.'

Lucchino eyed his host across the table. 'Why not call Sarah by her name?' he suggested quietly. 'I'm glad the *padrone* made her feel welcome – it's more than you did this afternoon. She was bound to think you didn't want her here.'

'I *didn't*; still don't!!' It wasn't quite a shout, but sounded much too vehement all the same. With Lucchino's astonished eye upon him Giulio managed a wry smile. 'Take no notice, Luc, it's been a long day and I'm tired. Sarah Cavanagh will go back to Venice, back to England in due course, and soon we shan't remember that she was here at all.'

Lucchino chose not to comment on that. 'Laura's breakdown has upset you,' he said instead. 'But none of the muddle was your fault – you just got trapped into helping her.'

'Into *trying* to help her! I think I made matters worse in the end.'

Lucchino hesitated for a moment, then risked a snub by going on. 'You know me – the fool who rushes in with good advice for a man who's more than capable of running his own life! But I'll say it anyway. Laura is Fabrizio's responsibility now; fear of upsetting *her* mustn't spoil your future with Zoe.' He examined his friend's face but found it unreadable. 'She *is* the future, isn't she, or do you have a strong desire to tell me

167

to mind my own business?'

'Would I be that rude to a fool who only wishes me well?' Giulio's rare smile shone for a moment. 'Yes, I think Zoe is the future, Luc ... It's high time I had one, after all, and she seems very happy here.'

It seemed a strange way to phrase his intention to take a wife, but even Lucchino knew when probing had gone far enough.

'You'll both be happy,' he said instead. 'Zoe is as pretty as a picture, but she's much more than that – intelligent, lively, vivid, and ready to lavish her whole loving heart on you. What more could a man ask?'

'What indeed?' Giulio agreed, then put the subject aside. 'Bedtime, I think. Your first task tomorrow is to guide our guests round the estate, and something tells me that they will rise with the dawn!'

But when Lucchino had said goodnight and left the room, he still sat there alone – not thinking of Laura and the past, and not even of Zoe and the future. Instead, he was remembering a moment when he'd walked round the side of the house and there, before he expected her, a slender, fair-haired woman had been standing looking at the house. The moment didn't last, of course but, just for as long as it did, it had been his absolute, entire conviction that Sarah Cavanagh belonged there.

Thirteen

It was Lucchino who went in search of the children the following morning, not the other way round. He found them in the little room Domenica had said was 'theirs' while they were at Belmonte, but instead of the geography lesson Sarah had proposed, they were writing letters – Highfold had to be informed where to send their next correspondence.

'I've come to offer the guided tour,' Lucchino explained, 'but my customers don't look ready for it.'

'The customers must suit *your* convenience,' Sarah said, smiling at him, 'and in any case, I expect they'd rather be out of doors.'

'Then follow me, ladies and gent – we begin outside this very room and cross the yard to the cantina.'

They went out into the lovely, sunlit morning and he explained about the cantina – a place where small children couldn't roam freely, because serious work was done there when Giulio's grapes were brought in at harvest-time and the complicated business of making them into wine was begun.

The cantina *was* interesting, and the orchards and vineyards were beautiful in their spring green and blossom, but Emmanuele's heart was given to the livestock, especially to a pair of enchanting donkeys that James and John must hear about. For Beatrice, the high moment of the tour came with what they arrived at last, a secret garden hiding within its walls a splendid swimming pool – there'd been no mention of such a thing at Highfold!

Lucchino explained, as he had in the cantina, that here the children shouldn't come on their own.

'Certainly not,' Sarah agreed, 'they aren't able to swim! I know it's all wrong; they live surrounded by canals and don't even know how to float.'

'Then why shouldn't we teach them? The pool temperature isn't up to Mediterranean levels yet but Giulio is swimming already. If you're brave enough to suffer in a good cause, I shall steel myself to join you.'

'Let us shiver together by all means! But our first problem is that the children don't have any swimwear. If Castelfranco has the sort of shop we need, is there a bus we can catch?'

Lucchino looked pained. 'Of course

there's a bus – this is rural Italy. But my *macchina* is at the door. It would be even easier to go in that. We could see the sights of Castelfranco at the same time.'

She doubted if a morning spent trailing round a small town he already knew very well could be reckoned much of a treat, but he was smiling at her now and she remembered what he'd said – the object of his life was simply to spread pleasure.

'Then we accept gratefully!' she said. 'All I need is to fetch some money and let Domenica know we're going out.'

Installed in Lucchino's cream-coloured Alfa Romeo – Emmanuele, bursting with pride, allowed to sit in the front seat – they set off for a little walled town that looked even more attractive at close range, with its surrounding empty moat now converted into a charming park.

The shopping took longer than it might have done, owing to Beatrice's inability to choose between pink frills and blue and white polka dots, but at last Lucchino was able to offer refreshment at a café in the piazza. Sitting there, he intercepted Sarah's wistful glance at the cathedral.

'Giorgione's "Madonna and Saints" *is* stunning,' he said, 'if that's what you're longing to see. But we shall have to come back another time; the *duomo* will be closing soon.' Then he smiled at the look of surprise in her face. 'I'm afraid you don't expect me to know that a strange and wonderful artist was born in this little town, much less that the cathedral altarpiece is probably the most flawless thing he ever painted!'

'I had no reason to be surprised,' she admitted, 'except that you *do* rather like pretending to be an amiable drifter with nothing serious on your mind at all. But the disguise is wearing rather thin!'

Lucchino gave a shout of laughter in which Emmanuele delightedly joined, not because he really understood the conversation; he knew very well when the people he was with were happy in each other's company.

Sarah smiled too, but took pity on the children. 'The cathedral can wait for another day, but not the pool, I think. Let's go, shall we?'

It was too close to lunch time, all the same, when they got back, and the terrace table was already laid – for five places, Sarah noticed. Guests were obviously expected, and she went in search of Domenica to ask where the children should eat.

'Outside of course, signorina, with Signor Lucchino and the *padrone* himself. Imagine it, he wants to meet the *bambini*!' The housekeeper smiled at the thought of it – for once her dear, elderly friend wasn't going to stay alone in the library.

Sarah tried to look equally pleased, but she hurried the children upstairs to tidy themselves for the presentation with a twinge of anxiety. Beatrice would probably want to hog the limelight and chatter far too much, and Emmanuele was still equally capable of saying nothing at all.

Out on the terrace again they found the *padrone* already there, and Lucchino waiting to make the introductions. There was nothing to blush for so far – Beatrice's curtsey erred on the theatrical perhaps, but she'd learned at her dancing class how to do it very nicely. Emmanuele made the bow copied from his father and then offered a charming, shy smile as well.

Lucchino, adroit as usual, got the conversation started, and soon the children's awe of an elderly relative disappeared, and the *padrone* discovered how easy it was to talk to them. When lunch was over Emmanuele ran indoors to fetch the all-important atlas, so that his parents' route could be traced on the map, but he was at pains to make something clear.

'We like it *here*, Zio Luigi,' he said earnestly, 'don't we, Bea?'

She might once have insisted that *they* should have been on the marchese's yacht as well, but lunch on the terrace with grown-ups had been a great improvement on the nursery routine at home, and there was the pink bikini still to come! So, with Sarah's eye upon her, she agreed that her brother was right and smiled engagingly at a white-haired relative who seemed much more interested in what they had to say than most of her parents' friends.

At this appropriate moment Sarah hauled them indoors to recover from lunch before their first swimming lesson, and Luigi Leopardi smiled at his remaining guest.

'Nice children! I wonder why Giulio didn't want them here?'

'Because he remembered them as they were. Now, they're really very pleasant to have around.'

The *padrone* considered this for a moment, then ventured on to what Lucchino thought of as more difficult ground. 'I hope that Laura can recover from whatever ails her. Sarah Cavanagh won't always be here to take her place.'

How much, Lucchino wondered, did a very intelligent but reclusive man know of the world he'd chosen to retire from? More, probably, than the rest of them suspected. 'I don't think Fabrizio's wife has been physically ill,' he suggested with caution. 'The problem's been more mental ... more emotional. But the cruise with my parents is sure to do her good.'

'Laura is a taker, I fear,' the older man said quietly. 'Perhaps it's what we have to expect

174

of artistes – they must draw their creative strength from other people.'

Lucchino nodded, but didn't answer, and the *padrone* then disconcerted him with another change of subject.

'Giulio's young American friend seems to like being here. I can't find anything to say to her, but that doesn't matter. He hasn't been happy since he was a boy. That's all I want now – to see *him* happy.'

'Zoe has the same ambition,' Lucchino suggested gently. 'I think she'll achieve it.'

Sarah didn't hesitate that evening about going downstairs, but she made sure of arriving on the terrace at the right time. Permission to play the piano in the salon might have been given, but not in a way that encouraged her to take advantage of it.

As it turned out, the man she preferred to avoid arrived only as Domenica called them in to supper. For Sarah it was a reprieve, because she couldn't feel at ease with him or help suspecting that he *wanted* her to feel uncomfortable. She would have liked to offer him the truth: her discomfort was only with him. Between the *padrone* and Lucchino and herself there was the shared contentment of friends.

Their talk that evening was of Florence and the extraordinary flowering of art and architecture under the Medicis. Encouraged by Sarah's deep interest in the subject, Luigi Leopardi dipped freely into his store of knowledge, and only when the long, leisurely meal was over did he ruefully apologize for having talked too much.

'But I shall blame it on our English guest,' he said, smiling at her. 'She listens too intelligently.'

His other guest made a face at Giulio, across the table. 'We do *not*, is what your father is saying, my friend. But she has the unfair advantage of a pair of very speaking grey eyes!'

'Not to mention close acquaintance with a noted historian, I believe,' Giulio pointed out, then wanted to apologize for the snide remark.

Sarah answered coolly. 'Yes, it's true – I had that privilege.' Then she ignored him and spoke only to Lucchino. 'Thank you for looking after us today. The children loved the swimming lesson, but you mustn't spoil them with too much attention. We can muddle along on our own now.'

Lucchino shook his head. 'Unless my friend has some disagreeable task for me tomorrow, I shall be there. I'm sure the exercise is very good for me!'

A lovely smile lit her face for a moment, then she said a general goodnight and left the room. Soon afterwards the *padrone* did the same, explaining that he felt a little more tired than usual.

When his father had gone, Giulio poured more wine and looked across the table at Lucchino. 'I get the impression that I missed something by not being here today. Why should my father be tired?'

'Perhaps because he's had a more sociable time than usual. He shared our lunch on the terrace, and then wandered out again to watch us cavorting in the pool. The children can't swim, and it's time they learned.' He grinned suddenly at the look of disbelief on his companion's face. 'I'm not making it up – and I'll offer you a small wager that the *padrone* won't lunch alone in the library for as long as Sarah and the children are here; he enjoyed himself!'

There was silence in the room for a moment, then Giulio spoke in a quiet voice that was nevertheless tinged with pain. 'I was right not to want them here.' He saw Lucchino about to protest, but went straight on. 'If you think I begrudge my father pleasure, you're wrong. The peaceful routine he had here suited him; how does it help him to get used to a different life that can't possibly last? Fabrizio will bring Laura home and, whether she's restored or not, Sarah will take the children back to Venice. At that point your own enthusiasm for Belmonte will suddenly wane and my father will be left lonely again.'

Lucchino's nod accepted the truth of it, but he pointed out something else. 'The *padrone* is more concerned about *you* – rightly so. You work much too hard and you look tired to death, my friend.'

The room's soft candlelight was kind, but it showed him Giulio's brown face clearly enough: its bones too prominent under the taut skin and the sprinkling of silver in his dark hair. He wasn't forty yet but he looked older, a man whose youth had been spent saving Belmonte for the people whose lives had depended on it. At last he replied to what Lucchino had just said.

'Hard work isn't exhausting; uncertainty is! Today I made up my mind to stop shilly-shallying, and I'm very glad I did.' There was another small pause before he went on. 'On my way home this evening I called at the Villa Mara.'

'Where Zoe and Elsa Vandenburg are staying,' Lucchino commented.

'Yes, though not for much longer. Elsa is going back to Venice the day after tomorrow, and then straight on to some other visit. Zoe could stay on with the Lambertinis, but doesn't want to – understandably; they're very boring people! She could also return to Venice, but she'd be alone there.'

'So you've invited her here?' Lucchino guessed.

Giulio nodded. 'She jumped at it. Wants to

see Sarah Cavanagh in any case but also hopes, I think, that with other people here it will be easier to get to know my father. They haven't been very successful yet at understanding one another.'

He wiped a hand across his eyes, as if the gesture could remove whatever uncertainty still troubled him, and smiled suddenly at his friend. 'You may have to bribe me not to tell your Roman friends how you spend your afternoons at Belmonte!'

'I'm enjoying myself,' Lucchino answered with unexpected seriousness. 'They're nice children now, but even if they weren't I'd do much more than put up with *them* to help Sarah.'

'Yes, I gathered that,' Giulio said briefly. 'I shall be out early in the morning, so perhaps you'll tell her about Zoe coming, the day after tomorrow. Now I'm going to turn in. What about you?'

'Not yet – there's a late film I might watch.'

But when Giulio had left the room he stayed where he was, thinking about their conversation. A decision had been taken about the future – that much was clear. His friend wouldn't have gone out of his way to invite Zoe to Belmonte otherwise. There'd been a worrying lack of joy in his announcement, but Lucchino at last worked out the simple reason for it: Giulio had to learn to be happy. He'd got involved with Laura as a very young man, when she was a beautiful and celebrated diva. With little to offer her then, he'd lost her eventually to Fabrizio and a marriage that hadn't worked out. Laura had reclaimed his allegiance and become dependent on him. Since then, he'd grown steadily more reserved and more wary of emotions. That sort of reticence couldn't be melted overnight, but Zoe would manage it in the end – with perhaps a little guidance from himself, Giulio's oldest friend. One way or another the amiable drifter – he remembered Sarah's phrase with a wry grin – was being kept busy at Belmonte, but he didn't begrudge the effort. He was even beginning to feel quite useful, which was something he never did in Rome.

Fourteen

Even by the following day it was clear that a pattern had been set: the small amount of school work that Sarah still insisted on; then a long walk; lunch shared with the *padrone*; and after a brief rest, a swimming lesson when the afternoon sun was warm on the pool and the walled garden was sheltered from the breeze.

Already the children looked different. Beatrice, no longer overweight, showed signs of the slender long-legged teenager she might soon become. She wasn't by inclination a country child, but a seam of sweetness was surfacing that made her share Emmanuele's deep pleasure in everything that went on at Belmonte. The change in *him*, Sarah thought, was even more astonishing. He walked as far as they did now, without flagging, and instead of avoiding the other children on the estate, he reckoned it would be nice if Cousin Luc could teach them *all* to swim in the pool.

181

The news that another guest would soon be arriving pleased neither child very much – Emmanuele because he was very content with life as it was now arranged, and Beatrice because she suspected that the American signorina would want to become the centre of attention, a role that she still liked to play herself.

Sarah couldn't help sympathizing with both children privately. Zoe was a likeable engaging companion, but she would change things just by being there. Either Signor Luigi's quiet life would be encroached on even more, or he would retire into his library again to wait until he was left in peace.

That evening, when she went downstairs there was already a change because he was in the salon, not sitting on the terrace.

'Giulio tells me that you play the piano very beautifully,' he said. 'Play something for me please, Sarah. A Chopin nocturne if I'm allowed a choice.'

The music was already propped up on the piano, seeming to insist that – whether it would cause him pain or not – he wanted to hear it again. So she sat down and did as she'd been asked, and the sad, haunting melody filled the quiet room.

'Thank you,' he said when the last note faded into silence, 'thank you very much, my dear. Now I want to show you someone

– come with me, please.'

He led her across the wide hall into the library, flicked on a lamp, and gestured to the portrait that hung above the fireplace. 'My beloved wife – Eleanora – who played Chopin almost as exquisitely as you do.'

Sarah saw in the painted face looking down at her all that the *padrone* had lost when his wife was killed: kindness, warmth, generosity and, judging by the faint smile on Eleanora's mouth, humour as well.

'She was lovely,' Sarah said quietly.

'Yes, she was … and it was I who killed her. Perhaps you didn't know that.'

Even after all the years since then she could hear the anguish in his voice. Grief hadn't faded with time, but stayed his constant companion.

'I knew about the accident,' she managed to say at last. 'Lucchino told me, very briefly.'

The distress in her face silenced the *padrone* for a moment, then he spoke in a different tone of voice. 'Forgive me for being melodramatic just now, and upsetting you. The accident happened when we were coming home from the mountains. I couldn't see the black ice on the road and the car skidded out of control into a wall. Eleanora was killed outright; I was merely bruised and scratched. It *was* an accident and somehow Giulio managed not to hate me for depriving him of such a mother, but the waste of it still haunts me.'

'It's not all waste,' Sarah murmured. 'Eleanora still lives in your memories of her, and in your son; she will even live in *his* children some day.'

Luigi nodded, either too courteous to deny what she'd said, or perhaps a little comforted. 'I've been selfish, keeping you here talking, but tomorrow our little quartet will change, I understand. Thank you for the music, Sarah.'

He held the library door open for her and she walked out into the hall just as Giulio Leopardi came down the stairs. She couldn't accuse him of showing resentment that she'd been invited into his father's sanctum – he was too self-controlled for that – but she was conscious again of how little he wanted her there. It was an odd feeling, to know that she aroused such hostility, but not to know the reason for it. Their initial brush over Franco had been sharp but surely trivial?

In the dining room, though, he joined in the conversation with his father and Lucchino, and when Sarah mentioned that it would be Emmanuele's seventh birthday in a week's time, it was he who suggested a party.

'It must include *all* the children on the estate, of course, supposing that Emmanuele wants a party at all.'

Sarah considered this for a moment. 'Only a few weeks ago I'd have said it was the last thing he'd want. Now, I have the feeling that he'd love it – he's very much in favour of sharing things.'

'Then I'll speak to the *fattore* and Domenica; after that it will be up to them and you.'

It wasn't the most cordial suggestion she'd ever heard, but at least he'd offered it and she tried to sound adequately grateful. Then they talked of other matters: the prospects for the grape harvest, and the whereabouts of the house Lucchino thought of buying in the north; but the conversation didn't flow as easily as it had done before. They were trying too hard, it seemed to Sarah, to make up for the fact that Giulio Leopardi was saying almost nothing at all. She decided that Zoe Hartman couldn't come soon enough. Awkwardness wouldn't survive in her bright company, and with her there even the most taciturn host would have to make an effort.

Zoe arrived in time for lunch the following day, delivered by her godmother who agreed to stay and eat with them before continuing on to Venice. The *padrone* greeted them very courteously, but then excused himself from lunching with them on the grounds that he was in the middle of an important piece of work in the library. He looked solemnly at Sarah as he said this and, just as gravely, she looked back. But his absence didn't offend Elsa Vandenburg, who considered him too unworldly to be interesting; and since his conversation always nonplussed Zoe, she was very relieved to see him go.

But still the lunch party on the terrace had its anxieties, mainly because Emmanuele fixed Elsa Vandenburg with an unblinking, fascinated stare that even she found trying. Sarah suspected him of wanting to work out whether being Zoe's godmother made her immensely old or immensely holy; but neither possibility seemed to match her beautifully made-up face and elegant cream trouser suit. Rather than give him time to put his question into words, it was safer to explain that the children must return to writing invitations to his birthday party, and leave the foursome on the terrace.

The evening meal was over and the children were settled in their rooms, reading themselves to sleep as usual, when Zoe tapped on Sarah's door. She was already dressed for the evening, ravishingly pretty in a sleeveless silk dress in her favourite shade of pink. It was the perfect choice against her dark hair, and Sarah was glad to tell her so.

'In fact, you look wonderful altogether, and radiantly happy. Belmonte agrees with you more than the Villa Mara did, apparently!'

'I can't tell you how God-awful and stuffy *that* was. Dear Giulio's home is something else!'

'Because it contains him?'

'Well yes, of course,' Zoe agreed with an enchanting blush that made her look seventeen again. 'A tent in the desert would do if *he* was in it ... in fact it would do very well!' She fingered the odds and ends on Sarah's dressing table, not really seeing them at all. 'You know, I was beginning to think I was mistaken ... that it wasn't a two-way thing after all; just *me*, falling for someone older and more experienced and, because of Laura, almost certainly out of reach. I got very down, and reckoned that when we left the villa I might as well go back to New York. I couldn't take Italy any more, not without Giulio.'

'So what brought you here?' Sarah asked, knowing that the question was required.

'*He* did – my darling knight on a white charger rode up and ... well, he didn't quite throw me over the saddle, but he said I was to come here!'

'Satisfactorily masterful,' Sarah agreed solemnly, and heard the American girl's trill of laughter.

'Oh, I've missed you,' Zoe said happily, 'and I'm so *glad* you're here. I got the feeling before lunch that you and old Signor Luigi understand each other very well. You've got to teach me the trick, Sarah, because at the moment we're not on the same wavelength at all; in fact, I wouldn't be surprised if he winces every time I open my mouth!' She said it lightly, but her expression had grown serious. 'It's important, because Giulio adores his father; so I've *got* to get on with him too.'

Sarah hesitated for a moment, then took the bull by the horns. 'Are you sure that Giulio and Belmonte are what you want, Zoe? I don't think you need worry about Laura any more – she's Count Fabrizio's responsibility; but Giulio Leopardi is almost twice your age, and his life is here. It may look idyllic on a morning in May, but the winter can be long and harsh this far north. A little skiing up in the mountains may be all the fun you'll get.' She was tempted to say more – that Giulio himself would be a difficult and demanding husband – but she stopped herself in time. Zoe knew him better, and no doubt knew a side of him that hadn't been on offer to his cousins' governess.

As if she guessed what Sarah hadn't asked, Zoe answered the question anyway. 'Being married to Giulio will be all the fun I need, and I think – no, I guess I'm sure – that's why he asked me to come, so that I could make up my mind.'

'Then I wish you very happy,' Sarah said gravely. She looked at the time and made a little face. 'You're dressed but I'm not. See you downstairs.'

But when Zoe had blown her a kiss and floated away, she didn't immediately do anything about getting ready for dinner. She was remembering what had been said about the *padrone*, who now had no difficulty at all in talking to a not quite seven-year-old child, but seemed to find pretty, vivid, sophisticated Zoe too much for him. He just needed practice, Sarah decided, and Zoe needed patience; they had their love of Giulio in common and that would be all the trick Zoe needed.

The evening that followed convinced her. Luigi Leopardi didn't find much to say to his new guest but he smiled at her most kindly, and this time Giulio exerted himself to such an extent that Sarah glimpsed the young, carefree man he might have been. He could match, and even top, Lucchino's performance as a raconteur, it seemed, when Zoe's sparkling eyes were upon him. Her American pizzazz combined with his Italian brio were all Belmonte needed to bring it out of the shadows of tragedy. 'For lo, the winter is past ... And the voice of the turtle dove is heard in our land' – the Song of Solomon's lovely words echoed in her mind, and she smiled at the *padrone*, hoping he saw that same hopefulness in Zoe Hartman and his son.

From the following day onwards a slightly different pattern established itself, in that the afternoons spent around the pool now included Zoe as well, sporting – to Beatrice's private grief – a wonderful variety of swimwear. Sarah still insisted on the children working in their room for the first half of each morning, and after that they went walking about the farm once the obligatory visit to Emmanuele's donkeys had been made, with titbits wheedled out of Domenica. She was determined to keep to this routine, because it suited the children, but also left Lucchino free to look after Zoe when Giulio couldn't abandon work in order to entertain her. Governess and children were not invited guests – she was very clear in her mind about this – and it behoved them to be as little nuisance as possible. This led her one morning to set off to catch the bus to Castelfranco, once the children had been handed into the *fattore*'s care, for the purpose of delivering their invitations around the estate.

She had walked the length of the drive, and most of the half-mile along the road to the bus stop, when an unfamiliar car pulled up beside her. The door was opened, and

190

Giulio leaned over to instruct her to get in. She was past the age of cutting off her nose to spite her face so – temper rising nevertheless – she did as she was told.

'To save you enquiring,' she said with heroic calm, 'I'm going to Castelfranco, to see Bianca and her grandparents.'

'I know, Domenica told me.'

'And the children are in the safe hands of Signor Bruno.'

'She told me that as well.'

'So, I don't understand why *you* have a face like thunder and I'm made to feel like an erring housemaid.'

He accelerated with more violence than she thought his car would like, but decided not to mention the fact. It might mean that they drove to Castelfranco in complete silence, but that seemed safer than offering any more provocation. At the end of another mile he spoke again himself.

'You do *not* have to stand waiting in the road for a crowded, uncomfortable bus if you want to go somewhere; you simply ask to be taken.'

'We've had this conversation before,' she pointed out gently, because irritation had died in the sudden knowledge that she'd offended some deeply ingrained code of what was due to anyone living under his roof. 'I'm not used to being looked after, and even an uncomfortable bus ride

191

wouldn't be much of a hardship – I should probably enjoy chatting to the other passengers if I could cope with the dialect they speak.'

He glanced briefly at her, then returned his attention to the road. 'You can have that pleasure another time. For now, I'll drop you at Emilio's door, and collect you in time to get us home for lunch.'

'I was planning to go on to the cathedral after seeing the Rasinis.'

Between gritted teeth, she thought, he adjusted the arrangements. 'I'll collect you from the cathedral at noon – it closes then.'

Nothing more was said until he stopped the car at the entrance to a narrow alleyway.

'The second door on your left. They're nice people, Bianca's family. You'll like her grandmother especially – she's as stubborn as you are!' And with that he drove away.

But he was right about Emilio Rasini, and his roly-poly wife Jane, whose blue eyes still marked her out from the people she lived among. They welcomed Bianca's *signorina inglese* with the kindly warmth that seems to come naturally in Italy, pressed coffee on her which she enjoyed, and wine which – at ten thirty in the morning – she refused; and then Emilio promised to deliver his granddaughter to Belmonte, in good time to help with the birthday celebration.

Bianca herself kept smiling at the thought

of the party. 'Imagine it,' – Domenica's phrase too, Sarah remembered – 'little Emmanuele *wanting* a party!'

'He's not quite so little now,' Sarah explained. 'The swimming lessons are making him grow, I think.'

It was difficult to get away from such hospitable people, but she hurried to the cathedral with half an hour to spare – time enough at least, to look at the altarpiece Lucchino had spoken about. She stood in front of it, filled with the delight that any true masterpiece can't help but inspire. The Madonna, serene and lovely, with her attendant saints, set in the spacious, sunlit landscape of the Veneto in which Giorgione had grown up.

'It's beautiful, *non è vero*?' enquired a quiet voice beside her.

She turned to see Giulio standing there, as if he'd also been looking at the painting for some time.

'Beautiful beyond words,' she agreed. 'I shall have to come again, but I'll bring the children next time in case they don't get another chance to see it.'

With nothing more said, they left the cathedral and walked to where his car was parked. The drive back to Belmonte was equally silent, but some of the serenity of the painting seemed to have stayed with them, because for once she could feel no tension in the air; they might have been friends, who knew each other well enough for conversation to be unnecessary. It wouldn't last, but it was very pleasant while it did.

Fifteen

Postcards from several Aegean stopping places had given the children the pleasure of knowing that their parents still remembered them. The atlas had been duly consulted, and Emmanuele's map duly marked up to show the progress of the marchese's yacht. But there'd been no mention of his birthday, and Sarah knew that no party, however magnificent, would weigh against a simple message from his mother and father.

Even when the day itself dawned, in the pearly haze that promised a cloudless sky and heat to come, still nothing had been heard. There were presents from everyone else, including a magical globe that spun round and round from the *padrone*, but none of them had the name on it that Emmanuele's heart was looking for.

Then, just as Sarah was inwardly berating a cruelly selfish couple who didn't deserve a child at all, much less the one they'd got, Lucchino walked into the room with two more parcels. One, from himself, contained a music stand of just the size a small boy would require. The other, coming from his 'loving parents', held a black leather case into which a gleaming flute had been carefully fitted. Emmanuele lifted it out, scarcely listening to what Lucchino was saying.

'I shall blame Sarah if you don't like it. She said you wanted to learn to play this thing, so I knew what to suggest when your parents telephoned.'

'That's why you weren't here yesterday,' Beatrice said accusingly.

'Quite right, sweetheart. Castelfranco doesn't run to musical instruments. I had to make a dash back to Venice for it.'

Speechless with delight, Emmanuele went to hug his cousin, and then stood stroking the little silver flute with gentle fingers. Sarah watched him, thinking that any other child she knew would have insisted on blowing into it at once. Emmanuele was content to wait, understanding that he must be taught how to use it properly. Till then, he had his splendid globe, and the adventures of Badger, Mole and Ratty to read about in the beautifully illustrated copy of *The Wind in the Willows* that Sarah had given him, and all his other presents.

By early afternoon everything was in readiness for the party. Long trestle tables had been set up on the terrace, with a place for every child on the estate. There was a magician to entertain the guests, and a sumptuous tea provided by Domenica, with the help of Bianca, who was now installed at Belmonte.

Nearly thirty children of assorted ages required a lot of looking after, and Sarah was too busy to notice the late arrival of Giulio who – after a hasty shower and change of clothes – slipped into the place Beatrice had been keeping for him against all comers. He smiled at her and accepted a slice of birthday cake, then looked with astonished disbelief at the sight of his father, not only present but deep in conversation with the curly-headed imp who belonged to the *fattore*'s daughter. Next to them, and joining in whenever there was a communication problem, Sarah serenely shovelled ice-cream into the mouth of Domenica's youngest grandson.

It was only towards the end of the afternoon, when the guests were reluctantly beginning to go home, that she realized that someone unexpected was also there. Franco di Brazzano was sitting with Zoe, whose Italian had been under great strain with children who spoke no English at all.

196

'Nice of you to remember Emmanuele's birthday,' Sarah said, determined to give the devil his due. 'He's been rather missing his parents.'

Franco looked pleased to be able to correct her. 'I'm afraid I *didn't* remember, but Giulio invited me. Now that I'm here, though, I find it very interesting. The *padrone* doesn't make a habit of sitting through an afternoon like this, and Lucchino normally runs a mile from squalling children! I can see that I underestimated the English after all!' It was said just lightly enough for anyone overhearing them to imagine that Franco spoke in fun, teasing the *Inglese* he was fond of. Sarah felt certain that Franco's usual insolence had been intended.

'Signor Leopardi and Lucchino are both kind enough to want a small boy to enjoy his birthday,' she remarked calmly. 'You must be glad about that – you're his brother after all.' Then she gave him a sweet smile and walked away.

She was intercepted by Zoe, with what the American girl thought was good news to impart. 'Dinner out tonight, Sarah – in Treviso – to give Domenica a rest. Well, to give *us* a rest as well! Signor Luigi doesn't want to come, so we can have a light-hearted evening for a change. After an afternoon of sign language with these kids, I can't tackle another two-hour conversation about the Italian Renaissance!'

'You try too hard with him,' Sarah suggested. 'If *you* would relax, so would he.'

'I *can't*; I'm too busy trying to find something intelligent to say. But tonight, thank God, we'll just gossip and have fun.'

'Who are "we"?'

'Giulio, Lucchino, Franco, you and me, of course.'

Sarah shook her head. 'Sorry, Zoe, but *not* me. I'm full of ice-cream and birthday cake, and I'm also rather tired.' It sounded a reasonable excuse, she hoped, whereas the truth – that food eaten with Franco would probably choke her – was better not said, even to the girl beside her.

Zoe didn't look entirely surprised. 'I thought you might say no. It isn't quite your thing, is it? Too lowbrow and frivolous!'

'You've been listening to Franco,' Sarah said lightly, and saw Zoe blush. 'Excuse me, now, there's a lot of clearing-up to do. Have fun this evening.'

She turned away, thinking that she could have guessed exactly what Franco had said. The governess was a soured, nearly middle-aged specimen of womanhood whose only enjoyment was in depriving others of the more natural pleasures she couldn't have herself. He wouldn't believe that she'd known more of passion and delight and pain than any of his own adolescent lusts had provided. If he'd said that she was lonely at her heart's core, *that* would have been true; but such loneliness was something he hadn't learned about yet.

It was also true that she *was* tired after the strenuous day, and she wasn't sorry to see that Beatrice was already asleep when she went in to say goodnight. But Emmanuele was still awake, with all his new treasures lined up where he could see them.

'Good birthday?' she asked, smiling at him.

'Lovely!' he agreed with great contentment. 'Even Zio Luigi said he enjoyed it and he doesn't like parties really – so that proves it.'

She'd noticed before that Emmanuele favoured proof of things he thought important – perhaps it meant that he was going to be a scientist of some kind. His arms hugged her tight when she bent down to kiss him, but he was already half-asleep before she turned out the light.

It was much too early to go to bed herself, but she was restless and disinclined to sit reading in her room. Then she remembered Eleanora's piano, needing to be played, and thankfully went downstairs. Not Chopin tonight – she wanted something less romantic, less heart-catching. A more astringent Frenchman would suit her mood better – Debussy or Ravel.

Sitting quietly as the last note of the piece died away, a voice spoke behind her, as it had done once before. Her heart's normal rhythm faltered for a moment but it wasn't Giulio Leopardi's voice this time.

' "The Girl with the Flaxen Hair",' the *padrone* said. 'I can just see her, can't you?' He stared at Sarah's lamplit face and wondered why it looked sad. 'I thought you'd gone out with the others. Why didn't you?'

'Mainly because I wasn't hungry.'

'And perhaps also because you were tired? You *look* tired, child.'

The kindness in his voice threatened to reduce her to sudden tears. She couldn't think why this should be so, unless it awoke an echo of the loneliness she'd acknowledged to herself earlier.

'Come and share a glass of wine with me,' Luigi said next. 'I think it will do you good.'

She followed him across the hall into the library, grateful for his gentle company. Unlike Zoe, she felt no need to shine with him, or even to hold her own; he wouldn't mind if she preferred to say nothing at all.

'I asked Giulio about the "noted historian" he mentioned one day,' the *padrone* said after a moment or two. 'He told me you were briefly married to him. Perhaps that still makes you sad, or perhaps you miss your dear father?'

'A bit of both, I expect,' she admitted;

then her mouth sketched a faint smile. 'And there's something else that's entirely my own fault! Governesses are not supposed to grow too fond of the children they look after!'

'Aren't you also afraid that Beatrice and Emmanuele will grow too fond of you?'

Her shoulders lifted in a little shrug. 'Not really. I'm important to them at the moment because I'm here; when I'm not, they'll forget me soon enough. Quite rightly so; of course they must.'

He nodded, but returned to the subject of Steven. 'Your former husband is in Venice, I understand. Does that upset you, Sarah?'

She smiled in spite of herself, thinking that whoever had imagined the *padrone* to have given up on observing the rest of the world was seriously mistaken. 'No, it doesn't upset me,' she answered after a moment's thought. 'My marriage failure was final and very complete. I don't have the slightest hope that Steven and I could do better if we tried again.'

Luigi nodded again. 'But it doesn't mean that you should expect failure with someone else. I know that I'm thought not to notice or understand what goes on, but I should have to be blind not to see the impression you've made on Lucchino.'

'He's a dear friend,' Sarah insisted, and then was startled by the *padrone*'s forgiving smile that said she wasn't being honest with him for once.

'And like the children, he's going to forget about you the moment you go away? I don't think so, my dear, and I know him very well.'

She felt obliged to go on arguing. 'He likes the company of women, and I happen to be here. Apart from that, kindness is his middle name and spreading happiness around is his charming philosophy. That's all there is to it, Signor Luigi.'

The *padrone* gave a mock bow, accepting defeat. 'What a pity – I thought I could see him keeping you in Italy!' Then, as if afraid of having embarrassed her, he spoke of Emmanuele's flute instead until she said it was time to go, and he escorted her to the door.

'Thank you for the wine and the company,' she said and, because it seemed natural to do so, reached up to kiss him goodnight. He returned to his armchair and spoke, as he often did, to the painted face of his dead wife.

'She's wrong about Lucchino, my dear one. I expect Laura has told her that he's overfond of ladies or some such nonsense, but he'll convince her in the end.'

In no hurry to go to bed, he was half-drowsing in his chair when Giulio walked in.

'I saw the lamplight and knew you were still up,' his son said. 'I'm sorry we left you alone – you aren't in the habit of that nowadays!'

'I wasn't alone,' Luigi said serenely. 'Sarah came down to play the piano; then we talked and drank a little wine together.' He glanced at his son's face. 'Perhaps I had a pleasanter evening than you did!'

'Perhaps,' Giulio agreed briefly. 'But now it's time we both went to bed. Let's hope the children are back in Venice before Beatrice has a birthday. I'm getting too old for all this excitement!'

It took him out of the room smiling, but the smile had required an effort, the *padrone* thought. He said as much to Eleanora, and finally turned out the lights.

After breakfast the next morning, when the children had left the table, Sarah asked how the previous evening had gone. Zoe tried to sound enthusiastic but, looking puzzled, suddenly confessed to the truth.

'I'm lying, of course, it was nearly a disaster. Giulio started out in a bad mood that he didn't recover from, even though he tried quite hard. Then Franco was fool enough to sneer at *you* and got a trimming from Lucchino. At that point I reckoned we might as well abandon ship, but your darling man took us in hand and sort of rescued the evening.'

'As darling as you like, but *not* mine,' Sarah said with unexpected heat. 'Lucchino is here, at a loose end; he's also exceptionally kind. But we are not in the middle of a Victorian romance where the governess ends up in bed with the young milord. Could you please remember that?'

'Well, all right; I hear you and there's no need to shout! But don't pretend that he isn't mad about you, Sarah Cavanagh, because he *is*, and any other woman I know would be thrilled to bits, not angry.'

'Sorry,' Sarah muttered after a moment. 'Forgive me for jumping down your throat. But something Franco said yesterday has made me touchy on the subject. Where is he, by the way – still here?'

'I don't think so; he said he had to leave early to go back to Bologna.' Zoe poured herself some more coffee, looking thoughtful. 'Just now and again I get a glimpse of someone who might be quite likeable – perhaps because he seems to value Giulio so highly! Then the next moment he's back to being an arrogant little monster.'

'Forget Franco,' Sarah suggested. 'I'd rather talk about you.'

'Well, that's another problem,' Zoe said, sounding wistful. 'I'm not really sure why I'm here! I thought Giulio meant me to get to know Belmonte, before I agreed to spend the rest of my life here. He must know how I feel about him ... certain that his people will be my people, and all that biblical jazz ... but *he* doesn't say: "Zoe, love me for ever or I'll die"; and I kind of get the impression that I had things the wrong way round. Belmonte is making up its mind about me!' She spoke with the wry New Yorker humour that was an attractive and rather unexpected part of her make-up, but it didn't conceal the fact that she was puzzled and hurt.

'He must know that you're just what Belmonte needs,' Sarah said gently. 'Be patient, Zoe, he's out of practice at expressing his feelings, I think. What was necessary self-preservation when his mother died has become a habit he has to learn to break.'

Zoe nodded, smiling more happily now. 'Yes ... I should have figured that out for myself, I guess.' She might have added that Sarah seemed to know a lot about a man she obviously didn't like, but Lucchino chose that moment to walk in, in search of breakfast. He smiled at them both, but then frowned accusingly at Sarah.

'*You* look fresh and beautiful – the unfair reward for not joining us last night. I expect Zoe's told you that it was a very joyless evening! Still, the tiresome Franco has his uses – he reminded me of something I didn't mean to forget.' Happy to be bringing them good news, he was smiling again now as he thanked the little maid who offered him fresh coffee.

'Even you ignorant Anglo-Saxon maidens will have heard of La Rotonda – the most beautiful Palladian villa that even the Veneto has to offer. You probably haven't seen it but I shall take you there next weekend. Anna Foscari's coming-of-age is being celebrated with a ball that we have to buy our way into so that the proceeds can go to charity – otherwise, of course, we should have been invited.'

'Of course,' Sarah agreed solemnly, earning herself another reproachful glance. 'Dear Lucchino, I shall want to hear about the villa afterwards, but please don't buy a ticket for me.'

'*Sarah!*' This was a wail of dismay from Zoe. 'How dare you *not* come? Lucchino means the four of us to go. You can't leave him without a partner.'

'Since he'll know just about everyone else there, I don't see why not,' Sarah pointed out reasonably. 'Apart from that, my first small problem is that I don't own a ball dress at all, and even if I had one it wouldn't be here. The other drawback – not so small – is that I'm employed here for the children, not to leave them to other servants to look after while I go gadding about in high society!'

With her back to the door, she wasn't

aware that Giulio Leopardi had come into the room in time to hear what she'd just said. Zoe, who *had* seen him, got up from the table and rushed across to him.

'Giulio darling, we *need* you. Explain at once to Sarah, please, that she's talking nonsense – she *has* to come with us to the Foscari ball.'

He smiled at her with the gentleness he seemed to reserve for the women who were important to him – Sarah had seen him smile at Laura di Brazzano in just the same protective way.

'*You* like the idea of a ball, *tesoro*; but perhaps Sarah doesn't. She seems to prefer staying here ... keeping my father company.'

It might have been kindly meant, but Sarah didn't think so. He knew she'd spent some part of the previous evening with the *padrone* and, for some reason known only to himself, he'd decided to resent her friendship with his father.

'This is a silly subject to argue about,' she said briefly, then smiled at Lucchino. 'Thank you for your invitation. If Bianca is happy to look after the children then I'll go with you, provided Castelfranco can provide me with something more or less suitable to wear!'

'Castelfranco almost certainly can't,' Zoe asserted very firmly. 'We'll go to Vicenza and do some shopping there. Sarah, let's go today. If I ask him very nicely, perhaps Lucchino will let us borrow his lovely car!'

'No such thing, sweetheart,' Lucchino said firmly, 'but he will be glad to drive you there.'

'May we take the children?' Sarah asked. 'Well, perhaps not Emmanuele – he'd probably be bored; but Beatrice will certainly want to give us the benefit of her advice.'

Laughing and arguing about the exact time they must be ready to leave, Zoe and Lucchino walked out of the room, leaving Sarah still there with their host. It seemed churlish to go away, leaving him to drink his coffee alone, but equally difficult to know what to say if she stayed. At last she thought of something.

'It was kind of you to give Emmanuele his party yesterday. I doubt if he's ever had such a birthday.'

'Thanks aren't needed. Domenica – and you, of course – did all the work.' The conversation ground to halt again, and Sarah risked a glance that showed him to be now deep in some different line of thought. His brown face looked tired, but she could see in its features a kind of masculine beauty that had nothing effeminate about it. No wonder, of course, that Zoe had been bewitched; this man had the sort of authority that Lucchino had never had to earn. His air of reserve challenged any spirited girl to break it down, but there was obviously, as well, some hidden sweetness for anyone he loved. Lucky Zoe! But the strange thought was disconcerting and she failed to notice that it was her turn to be examined.

'You take your duties too seriously, I think,' he said abruptly. 'Without a single day off in the three weeks you've been here, you can surely go to the ball without feeling guilty?' She didn't answer immediately, and he went on himself. 'What happens when this job comes to an end?'

She looked surprised at a question that seemed to answer itself. 'I shall go back to England, of course.' Then something in his expression provoked her. 'Unless I try to lure Lucchino into marrying me ... that seems to be the general view.'

'You could do it quite easily, I'm sure,' the man watching her replied. 'Unless you decide instead to return to the man you *were* married to.'

She half expected him to throw in for good measure the idea that she might even have designs on the *padrone* – a lonely, elderly man who could be persuaded that he need-ed a comparatively young wife. But the flash of anger in her eyes was warning enough, perhaps, and he didn't go on.

'Emmanuele won't go away to school until he's nine,' she managed to say quietly. 'All these men who are supposed to be lining up to marry me may not want to wait that long, in which case I shan't have to make a choice at all.'

She was tempted to point out that he should give some thought to his own future, rather than speculate about hers; but he would guess that Zoe had been talking about him, and so she said instead that it was time to go in search of the children if they weren't to keep Lucchino waiting.

He nodded, and stood up with his usual grave courtesy as she left the room, but she took with her the impression that he might have liked to go with them. His father had coped with loneliness by delving deep into the past. Giulio had immersed himself in work, necessarily if Belmonte was to survive; but Luigi wasn't the only one of them who'd been lonely.

Sixteen

Given the option of keeping Lucchino company in Vicenza while the serious business of dress hunting went on, Emmanuele elected to stay behind.

'I have to see to the donkeys,' he told Sarah, 'and Zio Luigi is going to show me how to work my globe.'

'Both important matters,' she agreed, smiling at him. 'Will you promise me not to go to the swimming pool on your own, or even with Bianca?'

'Could I go with Cousin Giulio?'

'Yes, but *only* with him. Is it a promise, *tesoro*?'

He agreed that it was, and she knew she could leave him without worrying; a promise was something he understood.

The expedition was waved off by him and the *padrone* only half an hour later than planned, and Lucchino congratulated his female cargo as he set the car in motion – it was better than experience had led him to expect.

Beyond arranging to meet them for lunch, he took no part in the rest of the morning's programme, and went off to inspect the famous Teatro Olimpico instead. Left to herself, Sarah would have bought something in the first dress shop she came to, and asked to go with him. But Zoe and Beatrice were made of sterner stuff, and it wasn't until they'd inspected three establishments that they were ready to get down to the serious business of making purchases.

'The morning has gone well, I can see,' Lucchino said when they met him at the restaurant, nearly on time, and carrying packages. 'Otherwise you wouldn't be looking happy; in fact you wouldn't be here at all.'

'We shan't disgrace you on Friday,' Zoe confirmed. 'That's the habit of English unerstatement I'm catching from Sarah; in good, plain American it means that we shall knock your eyes out!' Then she gave a dazzling smile. 'Be warned – now, I'm ravenous! Shopping always has that effect on me.'

Apart from the theatre which Sarah would have dearly liked to see, the town was full of other lovely buildings, especially the town hall, reckoned to be Palladio's masterpiece. But she could get little enthusiasm from Beatrice for a stroll round, and none at all from Zoe for whom Vicenza was simply a small, provincial city not worth lingering in; with their shopping done, they might as well go home and spend what was left of the afternoon by the pool. It was an attitude that Sarah found disappointing – more forgivable in a ten-year-old than in Zoe herself, who would surely need to discover things of value in provincial life if she was going to stay happily at Belmonte. It didn't seem likely that Giulio would spare the time to escort her to Venice very often, much less to Rome or New York.

With Beatrice installed happily in the front seat for the journey home, and Zoe engaged in wondering whether, after all, she'd made the right choice of dress, there was nothing for Sarah to do but watch the lovely Veneto landscape flash past. Matthew would have enjoyed it, she thought, would have appreciated how carefully, lovingly, it was tended. And before she left Venice for good, she would persuade him to bring Meg and the children out for a visit. She wanted them to make friends with Beatrice and Emmanuele, as well as to see a city that was uniquely itself, like nowhere else on earth.

For no reason that she could think of, she was reminded of her conversation with Giulio at the breakfast table that morning. The months would fly past, and when it was time to leave she'd be far too unready to say goodbye to this strange Italian interlude that seemed to be blotting out the memories of a different life. The rectory at Pendock had slipped into the past, only to be brought to mind with an effort; and even Highfold seemed misty and unreal.

Lulled by the motion of the car and the afternoon heat, Lucchino's other passengers were dozing when he suddenly spoke quietly into the rear-view mirror at Sarah.

'A penny for your thoughts, *amore*, you're looking *triste*. Is that how you feel?'

'Not *triste*; anxious,' she said, making an effort to smile at him. 'I was trying to imagine Emmanuele's donkeys in Venice! Something tells me that it's going to be my job to explain that they'll have to be left behind when we return to the palazzo.'

'True, I'm afraid! Still, perhaps his flute will take the place of the donkeys – not so strokeable, I know, but something to keep him busy.'

Sarah nodded, then asked the question that now occupied her mind. 'When you spoke to his parents, did they say anything about coming home? We've been here already for the month that Donna Laura mentioned.'

'I think I gathered that they're on their way home – nothing definite, though.'

Sarah looked at her snoozing companions, and risked another question. 'How did they seem?'

'I only spoke to my uncle, but he sounded cheerful, and he said that they were all well. I think the cruise has been successful. They've met someone who wants Laura to take up teaching, even if she won't perform herself, and she seems keen on the idea.'

'It's what she'll need,' Sarah agreed, 'something worthwhile to do.'

Then Zoe stirred beside her and the brief conversation was over.

It was a relief to get back to their quiet, ordered routine after the upheaval of the party, but Sarah suspected that the time hung heavily again for Zoe. She saw too little of a man for whom the working day was never quite long enough. His absence didn't matter for as long as Lucchino was there to keep her entertained, and it might not matter in the future, because as Giulio's wife she would have her own duties and responsibilities to keep her occupied. It was the present in-between stage that was so difficult for her to manage. If it lasted much longer Sarah could imagine herself telling Giulio Leopardi that it wasn't enough to love Zoe; he must understand what her needs were as well.

It was in this frame of mind that she dressed for the ball at La Rotonda. There was no use in pretending that the evening ahead didn't look exciting – she knew it did; but

215

she was apprehensive as well, conscious that she was doing something her employer would deeply resent. The fact that Laura di Brazzano was a thousand miles away and would never hear about it didn't alter anything.

But dressed and ready, she went in – as promised – to say goodnight to the children. Emmanuele, already half-asleep, simply smiled at her and muttered, '*Bellissima*, Sarah.'

Beatrice needed to get out of bed and walk slowly round Sarah before she finally delivered a verdict. Yes, although her *cara inglese* wouldn't have managed it alone, together they'd made a choice that was satisfactory.

'I shall have a dress like that when I grow up,' Beatrice decided, sounding wistful now. It seemed a long time to have to wait.

'And you'll look much prettier in it than I do, sweetheart,' Sarah suggested. 'Now, hop back into bed, and I'll tell you all about it in the morning.'

Her last call, at the library door, produced no response because she found the *padrone* with the others in the salon. Giulio and Lucchino were in the conventional black and white of men's evening dress, Zoe in the gown she'd bought in Vicenza, a cunningly swathed white satin that made a wonderful contrast with her dark hair and tanned skin.

The dress was beautiful but it wasn't only that; she seemed to be alight with excitement and happiness.

Luigi Leopardi lifted the glass he held in a little gesture of salute. 'A sun-maid and a sea-nymph, each of them lovely!'

Lucchino smilingly agreed, but although Sarah was very conscious of Giulio's intent stare, she noticed that he said nothing at all. She supposed that he'd already complimented Zoe and saw no reason to think that anything else was needed. He probably thought his father's comment, untypically fulsome, had been adequate for both of them. Perhaps, since his stare was now making her nervous, she and Beatrice had made a mistake after all. But the aquamarine of her drifting chiffon skirt and beaded top *was* the colour of the lagoon at dawn, and the effect was as delicately lovely as spindrift.

'We shall make a stir,' Lucchino predicted confidently. 'Two undeniably handsome men–' across the room Giulio bowed – 'and two incomparably lovely women!'

'And we shall undoubtedly be the last as well as the most beautiful of the Foscaris' guests if we don't leave now,' Giulio pointed out.

With their goodnights said to the *padrone*, they were led a moment later to *his* car; having done nothing to organize the evening, he was nevertheless in charge. He had that sort of authority and it was obvious that Lucchino accepted it without the least resentment. It said, Sarah reflected, something about both of them.

La Rotonda, when they reached it, looked magnificent – not chillingly classical and formal as imitations of Palladio's style tended to seem in England. Ablaze with light, and thronged with all the high society the Veneto could muster, it was a spectacle that Sarah was grateful not to have missed.

They made their way up the great staircase to be greeted by their hosts, then merged with the crowd in the *portego*, most of whom Giulio and Lucchino seemed to know. Sarah could even recognize one couple herself – Elsa Vandenburg, stunning in silver lamé, was flanked by her English professor. Both of them, she thought, looked astonished to see *her* there, but at least Elsa sounded pleased when she greeted her god-daughter.

'I should have known *you* wouldn't miss a good party,' she said approvingly.

'It's due to our dear Lucchino that we're here,' Zoe explained. 'He's got more time than Giulio to keep an eye on what's happening!'

The men were introduced to Steven Harding, whose glance seemed fixed on Sarah, and then Elsa took charge – the society *grande dame* in her true element.

'You must all come and share our table – so much more comfortable, don't you think, than not belonging anywhere!'

She was right, of course, and no doubt large amounts of lire had changed hands to secure the favoured table she led them to; but Sarah could read no pleasure in Giulio's brown face, only polite acceptance of a situation he could do nothing to avoid. Mrs Vandenburg was Zoe's godmother; she was almost part of the family, whether he liked her or not, and must be accepted as such.

Sitting at the table, sipping the chilled champagne that immediately appeared, Sarah suddenly found herself wishing that she wasn't there. This glittering, artificial display of wealth and extravagance might be benefiting a good cause, but how much would she rather have been at Belmonte, enjoying the reality of its quiet, shabby grace.

'You aren't happy. Why not?' Steven asked quietly beside her.

She turned to smile at him. 'I expect because I feel out of place – unlike you, who can outdo the chameleon and look at home anywhere!'

'Which is a charming way of saying something that does me no credit at all.' He took a sip of wine and then attacked on a different front. 'Why didn't you let me know you were leaving Venice? I called at the palazzo and found it shut up.'

'We had only a day's notice because the di Brazzanos decided very suddenly to go away themselves.'

'But you weren't sorry to leave, I think. Does it irk you as much as all that to have me around?'

She stared at him, surprised that he sounded hurt. He would have concealed it better in the past. But it was very like him, though, to assume that she was still affected by his being there.

'I *was* sorry to leave Venice,' she corrected him firmly, 'because we were being foisted on people I thought didn't want us. Despite that, Belmonte has become a place we all love, and the children will certainly be reluctant to go home. But it won't "irk" me to bump into you occasionally; how could it, when it was you who introduced me to Venice in the first place?'

'At least you remember that,' Steven said, but got no chance to say anything else because Lucchino interrupted them by asking her to dance.

The evening after that became a blur of rather feverish gaiety. There was too much of everything, Sarah thought: music, chatter, wine, and a long, elaborate supper. There were even too many undercurrents of emotion: Lucchino and Steven were engaged in some private contest that should have seemed amusingly pointless, but didn't; Zoe was seriously at odds with her god-mother for some reason, despite surface affection; and Giulio Leopardi was tender towards Zoe, politely attentive to Elsa, but left Sarah to be looked after by Lucchino and Steven. She didn't care, she told herself; didn't in the least want to dance with a man who might have been unaware that she was even there, except that occasionally when she looked in his direction she found him watching her.

But there came at last a moment when the others were away from the table. She gazed round the huge, crowded room, determined to sit in silence if he couldn't be bothered to find something to say. But his opening gambit when it came was unexpected and disturbing in its gravity.

'Are sea-nymphs allowed to dance with mere mortals?'

'For one night in the year,' she agreed, not quite steadily. 'We're not supposed to make a habit of it though.'

His sudden smile was sweet, wiping away sternness and care. 'Then we mustn't waste any more time.'

It came as no surprise that, within the circle of his arms, she should feel entirely secure. What she couldn't have expected was the sudden, drowning wave of delight that flowed over her. She would pretend that it wasn't so, but here, said her heart with complete certainty, was where she belonged, and her struggle not to recognize the fact was what had underlain all her difficulties with him.

They didn't speak as they danced slowly round the ballroom. There wasn't anything to say ... She could only savour, for as long as the music lasted, and his arms enfolded her, this feeling of unimaginable joy. Even so, it was interrupted too soon because now, dancing alongside them, was someone else Sarah recognized. Franco di Brazzano was not safely in Bologna, poring over the books that would earn him a law degree. He was *here*, watching her again with the sly, knowing smile that she found so intolerable.

The music stopped, and Giulio's arms relaxed their hold as he looked down at her.

'You're pale, Sarah, it's too hot in here. Shall we step outside for a moment?' He led her to one of the long windows that opened on to balconies, and she stood looking out over the floodlit gardens, grateful for the cool touch of the wrought-iron railing beneath her fingers.

'The sight of Franco in there upset you,' Giulio said quietly. 'If you're afraid that he'll make mischief, don't be. I can deal with him. You've done nothing wrong in being here.'

Nothing wrong, just something incredibly stupid, she thought, but it was God's mercy that He'd put into Giulio's mouth the excuse she needed. The discovery she'd made about herself could be buried deep in some largely imaginary agitation about Franco. But to make sure that concealment was complete, she added still more embroidery.

'It's not just Franco. I knew all along that I shouldn't have come. It seemed churlish to refuse when Lucchino wanted to give us all pleasure, but the truth is that I can't really cope with this sort of extravagant splendour!'

'Like me, you'd rather be at Belmonte,' he suggested.

It was an unfair path to lead her on to, but she could see how to avoid danger. 'Well, I was thinking of my brother's farm,' she lied heroically. 'Highfold is tucked into a corner of the Malvern Hills in Gloucestershire. It's green and very peaceful – the loveliest place I know.'

She couldn't look at him to see what he made of this slight to his own home, but suddenly his hand covered hers where it gripped the balcony railing. Heart beating too fast, she managed to hear what he said next.

'Before we left this evening I asked Zoe to marry me.' His deep voice halted, then went on a little more roughly than usual. 'I've

223

waited to be sure that she knows what she's taking on, but she doesn't seem to doubt that we can make her happy.'

'We' seemed an odd word to use. Sarah vaguely wondered, while she waited for some huge onrush of pain, who else was thought to be involved beside himself. But all she felt instead was the light-headedness of relief. Five minutes ago she'd been floating in a fantastical dream; now she was back in the real world and no one need know how insanely stupid she'd been just now to stray out of it.

'That explains why Zoe has been looking so radiant all the evening,' she said calmly. 'I hope you'll be very happy together. She's been footloose long enough; I'm glad that she'll be able to settle down.' Then she withdrew her hand, still warm from the clasp of his. Soon it would forget the feel of his fingers, and quite soon she might even be able to remember that for most of their acquaintance she hadn't liked him at all.

'My father doesn't know yet,' Giulio said quietly. 'We must tell *him* before it's announced.'

'When it is, Beatrice will insist on being a bridesmaid at your wedding – you must warn Zoe of that!' She said it with a smile, and told herself that she was doing very well, but she hoped the conversation wouldn't last much longer; the strain was too great.

Then Giulio suddenly changed tack. 'Steven Harding still cares about you, but I expect you know that.'

She managed a little shrug. 'It's only a memory of affection, I think ... that remains, just as other memories do.' The night air was growing cool and she shivered suddenly.

'We'd better go in. You're getting cold,' he said abruptly.

She'd have been much more grateful if he'd suggested going home, but it was unlikely that Zoe would be ready to leave yet, and nor would Lucchino.

For the rest of the interminable evening she danced when asked to, sipped wine she didn't want, and chattered too much, but it came to an end at last; there was only the homeward drive to get through. They were all tired and untalkative, and even Zoe, to Sarah's great relief, seemed disinclined for conversation.

Back in the haven of her own room, the aquamarine skirt was hung up with care – unnecessarily, she thought; it was unlikely that she would ever want to see it again, much less wear it. Tomorrow she would have to make good her promise to Beatrice and report on the evening's pleasure, but for the moment she need only climb into bed and try to think of nothing at all.

Seventeen

Only the children were at the breakfast table with her the following morning. She survived the interrogation quite well, and if Beatrice thought the flow of information lacked anything, she was kind enough to overlook the fact.

'I expect there was too much dancing for you,' she suggested, generously not harping on the possibility that their ageing governess might have found the evening too strenuous. With more affection than she was usually prepared to show, she wound her arms about Sarah's neck. 'You don't have to swim with us today ... We'll ask Lucchino and Zoe instead.'

'They're even tireder than Sarah – not up yet,' Emmanuele pointed out. 'Why do people do dancing at all if it wears them out?'

'It's generally reckoned to be enjoyable,' Sarah explained, smiling at his puzzled face. 'You might enjoy it yourself when you grow up.'

'I don't think I shall.' As usual he was polite, but very firm. 'It seems rather silly to me.'

Sarah thought of the few minutes when she'd drifted round the ballroom with Giulio – a heart-stopping memory she might wish she could be without; but, dear God, *not* silly. She was about to lead them on to a safer subject when Lucchino tottered into the room, shielding his eyes from the bright sunlight.

'Not enough sleep?' she asked kindly.

'Too much champagne, I fear, but some of Domenica's coffee might help.'

'You probably need a swim,' Emmanuele suggested, and grinned when Lucchino closed his eyes in pain. But they wrung out of him the faint admission that he might feel strong enough later in the morning to join them at the pool, and then hurried out of the room. It had become their habit now to follow Giulio about the farm buildings and, much to Sarah's surprise, he showed no irritation at this daily shadowing.

Left alone with Lucchino, Sarah smiled ruefully at him. 'They're beginning to believe that this is home. Venice could have floated out into the Adriatic Sea for all they think about it.'

'Worry when the time comes to leave,' Lucchino advised, now sufficiently restored to help himself to a breakfast roll. He glanced at Sarah but didn't comment on the fact that she was looking pale. 'I think you know what happened last night. The *padrone* knows as well now, so we're free to talk about Giulio's engagement to Zoe.'

'Was he pleased – the *padrone*, I mean?'

'Glad to have it settled, I think. He reckoned that Giulio was making it difficult for Zoe to go on staying here. Now we can stop worrying.'

Sarah smiled in spite of herself, unable to see Lucchino racked by anxiety of any sort, but he guessed what she was thinking and looked hurt.

'I'm afraid you'll never take me seriously,' he said sadly. 'I'm the well-intentioned fool who skims along the surface of life like some gaudy dragonfly, never getting involved in the things that trouble other people.'

'You're well-intentioned, but never a fool,' she insisted, 'and no one could be as kind as you are without getting involved with the rest of us. But you're very well proportioned as well; nothing is allowed to seem more important than it really is. It makes you wonderfully restful to be with!'

He smiled at her with a rueful sweetness she didn't understand. 'You dug yourself out of that hole very neatly!' He could have insisted that his involvement was much greater than she knew, but he realized that it wasn't the moment for that confession; his own great matter would have to wait. Instead, he lifted his coffee cup. 'Shall we drink to Giulio and Zoe's happiness?'

Accustomed now to the shades of colour in his voice, something in the way he'd spoken prompted a sudden question. 'It's a good thing, don't you think – for them and for Belmonte?'

He hesitated long enough to make her wonder whether he was about to disagree, but at last he nodded. 'Yes, Giulio will take great care of Zoe, and she'll bring gaiety back to Belmonte; it's been missing for a long time.'

Sarah would have liked to know whether Zoe would describe the future in those terms. She was never reluctant to talk about herself, so whatever she *was* feeling would come tumbling out: excitement at the prospect of becoming Giulio's wife, the wonder of being the woman he wanted and loved, perhaps even the anxieties attached to sharing his life – all of this she'd be ready to confide to a friend.

But for once she was in no hurry to do so, or even to come downstairs. It was lunch time when she finally appeared, and by then the *padrone* had summoned the servants to drink the health of the engaged couple. The chance to talk only came after lunch when Giulio had left them to visit a farm on the estate.

229

'All is well then,' Sarah said. 'You're going to stay here and live happily ever after, just as all the best fairy tales say!'

Zoe nodded gravely. 'I still can't believe it. I have to keep looking at Giulio. When he smiles at me I *do* believe it.'

She relapsed into silence and Sarah tried again. 'Does Mrs Vandenburg know?'

'Yes, and so does my father – I rang New York just before lunch. He thought he'd be able to come over for the wedding, but my mother won't bother. She lives in California now ... doesn't trouble herself about me.'

It shed such a bleak light on Zoe's family life that Sarah no longer wondered why Elsa Vandenburg, no cosy mother-figure herself, had been so valued.

'I hope your father, at least, was pleased,' Sarah suggested, anxious for *some* normal parental reaction.

'Glad to see me so respectably settled,' Zoe said frankly. 'I think he always reckoned I'd make a mess of my life! He's very sharp in business, and – like a lot of ugly men – very sought after by the opposite sex; but you'll enjoy meeting him – women always do. I can't blame my mother for getting tired of waiting for him to keep returning to the fold. He's remained friends with Elsa because she's never tried to get him to change.'

'And nor have you,' Sarah suggested; 'I

think you like him the way he is.'

Zoe nodded. 'I take after my mother in looks, which is just as well, but otherwise I'm Jacob Hartman's daughter – a chip off the old block!'

'You said he'd come over for the wedding. It *is* going to be here?'

'In Venice. Elsa's already working on it, of course. According to her there isn't a moment to lose. We have to make lists, apparently, though what will be on them I haven't the faintest idea. But it's going to be a wedding Venice won't forget – she's made up her mind to that.'

'It's yours and Giulio's,' Sarah pointed out. 'You *could* thank her very much but say you don't really want an extravaganza that brings the Serenissima to a halt.'

'No, she'd be hurt,' Zoe replied slowly. 'In any case I quite like the idea of an extravaganza myself!'

It was tempting to ask whether Giulio Leopardi's views were going to be consulted. Sarah thought she knew what his own choice would be – to go before a priest one morning with a handful of his family present. But the chances were that she was wrong; it was a luxury she must do without to imagine that she understood him better than the girl he was going to marry did. She found a different question to ask instead.

'Will you let Beatrice help? She'll want to,

I'm afraid. In fact, she's probably considering the matter of a bridesmaid's dress right now!'

'I shall want you both to help,' Zoe insisted. Then her smile faded. 'Beatrice probably won't be allowed to. If *you* can see Laura di Brazzano congratulating me on marrying Giulio, I can't. She's more likely to be sticking pins in a wax doll that looks like me and muttering spells over it.' Despite the warmth of the day Zoe shivered slightly, then shrugged superstition aside. 'So what! She can't really do us any harm.'

'Nor will she want to,' Sarah said firmly. 'I don't think she's emotionally dependent on Giulio any longer, and spitefulness for its own sake isn't part of her nature.' But Zoe looked unconvinced, and it seemed better to change the subject. 'What happens now? Are you going to stay on at Belmonte?'

'For a bit – getting to know people here before I go back to Venice to help Elsa.' Zoe hesitated for a moment then went on more diffidently than usual. 'I'm glad *you*'re here, and Lucchino too. I've got to learn how to fit in ... how to cope with this strange place! It's easier with the two of you around.' Her little frown of worry melted suddenly. 'The truth is that I may always need you. Life would be perfect if you'd marry Lucchino and live with him somewhere nearby – a little palazzo in Castelfranco, say!'

Sarah shook her head. 'Don't bank on it, I'm afraid; it isn't going to happen.' But although she answered lightly, to make a joke of what Zoe had said, there'd been an underlying anxiety that seemed to need reassurance. 'With Giulio beside you, I doubt very much that you'll need anyone else at all,' she suggested gently. 'If you do feel nervous, it's because you can't always grasp yet what people are saying. Leave Elsa to get on with her lists, I should, and take an assault course in Italian yourself!'

'Spoken like a true governess!' her friend agreed with a faint grin.

They didn't return to the subject and dinner that evening was the most light-hearted Sarah had known at Belmonte because her elderly friend, with no trace of stiffness in his manner, went out of his way to include Zoe in a conversation that had nothing to do with the past. They talked of present-day Venice, about which – thanks to Elsa Vandenburg – Zoe was quite well-informed. But Giulio also unobtrusively encouraged her to tell them about life in New York, surely with the object of letting her know that, in marrying him, she needn't cease to feel American.

Watching him occasionally across the table, Sarah tried to remember a time when she'd thought him arrogant and cold and unfeeling; the truth was that he was none of these things. She knew that however far away from Belmonte she travelled in time and space she wouldn't forget the lovely, shabby room they were in, she'd remember Giulio's gentle way with his father and his teasing affection for his friend; these were memories to cherish. But she'd blot out, if she could, the image of him smiling at Zoe.

It would be easy to hate a girl who, having been offered the rich treasure of a life with him at Belmonte, needed to *learn* to enjoy it properly. That seemed to be one of fate's crueller ironies. But James Cavanagh's teaching still held, and she knew that Zoe wasn't someone to hate. For as long as the children had to remain at Belmonte, she would have to watch Giulio and Zoe together, but once back in Venice life would get easier. Her garment of contentment might be a bit tattered for the moment, but she wasn't without practice in the art of patching and making-do.

The following morning Emmanuele was explaining to her how the world – his precious globe – spun on its axis, and Beatrice was drawing bridesmaid dresses, when Domenica appeared in the doorway to call her to the telephone.

Fear that something was wrong at Highfold made her opening *'pronto'* husky; but it was Laura di Brazzano's voice that she heard at the other end of the line.

'Sarah, we're back in Venice – arrived last night. The cruise was splendid, but we're rather glad to be home. The children are probably longing to come back, too.'

Sarah searched for something truthful to say. 'Emmanuele was sad not to see you on his birthday, but your wonderful present saved the day. He can't wait to learn how to play it.'

'Good, now he needn't wait any longer, Michele is coming over tomorrow to collect you. Can you be ready to leave straight after lunch?' There was no immediate reply and she repeated the question more sharply. 'Can you be ready tomorrow? It shouldn't take long to put the children's clothes together.'

Sarah hesitated, wondering how to explain things to a woman who saw the world exclusively from her own point of view. Would she be able to understand without feeling hurt that Emmanuele was completely happy where he was, that Beatrice had a wedding to discuss exhaustively with Zoe, and that both children now doubted whether Belmonte could survive without them?

'There are things ... small treats ... that Beatrice and Emmanuele are looking forward to,' she began diffidently, only to be interrupted by the countess.

'And perhaps *you* have more balls to go to.'

So Franco had already reported her presence at La Rotonda. Stung by Laura's tone of voice, Sarah nevertheless managed to hold on to her own temper. 'There are no more balls to attend. The children *have* been very happy here, but they'll forget about Belmonte when they're back in Venice.' She hoped it was true, and thought there was a good chance that it was. Unlike adults, always yearning for what had been loved and lost, children lived in the present moment. Anxious to end the conversation, she made one last effort to sound calm and unconcerned. 'We shall be ready for Michele tomorrow.' Then she hung up, feeling angry, sad, and slightly sick.

The library door was half-open as she crossed the hall, and she heard the *padrone*'s voice call her name. He was standing by one of the long windows when she went in, apparently watching the daily watering of the flowers on the terrace.

'Perhaps you know already,' she said as he turned round. 'The children's parents are home. We have to leave for Venice tomorrow.'

'Yes, I know,' he agreed quietly. 'Laura seemed to think we should be relieved to see you go. I was pleased to be able to correct her.'

It had probably been his gentle reprimand that had put the frostiness in the countess's voice. She wouldn't have enjoyed being told that she was removing his guests with ill-mannered haste, and Sarah thought the *padrone* was capable of having suggested that as well.

'We've loved being here,' she said simply, 'but you know that! Now I must go and break the news to the children, and although Emmanuele may grieve in silence, Beatrice won't!' It meant that she could smile as she went out, but she found it hard work to sound cheerful when she went back to the children.

'Guess what, your parents are home! That means we can go back to Venice, too.'

Two pairs of dark eyes stared at her, but Beatrice, as usual, spoke first. 'Go back when ... next week?'

'Sooner than that – Michele is coming for us tomorrow.'

'We *can't*. Bella's puppies aren't ready yet.' This was Emmanuele, pointing out that Giulio's beautiful cream labrador wasn't due to produce her offspring for at least a fortnight. He looked at Sarah and under-stood from her expression how serious matters were. 'We have to help pick the grapes,' he added desperately. '*They* aren't ready yet, either.' He couldn't really believe that for the first time since he'd known her, his dear Sarah was going to let him down, but her face looked sad and somehow he knew that they *were* about to leave Belmonte.

She put an arm round both of them and gave them a little hug. 'Listen, please! We've always known that we were only visiting. Now, it's time to go home, because Mamma and Papa are there, feeling unhappy because you're still here.'

'But couldn't we go later ... Sarah, the *donkeys*...?' Bella's unseen puppies were bad enough, but the thought of his special friends made Emmanuele's eyes fill with tears.

'We'll ask Giulio to say hello to them every day,' she suggested, 'and when it's time to pick the grapes he's sure to want you to come back and help.' He nodded and smeared away his tears, but Beatrice was shaking her head.

'I *have* to stay here ... I'm helping Zoe.'

Sarah tried to sound regretful. 'But you won't be much help at Belmonte. Zoe will soon be back in Venice herself – that's where her wedding is being planned. You've met Mrs Vandenburg here, I know, but she lives almost opposite you, across the Grand Canal.'

Beatrice considered this unexpected fact for a moment, then regrouped her forces. 'Well, all right, I suppose we'll have to go, but we must make sure Giulio knows we're coming back. We'd better go and look for him now, I think.'

She ran out of the room, followed by Emmanuele, and Sarah let out a little sigh of relief. When the moment of departure came they'd be tearful all over again, but the idea of going home had at least taken root. She was collecting together their books and games scattered round the room when Lucchino walked in. His expression said that he, too, had already heard about the phone call from Venice.

'Dear Laura, we can always rely on her – minimum effort and the maximum amount of upset achieved!' Aware that Sarah was about to try to excuse her, Lucchino went firmly on. 'The *padrone's* seriously upset – he hates discourtesy – and he knows that you'll have a job to talk the children into going.'

'They've been told, but I've disappointed them,' she admitted. 'I was supposed to wave my magic wand and keep them here, at least until the *vendemmia*. I've bribed them with a promise that Giulio will invite them back for it.' She hesitated for a moment. 'Can *you* stay on? Zoe still needs some help in getting used to Belmonte. Giulio's the one to give it to her, of course, but he has too little free time.'

'He might also think he should have his fiancée to himself at last. Doesn't that occur to her?' If the question needed an answer

Sarah hadn't one to give. She went on piling books together instead, and Lucchino watched her, thinking how hard it was to remember a time when he hadn't known her. The weeks at Belmonte had made a change – her light-brown hair was dusted with the gold of sunlight now, and her bare arms and legs were a smooth, even brown; she looked younger, and more beautiful. He wished he knew what she was thinking.

'What about you, Sarah?' he asked suddenly. 'Will *you* be sorry to leave?'

This time she had to reply, and the words needed to be chosen carefully. 'I've loved being here, but I shan't mind going back to Venice – in fact I think I'd rather go than stay.'

He nodded as if this was what he'd expected, but since he might never have another chance to say what was filling his mind, he must speak now, whether it was the right moment or not.

'My own choice would be to always go with you.' He saw her startled expression but gave her no chance to interrupt. 'I know what you think – you've explained it very nicely! But you're wrong, *amore*. Where you're concerned I'm not well-proportioned at all. It's not what I expected – that I'd be slayed by a quiet, stubborn, English governess, even if she did have lovely grey eyes and a heart-catching smile! It happened and

I'm glad it did, even though I don't expect you to feel the same about me – why should you? But if you *would* marry me, my darling, I'd take such care of you.'

One way and another it was being an emotional morning, and she had to struggle not to weep, or give herself away. But she must do more than that – must swallow the lump in her throat and answer him.

'Dear Lucchino ... thank you for asking. If I had a grain of sense I'd marry you tomorrow – any sane woman would. But ... but...'

'Someone else gets in the way,' he suggested gently.

She nodded now, unable to trust her voice at all. He would assume that the 'someone' was Steven Harding, of course – the man she hadn't been able to stop loving – but that was much more bearable than having him guess the truth.

'It's what I thought,' Lucchino said sadly, 'you've been so careful not to give me the smallest encouragement!' Then he smiled at her. 'Don't look unhappy, please. Hearts can't be given away to order. If they could I'd have picked some dazzling Argentinian heiress by now, and made her and myself miserable for the rest of our lives.'

She managed to smile too, because he wanted her to. 'Forget the dazzling beauty – find someone kind, please.'

He walked towards her and took her

hands in his. 'Friends always, Sarah? We can't lose touch, because I shall need to know that you're all right.'

She nodded, finding words difficult again, and he leaned forward and gently kissed her mouth. 'There, now I've said goodbye. Tomorrow I shall merely wave you away!'

A moment later he'd walked out of the room, and she was left staring at the piles of books in front of her, trying to remember what she'd been doing with them.

At lunch with the *padrone* Lucchino was his usual even-tempered self, forbidding the children to spoil their last day at Belmonte with tears or tantrums. They spent the afternoon by the pool or in the water, for once without Zoe, whom Giulio had taken off for the day to meet friends further north. Sarah watched the children, wondering whether Laura di Brazzano would recognize them. Gone was the too-plump, overdressed and overbearing child that Beatrice had been, and in place of a pale, limping ghost called Emmanuele was a tanned, wiry boy quite capable of calling his sister to order.

The travellers returned in time for dinner, and the *padrone* announced sadly that Sarah and the children would be leaving in the morning. She looked, because she couldn't prevent herself, at Giulio's brown face and thought she read there a flicker of relief. It was only what she expected, of course, and it scarcely hurt at all. More surprisingly, Zoe showed very little sign of regret either – she was probably still so wrapped in the contentment of a day spent with Giulio that the future now looked to be nothing she need fear.

By the time Michele arrived the following morning the children's farewells had been said; Emmanuele's leave-taking of the donkeys made just bearable by Giulio's promise that they would be waiting for him when he came back to Belmonte to help pick the grapes. Beatrice had been assured that Zoe's wedding couldn't possibly take place without her, and both children discovered that they were glad to see Michele again.

There remained the *padrone* to say goodbye to – the so-called solitary, self-absorbed recluse whom Sarah now counted as a loved and loving friend. But she thanked him calmly for all his kindness, knowing that emotion would upset him.

'We shall see you here again, my dear, you will always be welcome,' Luigi answered. 'In fact you *must* come – who else is to play Eleanora's piano?'

She managed to smile and kiss him on both cheeks. Then after a hug for Zoe, only Giulio remained to be dealt with. Standing behind Emmanuele, she could smile a goodbye but not hold out her hand. To have him touch her wasn't possible.

'I've thanked Signor Luigi for all his kindness and hospitality,' she said. 'I'll let the children thank you.'

They did it very nicely, she thought, and there was scarcely time to notice that Giulio – now flanked by Zoe, whose arm was linked in his – spoke only to them. Michele was anxious to instal them in the car, and a moment later they were being waved off by everyone they knew at Belmonte.

Beatrice was able to turn round and wave back, but Emmanuele only stared at the road ahead. Sarah knew how he felt; it made two of them who couldn't bear to watch the lovely old house dwindle and disappear behind them.

Eighteen

There'd been a change in the city during the weeks they'd been away. Now, in mid-July, Venice was in the hot grip of the summer season. The Grand Canal teemed with tourist-laden *vaporetti*, every waterside bar and *ristorante* did a roaring trade, and the more serious-minded visitors dutifully trailed from one 'must see' church to the next. It was the time of year when true-born Venetians couldn't make up their minds – did they love or loathe the strangely-clad flood of *stranieri* that daily poured across the causeway and the lagoon?

Michele steered through the water traffic with the ease of long practice, and allowed the boat to drift in neatly to the landing-steps of the palazzo.

'*Eccoci,*' he said with a broad smile; '*ritornati a casa!*'

It didn't, in fact, feel as if they'd returned home – Belmonte had seemed much more dearly familiar, Sarah thought, than this tall, gothic building perched improbably on its bed of wooden piles in the mud of the lagoon. But Count Fabrizio *was* hurrying down the steps to meet them, and his welcoming smile suggested that perhaps Michele had been right after all. The children's Venetian life *would* soon blot out their memories of Belmonte, and Sarah told herself that she must simply learn to remember their stay there as a lovely, unexpected gift.

Climbing the steps behind the children and their father, she couldn't help wondering what Laura's reception would be – the countess's manner on the telephone hadn't been exactly cordial – but suddenly a worse worry occurred to her. There wasn't the faintest chance that Beatrice wouldn't blurt out the news of the forthcoming wedding. It was anybody's guess how secure Laura's recovery was; Zoe's engagement to Giulio could be all that was needed to tip her back into alcoholic despair. A more natural mother might simply rejoice to be reunited with two such enchanting children as Beatrice and Emmanuele now looked, but Sarah couldn't feel sure that this was what the countess's reaction would be.

But her appearance, at least, was reassuring. Gone was the haggard, distraught-looking creature who'd packed them off to the mainland. She'd put on a little weight and, more essentially, had recovered pride in herself; she'd even begun to look beautiful again.

She greeted the children, in fact, as if she *was* pleased to see them, and commended Sarah for having brought them home looking so well. When Emmanuele – no longer tongue-tied and awkward – thanked both parents for his beautiful flute, Laura smiled affectionately at him.

'We thought you'd be bored and lonely at Belmonte,' she said, 'until we discovered that Lucchino had stayed on as well.'

'It was lovely, Mamma,' Emmanuele explained earnestly. 'Cousin Giulio was very busy, but Lucchino helped Sarah teach us to swim; and Zio Luigi ate lunch with us every day – we weren't lonely at all. And of course I had the donkeys to talk to!'

'Important friendships were made,' Sarah confirmed with a smile, seeing the countess's astonished glance. 'Signor Leopardi might have preferred his peaceful library, but he was kind enough to keep us company.'

'Extraordinary – not his usual style at all,' Laura commented.

Now came the moment Sarah had been dreading. Beatrice's news couldn't be contained any longer. 'Mamma, the American *signorina* was at Belmonte too. Did you know she's going to marry cousin Giulio? She says I may be her bridesmaid.'

After only a small silence the countess answered her. 'We knew that Zoe Hartman was with you – Franco told us; we *didn't* know that a wedding was planned. Exciting for you! We shall have to see what Zoe wants you to wear.'

Obedient to Sarah's small shake of the head, Beatrice didn't insist that she'd got her dress already designed, and the count filled what might have been an awkward gap by suggesting that the children went with him to say hello to Claretta Vanni and Agnese.

When they'd gone, Laura gave a wry

smile. 'My husband is determined to turn over a new leaf. We're to see more of him in future!'

It was on the tip of Sarah's tongue to ask whether the children could expect to see more of *her*, but the countess spoke first. She sounded calm, though, as if no longer personally involved in what they were discussing.

'I told you that Zoe Hartman would get what she wanted; let's hope it's what she continues to want. Giulio won't neglect Belmonte, not even to please a young, demanding wife, and God knows his father won't be much of a replacement companion!'

It was a worse temptation to fly to the *padrone's* defence, but Sarah resisted it, knowing that safety lay in saying as little as possible. Laura duly registered the fact and added a tart rider.

'I gather from the rather stony silence that you like Luigi Leopardi.'

'Yes,' Sarah agreed briefly, 'I do.'

'But then you seemed to like everything about Belmonte, according to Franco!'

Sarah decided to meet the countess's oblique attack head-on. 'I expect *he* told you that I liked going to the ball at La Rotonda. If you think I shouldn't have gone you'll be glad to know that I *didn't* enjoy it very much.'

'Because you saw Lucchino in his true

colours, I suppose – everybody's favourite, the charmer that no woman should ever take seriously?'

'I see him always for what he is – a friend,' Sarah answered steadily. Her greatest pleasure would have been to explain just how seriously a proposal of marriage entitled her to take him, but that couldn't be done; instead, she returned to the safety of talking about the children.

'Emmanuele had a wonderful birthday party at Belmonte, but I must warn you that Beatrice will feel unfairly treated if *she* isn't given a party when the time comes. And there's one other thing: may I take them over to the Lido occasionally? They're used to swimming now. We don't need Michele – we can go on the *vaporetto*.'

'Do what you like,' Laura agreed impatiently. 'You're in charge.' She looked at her watch, and then at her reflection in the huge, ornate mirror above the fireplace. Satisfied that all was well, she turned to smile at Sarah. 'Forgive me for rushing off the moment you get back, but I've been rather swept into something very exciting. God knows I've waited long enough for it to happen, but now it has. Tell the children I'll listen to their chatter about Belmonte tomorrow.'

She swept out of the room, the operatic diva again, making her exit, and Sarah could hear her on the staircase calling to Michele that she was ready to leave. The leaf-turning process applied only to the count, it seemed; Laura might be different in some unexplained way, but her self-absorption hadn't changed. She was still as preoccupied with herself as ever.

It was a depressing thought, but Sarah was puzzled as well as she walked upstairs. On the telephone to Lucchino there'd been mention of a teaching job – interesting and worthwhile almost certainly, but could it really account for Laura's rejuvenation, and her apparent indifference to Zoe's engagement to Giulio?

She was still mulling this over while she unpacked books in the school room when Fabrizio di Brazzano walked in.

'The children are being given tea downstairs,' he said with a pleasant smile. 'Apparently the servants have got to hear all about their stay at Belmonte!' That seemed to be all he'd come to report, but he didn't go away, and Sarah felt that *she* was now expected to find something to say.

'The cruise has done Donna Laura a lot of good – she looks very well now.'

'Yes ... yes, she does,' he agreed. Again the conversation faltered, but he still stood there, fingering the books she'd left on the table.

'Lucchino mentioned the possibility of her

doing some music teaching,' Sarah ploughed on. 'Does that appeal to her?'

'Very much, it seems.' The answer couldn't have been briefer, but it gave something away this time. The count's voice now held an unmistakable note of sadness and regret.

'I'm afraid it doesn't appeal to you,' Sarah suggested gently. 'Are you going to tell me why not?'

Fabrizio nodded; it was what he'd come for, she realized. 'First I must tell you how it came about. We moored one evening in the harbour of Corfu Town, alongside a yacht owned by a Greek couple. They recognized Laura and invited us on board. She'd been miserable until then, but suddenly she came alive again. Our host, Stefan Demetrios, had often seen Laura perform at La Scala, Covent Garden, The Met in New York...'

Remembering that first evening, Fabrizio forgot to talk, and Sarah had to prompt him.

'Was it Mr Demetrios who suggested the job?'

'Yes – for a very tragic reason. His daughter, a gifted musician, was killed in an air crash when she was eighteen. Since then, in her memory, Demetrios has used his wealth to fund masterclasses to train young singers. He wants to start them in Venice now, with Laura as the teacher.'

'It sounds a splendid thing for a rich man

251

to do,' Sarah pointed out. 'Why be unhappy about it?'

'Because my wife reacts to people immoderately,' he said bluntly. 'I hoped we were going to do better as a family – be together more. But, having at last accepted that Giulio is out of her life now, Laura is clutching instead at a very charming Greek. The dependence cycle begins all over again.'

'It's *not* the same perhaps,' Sarah tried to suggest. 'Giulio was needed to take the place of the career Laura had given up. She is older now, and this time she's being made a present of something – a new interest. Mr Demetrios won't stay in Venice long in any case; he sounds like a world-traveller.'

Fabrizio shook his head. 'It's not how things actually are; it's how Laura imagines them to be. You've seen the difference in her – she's like a beautiful young woman again. I *should* be glad about that, because above all I want her to be happy. But I just hoped that this time we could be happy together.'

Sarah tried to remember her first impression of Fabrizio di Brazzano – a vain, slightly boring, rather self-important man? All wrong, she now realized; he was selfless and loyal, and he deserved a better wife than Laura had made him. But he hadn't stopped loving her even so.

'Wait and see what happens,' she suggested, unable to find any other advice to offer. 'There *is* an important difference this time – Mr Demetrios has a wife, and they've gone through the agony together of losing their child. Laura is very excited at the moment, but she's bound to be; the performance of music was at the centre of her life, and in a different way she's being offered it back. She's grateful to Mr Demetrios, of course, but that's not the same thing as saying that she's certain to fall in love with him.'

'And while we wait and see, we have *you* to keep us going. Our blessings on Hubert Crabtree!'

He smiled at her with genuine affection, and finally walked away, leaving her to wonder whether her own strange experience of life as a governess had the remotest connection with anybody else's. There was surely some sensible, self-preserving rule that said she should never get involved with the family that employed her; but the truth was that she'd long passed the point where she could walk away from the palazzo and not care what became of the people who lived there.

By lunch time the following day the children's thank-you letters to Belmonte had been composed, concluded in Emmanuele's case with an anxious reminder to Giulio to remember him to the donkeys, who would wish to know that he was missing them very much.

There was even more to miss, of course – Venice in mid-summer was a hot, over-crowded place full of bemused, demanding strangers. Even Beatrice, who generally preferred activity to a peaceful contemplative life, complained about the noise when they went out to post their letters. They returned to lunch by themselves in the school room on the top floor and that in itself underlined another difference which they found it hard to accept. They'd got used to a long, leisurely meal on the terrace at Belmonte, shared with whoever else happened to be there, but always with Zio Luigi. It was Beatrice, of course, who asked the question Sarah had felt certain would come.

'You said Mamma and Papa would be sad if we stayed at Belmonte when they were back at home. So why are we by ourselves up here?'

'You'll lunch downstairs quite often, I expect,' Sarah tried to explain, 'but not every day. Your parents are very busy. It's different for Zio Luigi; because he's much older he can do what he likes.'

It didn't sound very convincing even to her, and she foresaw all too many days ahead when the threadbare excuse would have to be trotted out for intelligent children who hadn't believed it the first time.

'I don't like Venice,' Emmanuele said firmly. 'Sarah, may we go back to Belmonte, please?' His large, dark eyes, fixed on her face, were asking an even harder question. Why had his mother not wanted to hear all the things they had to tell her – about the swimming lessons and Bella's puppies and Zio Luigi's globe, on which they'd followed their parents' Aegean journey every day? Even this morning she still hadn't come to see them.

Sarah took a deep breath and tried to answer calmly. 'Belmonte is Giulio and Zio Luigi's home, but you belong here, *tesoro*. Mamma is probably longing to hear all about it but she has some important work to do first. You know that we're going to find a flute teacher for you, well, *she*'s going to teach people to sing as beautifully as she does. It all has to be arranged, but once it is she won't have to be out so much.'

'And anyway we can't go back to Belmonte,' Beatrice pointed out, clinching the matter. 'Zoe's coming back to Venice soon for the wedding.'

'So she is,' Sarah agreed. 'But while we're waiting for her we'll have another picnic. You can choose between you which island we go to tomorrow.'

They hadn't made up their minds when

Michele went to collect Bianca and the rest of their luggage from the railway station. She reported to Sarah after the children were in bed that Belmonte had seemed very quiet when she left, because Signor Lucchino had already gone down to Rome to visit his parents.

'He makes laughter and fun, *non è vero?*' Bianca suggested, and Sarah had to agree that he did. It left Zoe alone at Belmonte with Giulio and his father, but this had probably been Lucchino's intention, so that the three of them could settle down to life together.

By the following morning the picnic spot was agreed; Murano this time, followed by a return visit to Torcello, so that they could lunch there again in the green piazza.

On the way downstairs they bumped into Franco who, for once, seemed inclined to stop and talk to them. He explained that he was just home, like them, but not for long – his long summer vacation wouldn't be spent in Venice if he could help it. He gave Sarah a civil enough nod, but she couldn't look at him without remembering that he'd reported her visit to La Rotonda to the countess. He was attracted to the idea of setting people against each other, she thought. He'd probably do well in a court of law later on, hammering some unfortunate witness into testifying against the defendant he was there to help.

'Where are you all off to?' he asked, seeing the picnic basket as evidence that they were going out for the day.

'To Murano first – we take the *vaporetto*,' Beatrice explained in a tone implying at the very least that they were about to board the Orient Express for Istanbul. 'We're quite used to it now and it's fun.'

'I expect it is if you like rubbing shoulders with the hoi polloi,' Franco agreed.

'Well, we *do* like it,' Emmanuele insisted with unusual belligerence. He had no idea what hoi polloi might mean, but suspected that some criticism of Sarah lurked in his brother's comment.

'Then, enjoy! *Ciao, bambini.*'

Dismissed, they went outside by the gate that led to a pathway bordering a small side canal. There, a surprise awaited them, because the tall, bearded man standing beside an idling motor launch smiled at Sarah as if he knew her.

'Steven! What in the world are you doing here?'

'I was coming to call on you – Elsa heard from Zoe that you were back. I have to go over to San Francesco del Deserto this morning. I remembered how much you loved it once upon a time and thought you and the children might agree to come too.'

It was true – when he'd taken her there on

their first visit to Venice she hadn't wanted to leave its bell-haunted peace. Reputed to be an island where St Francis had once been shipwrecked, it remained even now an enchanted, peaceful place immune from the summer plague of tourists.

'This is Professor Harding,' she explained to the children; 'English, like me, but he knows Italian very well. What do you say to a change of plan – an island almost to ourselves, and the professor's *motoscafo* instead of a crowded *vaporetto*?'

Both dark heads nodded, and Beatrice smiled as well – she liked the look of the fair-haired stranger, so different from the dark menfolk she was accustomed to. 'You can share our picnic,' she said kindly.

They were handed into the launch, and as the boatman steered them out of the side stream into the Grand Canal, from the top of the palazzo steps Franco watched them leave. So there'd been no question of a *vaporetto* journey after all – the governess had had it all arranged, and the Englishman that all Venice seemed to be besotted with had been waiting for them on the pathway. Franco didn't know yet how he would use the information, but it would be stored away for future use.

Nineteen

Sarah would have found it hard to believe that a visit to San Francesco *could* be anything but happy – so peaceful, tranquil, and completely resistant to the clamour of the outside world had it always been; even so, the day's rich enjoyment came as a surprise. Steven had been a brilliant teacher of students at an advanced level of education, but she'd never seen him with young children and always imagined that he'd be awkward with them, perhaps unintentionally patronising. In fact, that wasn't how it turned out at all.

He let the children talk, and even Emmanuele was prepared to do so, only explaining himself what the history was of the little island they were chugging northwards to. Watching his fair head bent towards them as he pointed out something else in the lagoon, she was pierced by the irony of discovering how easily he dealt with children after all when setting his face against having any had been one of the rocks on which their marriage had foundered.

He was obviously expected at the island because a gentle-faced friar in his brown habit waited at the landing stage to conduct them to the monastery buildings. They walked through the greenness of what might have been an English garden; it hadn't changed, she realized with silent gratitude. This small corner of the world, surrounded by Brother wind and Sister water, was still what St Francis would have insisted on – a haven of peace and prayer.

They parted company with Steven, who had an appointment with the abbot to inspect some ancient records. But there was the chapel to visit, and the beautiful fourteenth-century cloisters, and the gardens themselves to roam in, the friars' lovingly tended potager, and then the flower-filled meadows, shared with the resident peacocks and geese and even some quietly-mooing cattle. Even the cows, it seemed, knew better than to make a noise here.

They were opening up the picnic basket when Steven reappeared. He helped them demolish the cold chicken and cheese and fruit that Claretta Vanni had provided, and then sat sharing the coffee thermos with Sarah while the children went off to watch the peacocks who'd chosen this moment to spread their magnificent tails.

'A nice couple,' he said when they were out of earshot. 'They're lucky to have *you*; according to Elsa, they don't see much of their parents.'

'I doubt if Mrs Vandenburg really knows much about their lives,' Sarah felt obliged to point out, 'and I suspect her of not liking Laura di Brazzano very much.'

Steven smiled at her. 'And *you* don't like Elsa very much!'

It had always been one of his more irritating habits, she remembered, to put into her mouth words she hadn't said but might have wanted to. On the whole, though, he was behaving very nicely and she refused to spoil the lovely day by wrangling with him.

'I suppose Mrs Vandenburg's delighted about Zoe's engagement,' she suggested instead.

'Not delighted, exactly.'

Sarah stared at him in astonishment. 'Why ever not?'

'I think she'd have preferred Lucchino to be the bridegroom. So nice to have a god-daughter who'll eventually become the Marchesa Vittoria!'

'But doesn't she care about the happiness of a girl who happens to be head over heels in love with Giulio Leopardi?'

'Elsa's a pragmatist, my dear, not a dyed in the wool romantic like you.' But he said it without the condescending tone he'd once

261

have used. 'She'll make the best of what Zoe's got, all the same, and arrange a splendid wedding for them.'

'Which Giulio will hate.' She saw that it was Steven's turn to look surprised, and hastily amended what she'd just said. 'Which I'm *guessing* that he'll hate – I don't *know* anything about him, of course.' She managed to hold Steven's blue glance for a moment, pleased with herself for the unblushing lie; but it was a relief when he returned his attention to the children.

'Beatrice's a taking child, but she's going to be a handful before she's very much older.'

'By then she won't be my responsibility. In less than two years' time Emmanuele will go away to school. A governess won't be needed then.'

There was a little silence, which he finally broke, sounding more diffident than usual. 'When we discussed your job once before, I think you got the impression that I was sneering at it. If that's how it seemed, I apologize. The truth is that I was concerned about *you* – still am; it matters to me to see you happy, Sarah.'

She couldn't doubt that he meant what he said; he hadn't ever lied to her. 'Thank you,' she answered quietly. 'I still have a painful scar or two, but I *am* happy. I shall miss the children very much when it's time to leave, but that will be the price of loving them, I'm afraid.' She hoped that it was all that need be said about herself; now they could talk about *him* instead, which he'd never been loath to do.

'I should have asked before how your work is going?'

'Very well, I think. The lectures are finished for the moment, although they're trying to persuade me to do some more in the autumn. Now I'm pressing on with research for the book. The Marciana Library is full of treasure trove, and there's enough material hidden away in the city's archives to produce a hundred books. But I need to see the places where St Mark's winged lion is still visible, all round the Adriatic and the Aegean.' Steven leaned over suddenly and reached for her hand. 'I shall be in and out of Venice for the next few months. When I'm here, will you let me see you occasionally?'

She thought that if he'd made the mistake of pressuring her, and especially the mistake of referring to the past, she'd almost certainly have said no. But the simple question wasn't something to resent, and the truth was that it would be very nice to have a friend. Content as she was with the children, there were times when life at the palazzo seemed lonely.

She smiled at him with the sweetness he remembered. 'I shall need to know about the lion – I think you'll find him in all sorts of unlikely places.'

'Good!' Then he released her hand as the children came back.

A fortnight later, Lucchino got back to Belmonte from Rome to find Zoe not there; she was in Venice with Elsa, Giulio explained. Over supper Lucchino told his hosts that two weeks in the city of his birth was as much as he could stand in one go.

'It's not the place itself – that's grand and beautiful,' he tried to explain, 'it's the people who live there, excluding my dear parents, of course.'

'Too proud, too self-satisfied?' Luigi suggested with a smile.

'Insufferably so! They'll concede that Florence has a few artistic treasures they haven't got, and Milan has the commercial drive they're *glad* they haven't got; apart from that, forget the rest of Italy. There's only Rome.'

'Where the women are supremely elegant,' Giulio solemnly took up the tale. 'The Pope resides in splendour, and the city's long history insists that it's still important in the global scheme of things.'

'Exactly so – Almighty God, the Government, and the gentle sex all where they should be. No Roman male will quarrel with that!' Lucchino took a sip of wine and then smiled happily at them. 'No wonder I prefer being here.'

Giulio shook his head. 'Not always, my friend. One of these days you'll have to become a Roman yourself, and when you're an elderly marchese I can hear *you* proclaiming that the only place for a civilized man to live is in the Eternal City ... such a pity about the rest of Italy!'

The *padrone* joined in the laughter, but then consulted his watch, and announced that he was going to bed. The other two men sat in the sort of companionable silence that Lucchino realized he could only share with Giulio, because their friendship was long and deep and entirely satisfying. It would change a little when he married Zoe – it was bound to.

'When will Zoe be back?' he asked, *à propos* of that.

'In a day or two. Elsa commanded her to return to Venice to discuss wedding plans.' The dry comment confirmed what Lucchino suspected.

'You don't like Mrs Vandenburg, I'm afraid.'

Giulio's shoulders lifted in a faint shrug. 'Not greatly, but it doesn't matter – she's not proposing to live with us. She and Zoe fight, but that doesn't matter either; they're very fond of one another.' He refilled Lucchino's glass and his own, then spoke again.

'I think Zoe was quite glad to have a break from Belmonte; Franco arrived to stay for a few days and she finds it hard to put up with him.' Giulio saw his friend's expression, and smiled. 'You're going to point out that most people do! I know, but I feel sorry for him, and with a little help I think he'll eventually improve.'

Giulio leaned back in his chair, apparently content to stare at the night sky above the terrace, lit by countless stars. A night for love, Lucchino reflected rather wistfully, but wasted on two men, consoling each other's loneliness. In the glow of the candles on the table he looked at his friend's face, registering its thinness, the skin drawn tightly over the too-prominent bones. He was used to seeing Giulio tired – the man worked too hard – but surely something more than overwork now ailed him.

'Is everything all right here?' he asked gently. 'You look a bit done in, my friend.'

Giulio didn't answer at once, then a faint, rueful smile touched his mouth. 'Tactfully put, but you mean, I think, is our future all right – mine and Zoe's!'

There was a little silence. 'All right, since you've put it into words yourself,' Lucchino finally agreed, 'are the two of you going to be happy?'

'I must try to *make* Zoe happy,' Giulio said sombrely. 'It's what I've promised to do. I'm

266

not sure that I shall succeed; it depends whether I can teach her to love Belmonte.'

Lucchino turned over in his mind what he was entitled to ask next; there were limits to what even a very old friend was permitted to say.

'She had enough time to discover what your life is here,' he pointed out. 'She didn't accept you imagining that you'd be able to take her to Paris or New York whenever she found Belmonte too peaceful.'

'I *hope* she had enough time,' Giulio amended quietly. He glanced at his friend's face and decided to answer the question Lucchino hadn't asked. 'You wonder about us, think we're a very ill-matched couple. So we are, of course.'

'And so are my parents, but they've had a wonderfully happy marriage. That's why *I'm* such a well-adjusted charming fellow myself!'

It wiped away the look of strain from Giulio's face, but he went on talking, as if wanting to convince himself as well as a friend he trusted. 'I'm very fortunate; Zoe is an enchanting girl – lively, intelligent, and a constant pleasure to look at!'

'She's also deeply attached to *you* – another virtue,' Lucchino suggested.

'Yes,' Giulio agreed slowly. 'That was something I couldn't miss, and nor could Laura. It meant that she finally had to face up to reality: *our* relationship was over. *She* had a husband, I had someone who was eager to become the wife I badly need. Put brutally, I saw Zoe as a means of making her accept the truth at last.'

'And then,' Lucchino said slowly, 'you felt committed to Zoe, of course.'

'Then at least it had to be *her* choice,' Giulio agreed. He managed to smile at his friend. 'It's not a hardship! What normal man wouldn't be more than grateful to have her as his wife?'

'I can't think of any,' Lucchino obligingly agreed. 'Nor can I imagine how any normal woman wouldn't be happy living here with *you*. So I shall now drink to you both and refuse to worry about you!'

'There's no need to worry; we shall manage very well.' Giulio took a sip of wine, then replaced his glass on the table. 'What about you, while we're swapping confidences like lovesick maidens? Was I right to think that you fell a little bit in love with Sarah Cavanagh?'

'I did much more than that. I offered her my hand, heart, and whatever expectations I have. She turned me down. We're friends for always, I'm sure, but someone else gets in the way of her seeing me as a husband.'

'I think I know who it is,' Giulio said quietly. 'Her marriage to Steven Harding broke down but perhaps he has learned something from that. Franco has seen them together in Venice, so whatever attracted them to each other in the first place is still there.' He smiled with great affection at his friend. 'I'm sorry if it hurts, *amico mio*, but Sarah will go back to England, with or without Harding. One day you'll be thankful you avoided getting a stubborn, argumentative English creature for a wife!'

'That's not how it feels at the moment,' Lucchino said wryly, 'and it seems strange to me that two people I happen to love very much – you and she – don't appreciate each other. On which deeply philosophical note I shall say goodnight and retire to bed!'

He smiled and went away, but turned to look round before going indoors. Giulio was leaning back in his chair, apparently staring again at the star-scattered sky. But he seemed to be seeing a different prospect altogether because, imagining that he was now alone, he no longer took the trouble to hide his desolate despair.

Twenty

A flute teacher had been found. Introducing
Emmanuele to the buxom, motherly lady
who opened the door to them at a small
house in the Campo San Vio, Sarah considered with quiet pleasure the change in
the count's youngest child. He might never
have his sister's bold approach, to other
people or to life itself, but even a total
stranger didn't now send him back into his
shell. He smiled shyly at Signora Artom,
and followed her up several flights of stairs
to a room on the top floor of the house. The
flute teacher was her son, Enrico, a
pleasant-faced young man who limped
towards them with one foot noticeably dragging behind the other. Sarah smiled at him,
imagining the child who, debarred from the
games that had gone on in the Campo
outside, had consoled himself with music
instead.

'I recognize you, signorina,' he said at
once. 'I was at the concert in La Pietà, and

you played with the contessa – *una sera meravigliosa!*'

'I was there also, with my sister,' Emmanuele piped up, obviously quite at ease with this gentle-looking musician. Then he looked round the room, empty except for a piano, some music stands and a few straight-backed chairs – yes, he felt sure he'd come to the right place.

Sarah explained the little that Emmanuele already knew – the musical scale that made up an octave: c, d, e, f, g, a, b, c; and the sharp or flat sign that made the notes slightly higher or lower.

'I was afraid to involve him in the piano too much,' she explained to Enrico, 'because teaching a wind instrument is probably quite different.'

'What he knows will be very useful,' Enrico kindly confirmed, 'but now I know where to begin.'

She stayed just outside the room for the first lesson, but decided that in future Emmanuele wouldn't at all mind being left with his new friend. It would probably even be better, less inhibiting, if she weren't there. She said this as they walked home afterwards, and Emmanuele thoughtfully agreed.

'I shan't be able to play for a little while, Enrico says; I have to learn something he calls theory first. But he's very nice ... he played something to show me how beautiful my flute sounds.'

At the palazzo, expecting to find Beatrice not best pleased at having been left to her own devices for most of the morning, they found her brimming over with excitement instead. Signora Vandenburg had called with Zoe to discuss the wedding arrangements with the countess.

'Sarah, it's to be just before Christmas – perhaps there will even be snow! And I'm to wear something much prettier than I thought of for myself – it's going to have a little collar of white fur.'

'Don't bank on snow, sweetheart,' Sarah suggested with a smile. 'It doesn't very often visit Venice.'

'I expect it will for us,' said Beatrice, having very little doubt in the matter. 'Zoe wanted to see *you*, but she couldn't wait and said she would telephone.'

The call came later that afternoon, suggesting a rendezvous in Harry's Bar, and Sarah set off to meet her there once the children were in bed.

As once before, Zoe was smiling from a corner table. 'Quite like old times, though our first supper here seems an age ago – you were scarcely on speaking terms with anyone at the palazzo, and I didn't dream of being married before the year was out.'

'Wedding plans forging ahead, I hear.

Beatrice is enchanted with what *she*'s going to wear, and I assume that your own dress will be gorgeous.'

Zoe nodded, then hesitated, for once not sure of what she was going to say next. 'I haven't asked you to be an attendant, Sarah ... I somehow thought you'd rather *not* be asked.'

'Quite right – I'd make a rather elderly bridesmaid, I think, and technically I don't count as a "maid" at all!'

It concealed her true objection very tactfully, she thought. She couldn't bear to take any active part in Zoe's wedding to Giulio. Being present at all would be painful enough, but she could see no way of avoiding that.

They ordered food and wine, and then it was Sarah's turn to feel her way into what to say next. 'I gather that Lucchino went down to Rome after we left Belmonte. You must have been glad to have Giulio and the *padrone* to yourself for a bit. Guests are all very well, but there comes a moment when you want to be rid of them!'

'We weren't by ourselves,' Zoe said rather shortly. 'Franco di Brazzano turned up, so I didn't mind in the least when Elsa hauled me back to Venice. In days to come I shall put up a sign: "Franco go home"!' Then she grimaced at Sarah. 'I shan't do anything of the kind, of course – Giulio feels sorry for him; a fellow-feeling, I guess, for someone else whose mother died young.' She stared at the food that had just been put in front of her, not really seeing it at all. 'You know, I'd never met a man like Giulio before, someone who naturally accepts responsibility for other people and feels passionate about the place he belongs to. I suppose that's an Italian thing – *companilismo*, don't they call it?'

'Yes, they do, and the feeling is certainly very strong here,' Sarah agreed, 'but my brother at home feels just as intensely about *his* "dear, dear land" – Shakespeare's words for it, not mine!'

'It's something else I have to learn,' Zoe said slowly; 'I've lived in cities all my life.' Her face looked strangely sad, and Sarah cast about for something that would make her smile.

'I haven't heard yet where your wedding is to be. Mrs Vandenburg's got her eye on San Marco, I expect.'

Zoe's merry smile reappeared. 'No, but only because she doesn't like it – too Byzantine, my dear! We're going to have the Frari instead.'

'I rather agree with her about the Basilica,' Sarah said thoughtfully. 'It's a robbers' cave filled with stolen loot, though no Venetian worth his salt would admit to it.' Personally, she'd have avoided the Frari as well; the

274

great Gothic barn of a church belonging to the Franciscans *was* where the fashionable weddings took place but surely it wasn't the intimate, friendly place its gentle saint would have wanted built in his name.

'Enough of me,' Zoe suddenly decided. 'What about you? I can't believe the handsome professor isn't glad to have you back in Venice.'

'A fragile new friendship is developing,' Sarah admitted. 'But it has nothing to do with what happened to us in the past, and we're not about to leap into a marital, or any other, bed together.' A smile touched her mouth as she looked at Zoe's expectant face. 'His *motoscafo* is a very welcome alternative to a crowded *vaporetto*!'

'Very rational, very English, and also, I suspect, very deceitful! He still fancies you, Sarah – that much was obvious at the Rotonda ball.'

A nearby clock chimed and Sarah signalled to their waiter for the bill. 'I've caught the Venetian habit of thinking that the day has lasted long enough by ten o'clock. And the children will expect to make an early start for the Lido tomorrow – they miss Belmonte's pool. Why not swim with us if you're tired of making wedding lists.'

'No can do, *amica*. I'm not sure that Giulio will be able to come, but Elsa's organizing a party to celebrate the Feast of the Redentore. She's hell-bent on observing every last one of Venice's traditions even if they *are* only kept up to please the tourists.'

'I'd forgotten the date, so tomorrow *won't* be a day for going to the Lido after all. But you aren't being fair, Zoe. The people here still live intimately with their past. To them it seems like yesterday that they were saved from a plague which could have wiped them out. So they make a bridge of boats from the Zattere to the Giudecca and continue to thank God in the church they built there.'

Zoe smiled at her with warm affection. 'Trouble is, I keep forgetting you're a clergyman's daughter! Don't ever go back to England, please, I need you here.'

They parted company at the Accademia bridge, Zoe to go across it and Sarah to walk on along the *riva*. But she thought as she went along about the evening's conversation. Brides did get het up before their wedding – that was expected of them – and a woman like Elsa Vandenburg wouldn't lose the opportunity that her god-daughter's offered her to turn it into a great social occasion. Even so, Zoe was under too much of a strain. It had been hard work getting her to smile, and her delight at marrying Giulio Leopardi seemed oddly mixed with dread.

The following morning at breakfast, Sarah

reminded the children what day it was – a visit to the Lido had to be postponed, but at least they'd have a grandstand view of the evening's firework display from the school-room windows. Fortunately, too, the morning's post brought letters from Highfold which needed answering, but they'd scarcely got started on the task when Sarah was summoned downstairs. Laura, looking displeased, reported a telephone call from Mrs Vandenburg.

'A party this evening – impromptu, Elsa says, but I doubt that. She's only decided to invite *us* at the last minute.'

'You don't have to go,' Sarah suggested, wondering what it had to do with her.

'Of course we do – Stefan and Angelina have arrived in Venice, and she hasn't lost a moment in getting hold of them. It's a sort of engagement party too, I gather – Giulio and Lucchino are coming over, and Zoe particularly wants *you* there as well. Be ready at eight o'clock, please. It's just a supper party, so don't dress up – something simple will do.'

'Something simple is all I have,' Sarah pointed out, trying not to resent her employer's way of passing on an invitation. It was tempting to refuse to go at all, but that would mean losing the pleasure of seeing Lucchino again, and in any case, she was very curious to meet Stefan Demetrios.

During the rest of the day she resolutely put out of her mind the thought that Giulio would also be at the party. It made no difference to her – he'd be where he now belonged, with Zoe and Elsa. She believed she'd made great progress where he was concerned – almost come to accept that she'd simply imagined the few moments when her heart had known its true home as surely as a compass needle pointed north. Imagination had lied then, but now she was almost herself again, and even having to meet Giulio was an ordeal she could survive.

With Bianca cheerfully agreeing to watch the fireworks with the children, there was no excuse left not to go to Elsa's damned party, but she put on with a certain perverse pleasure the grey dress that had already been seen at the Vandenburg palazzo. Let them see it again; she didn't mind. Her only addition this time was the one piece of jewellery she possessed – a delicate necklet of fire-opals whose gleams of colour echoed the shot silk of her dress. Ready to leave, she stared at her image in the mirror – neat but not gaudy! However inclined she felt to be bloody-minded, Laura could find no fault with that.

Then there came a knock at her door. Half-suspecting that Lucchino had come to fetch her, she found Franco there instead,

278

nattily dressed for the party in dinner jacket and black tie.

'My father asked me to escort you downstairs, signorina,' he said formally, for once managing to speak to her without his sneering smile.

'Thank you; how very kind.' They sounded, she thought, like characters out of a drawing-room comedy, but her heart warmed to Fabrizio, nevertheless, for a courtesy that was as charming as it was unnecessary.

The others were already waiting downstairs. Laura, predictably, not only 'dressed up', but stunning in emerald satin, with diamonds in her hair, waited beside the count. Lucchino came towards Sarah at once, smiling and kind as usual.

'My dear girl, how lovely to see you. We manage at Belmonte without you and the children, but you're sadly missed!'

Now it was necessary – she couldn't avoid it – to hold out her hand to Giulio and re-acquaint herself with that brown, self-disciplined face. But imagination hadn't lied after all; she knew at once, as surely as she believed in Almighty God, that what she'd felt at La Rotonda was true. Even if she never saw him again, she wouldn't forget him or make do with anyone else.

'My father asked me to give you his love,' Giulio said quietly.

'Is he well?' she managed to ask.

'As Lucchino says, a little lonely; otherwise he's well.'

The governess, Laura decided, had received sufficient attention. She glanced at her husband and he obligingly remembered that it was time they left, and Michele was already waiting for them beside the boat.

Outside, it was a perfect summer evening that would soon and suddenly become night. Sarah still missed the long, slow dusk that settled over the Malvern Hills at home, and wondered if Giulio remembered that magical transition from English day into night. He'd been there long enough to have become aware of it. But the thought had to be put away. She was lucky to be in Venice on a very special day; it was time to remember what she had, not weep in her heart for the treasure she had missed. It was time to feel the excitement in the air, and watch the crowds that were making their way in one direction, across the bridge, or on the water, all of them heading for the Zattere and the church of the Redentore on the neighbouring island of the Giudecca.

'You'd rather be going with *them* than to Elsa's party,' Lucchino murmured beside her. 'You're looking wistful, *amore*.'

'Then I shall be all a-grin from now on,' she promised. 'But I'll admit to a hankering to be inside the Redentore this evening – Palladio's church needs to be seen crammed with people, otherwise it's too severe. And I expect the singing will be glorious, too.'

'I'll take you next year,' he promised, smiling at her, as Michele steered them in towards the landing stage.

By Elsa's standards the party was a small one – no more than fifty or so people invited to celebrate the feast day and also, belatedly, her god-daughter's engagement. But this, she explained, with a forgiving smile, was because it was so difficult to lure Giulio from the mainland! A toast was drunk, Giulio replied to it very pleasantly on behalf of Zoe and himself, and then the evening's formality was over. Resplendent in a caftan of embroidered brocade, Elsa invited her guests to enjoy the lavish hospitality set out for them, until the sky outside the *portego*'s huge windows darkened and the firework display across the canal could begin.

Rather to her surprise, Sarah enjoyed the party. Steven, present of course, had been commandeered by Elsa, so there was no covert hostility to diffuse between him and Lucchino; and, watching Zoe with Giulio, Sarah decided that she could stop worrying about a girl who now seemed entirely care-free. No one who looked so radiantly beautiful *could* be anything but happy.

With that settled, she could take stock instead of the guest who was presumably troubling Fabrizio's peace of mind. At first glance there seemed to be little to worry about. Beside the count's elegant Venetian style, Stefan Demetrios looked at a disadvantage – powerful but slightly uncouth. His swarthy face was only redeemed from downright ugliness, in fact, by a pair of bright, intelligent eyes – true Greek eyes, Sarah thought, when she suddenly found them fastened on herself. Disconcertingly, she saw that he was shaking his head.

'There's something wrong here,' he said in fluent but heavily accented English. 'Traditionally, we're supposed to like each other, you and I, but you're not liking me at all. Why is that when we've only just met?'

There was, she thought, only one way to deal with Stefan Demetrios – meet him head on, with no care for the social niceties.

'I look after the count's children,' she said simply. 'He and they will miss Donna Laura very much if all her time is absorbed in giving masterclasses for you.'

He changed tack slightly, taking her by surprise. 'I know that you're a musician too. I asked Laura to sing for us this evening, which means that you have to play as well. Are you going to refuse because you disapprove of me?'

'What I think of you doesn't matter in the least,' she answered steadily. 'All that matters is that Laura can manage being both the performer you think she ought to be *and* Count Fabrizio's wife.'

'Well said, Miss Cavanagh; I hear what you're saying and I agree. Naturally, so does my wife!' An understanding smile changed his face, making Laura's captivation understandable, but at the same time less worrying. '*Will* you play, please?' She nodded and when he walked away she thought that some treaty had been struck between them.

Beckoned by the count a few moments later, she found the music of the songs Laura had sung at La Pietà lying on top of the piano. The reason for her dramatic choice of dress was now clear – she'd known about this musical interlude all along but chosen not to mention it. The room fell silent around them, Laura shot her a faintly apologetic, pleading glance and there was nothing to do but sit down at the piano.

They hadn't rehearsed together for weeks, so the performance was probably not as polished as the earlier one had been. Listening and watching them both, Giulio thought it still more moving because it was more spontaneous. Laura singing was unquestionably someone else – not the unreliably volatile and selfish creature they knew too well, but a woman released into her true element. There was silence when the last note died away, as if the people there were still collectively holding their breath. Then Demetrios stepped forward to kiss Laura's hand and wild applause broke out. Sarah stayed where she was at the piano, waiting for the moment when she could slip back into the crowd, but the Greek held out his other hand to her and she was obliged to stand up and accept a share of the applause.

Released at last, she found her way back to Lucchino, and begged him to find her a long, cold drink. But it was Giulio who brought it back to her, Lucchino, he said, having been temporarily purloined by Elsa.

'I'm afraid the recital was sprung on you,' he said quietly. 'It was unfair of Laura and Demetrios, but the songs sounded even more beautiful than before if that's any comfort to you. I even saw some women moved to tears by them.'

'Well, Mrs Vandenburg may not be pleased,' Sarah said ruefully. 'This evening is meant to be a celebration.' She sipped her iced *citron pressé* and cast around for something innocuous to say. 'Emmanuele will be sure to ask how the donkeys are, and how many puppies Bella had.'

'There were six puppies. Five will be given away when they're old enough to leave their mother, but I'll keep one in case Emmanuele wants it.'

'*Wants* it? Oh, if the count agrees he'll want it all right.' Awkwardness forgotten, Sarah's smile illumined her thin face for a moment. 'Poor puppy, though, in Venice – it would have a better life at Belmonte, I'm afraid.'

'But not nearly so much love,' Giulio pointed out gravely. 'Isn't that important, too?'

She had to agree, no longer sure that it was Bella's offspring they were talking about, because conversations with Giulio Leopardi were never quite what they seemed. Then, abruptly, he spoke of something else.

'Laura looks radiant and Fabrizio looks worried. I don't hesitate to say that because you're part of the family now. Is Laura's new enthusiasm something to be anxious about?'

Sarah remembered what Zoe had said, and thought how true it was. He did feel responsible for other people. So it was likely that he might always feel especially responsible for Laura.

'Laura won't be *content* to be only a wife and mother for years yet, perhaps never,' was Sarah's slow answer, 'and you can't help knowing why that is when you hear her sing. She's happy again now, and Stefan Demetrios understands that. But he's kind as well as clever, and I believe that he intends to manage things without doing any harm to the Brazzano family.'

Giulio accepted this careful assessment, knowing that the young man he'd been *hadn't* managed Laura nearly well enough.

That bitter failure had brought him to where he was now, but all he was free to do was promise himself that there mustn't be another failure – not with Zoe, who needed and deserved happiness. He longed to make this girl in front of him understand that, wanted to ask her to forgive him for the insuperable muddle that he'd made of things. But even if he could ever have found the words, it was too late. Zoe had discovered them and come to stand beside him, linking her arm in his.

Smiling too brightly at Sarah, she offered a half-serious protest. *'Amica mia,* you can have every other gorgeous male here, but not *this* one; he's mine!'

There was a moment in which neither Sarah nor Giulio found anything appropriate to say, and then the awkward pause was over because, with not quite impeccable timing, Steven Harding also arrived, to tell Sarah how beautifully she'd played her part in the recital. Relief made her smile at him too warmly, and for the man watching them it was confirmation enough of what Franco had once told him. Stupid of him a moment ago, insanely stupid, to have imagined that there was anything at all he wanted to say to Sarah Cavanagh.

Twenty-One

When Count Fabrizio was consulted the following morning he regretfully ruled against the puppy.

'Emmanuele would love it, I know – you don't have to persuade me of that,' he added, 'even if you think you do! But Venice is no place for what will grow into a large dog; and by then, in any case, Emmanuele will be away at school.' He looked at her disappointed face and asked a wistful question. 'Am I not right, Sarah?'

'Yes, I'm afraid you are,' she had to agree. 'Emmanuele won't know that the offer was ever made – otherwise there'd be real heartbreak.' She hesitated a moment, thinking that the man in front of her looked strained by more than his veto on the puppy. He might think that on the subject of his wife she should wait to be asked for an opinion, but she decided to risk it anyway.

'I'm glad Donna Laura was persuaded to sing last night,' she ventured, 'even though we hadn't rehearsed and I must have hit at least two wrong notes.'

'I didn't hear them,' he said. 'It sounded perfect to me.'

Not encouraged to go on, she nevertheless did so. 'I know the masterclasses will absorb a lot of the countess's time, but she can't *not* be involved with singing. Stefan Demetrios understands much more than that, though. He will deal with her, I think, so that no damage is done here.'

'You liked him, in other words; so do I,' Fabrizio admitted ruefully. 'We shall see what happens, *non è vero*? And, dear Sarah, I wish I could have said yes to the puppy!'

She went away to write a brief note to Giulio, and posted it when she and Beatrice escorted Emmanuele to the morning's flute lesson. It didn't really amount to something to grieve over in a world racked by much bigger tragedies, but all the same she felt sad and depressed, and Beatrice had to ask her twice before she agreed that the firework display the previous evening had indeed been *stupendo*.

Beyond another note, written to thank Mrs Vandenburg for her party, she had no contact with the palazzo across the canal. Giulio would certainly have gone straight back to Belmonte, but as the days passed she had no idea whether Zoe had gone with him or stayed in Venice. Lucchino, too, seemed to have disappeared and she was all the more grateful for Steven Harding's occasional suggestions of a meal together or a boat trip for the children.

On one of these outings, they chugged across the lagoon to Chioggia to see the fishing boats come in. While Beatrice and Emmanuele listened entranced on the quayside to the racket of the fish auction, Sarah asked the question that often exercised her mind.

'I don't think you invite us to come out with you purely from kindness, though that certainly comes into it; it seems to me that you enjoy the children's company. Am I right?'

He grinned at her with the affection she thought she'd lost a long time ago. 'It *could* occur to you that I have to accept their company in order to get yours! That's true of course, but it's also true that I find them likeable and interesting – much to my surprise and probably also to yours.'

She smiled at that, and he commented on the fact. 'That's the first time you've smiled this morning. Feeling blue, my dear?'

The question was gently put and she realized again how much he'd changed; time was when he wouldn't have noticed, being too concerned with his own affairs.

'Perhaps I am, a little,' she confessed, 'though not for any good reason I can think of. Something to do with the summer being soon over, maybe, or feeling a little isolated on the palazzo's top floor. Those are silly enough excuses, of course. I actually *prefer* Venice when the tourists have left her to herself again; and with the children on the top floor is where the governess properly belongs!'

'You're missing Lucchino, perhaps,' Steven suggested pointedly. 'Don't you know where *he* is?'

'No, but there's no reason why I should. He has a host of friends throughout the length and breadth of Italy.'

Then came another sharp question. 'So are you not going to marry him? I'm sure he's asked you to.'

'He has, but I'm not,' she answered calmly, and offered her lovely slow smile. 'I'm not marrying anyone, as it happens – *just* in case you felt obliged out of charity to suggest it yourself!'

'Didn't enter my head,' he lied with real heroism. 'I know it's only my *motoscafo* that attracts you.'

'And your kindness,' she added gravely. 'That's important too.' Then to move an awkward conversation away from themselves, she asked about Mrs Vandenburg. 'Still knee-deep in wedding invitations, I expect. I haven't heard from Zoe, so I assume that she's back at Belmonte.'

'She's in New York – flew out two days ago,' Steven astonishingly reported. 'It's odd she didn't let you know, but it *was* a very sudden decision to go. She'd got alarmed about her father apparently – reckoned he was ill but wasn't saying so. Elsa is displeased, of course – thinks Zoe was worked up about nothing.'

'She could try being sympathetic,' Sarah pointed out. 'Zoe *hates* aeroplanes – she wouldn't have endured a long flight if she didn't think it was necessary. Elsa's more than capable of organizing a wedding without the bride – she probably prefers it that way, in fact, only she isn't saying so.'

'Waspish, coming from you,' said Steven, grinning again. 'But women don't like Elsa much, I've noticed.'

'Just because men *do*, I expect,' Sarah suggested, smiling herself. 'Now, I think it's time we detached the children from all this market haggling. They aren't supposed to be learning the salty language of the fishwives.'

'It's what they'll hear along the Rialto any morning; still, by all means let's collect them and go in search of lunch – I'm getting hungry.'

They picked their way through the clutter of boxes, ropes, and nets littering the quay, Sarah holding on to Emmanuele and Beatrice happy to clutch Steven's hand. They might, she thought, have been any Venetian

291

family enjoying an outing together, if only the fair-haired, large professor had looked a little more Italian.

It should have been the di Brazzanos there with their children, of course, but with Laura so often over at the Cini Foundation on San Giorgio Maggiore now, Fabrizio was once again immersed in the preservation of his beautiful fragile city. They both managed to fill their days busily enough, but Sarah pitied them both. They had no idea what they lost by leaving Beatrice and Emmanuele to the care of other people.

Gradually, as the summer heat began to lessen, the swarms of people herded through the doors of St Mark's and the Doge's Palace dwindled as well. It was becoming possible to walk through the Piazza again without dodging the crowds, and board a *vaporetto* without queuing for it. The summer was dying in its usual magnificent blaze of sunsets over the lagoon; soon the first hint of autumn would chill the early-morning air.

Beatrice's dancing classes had resumed after the summer holiday, and Sarah was waiting for her one afternoon, sipping an espresso at Florian's, when Mrs Vandenburg walked by. She stopped, hesitating for a moment, and something in her pale face prompted Sarah's invitation to her to sit down.

'You look tired ... You're probably working too hard on Zoe's behalf,' Sarah suggested. 'I haven't heard from her, so I've no idea what's been happening about her father.'

'Nothing's been happening – that's *my* guess,' Elsa said tartly. 'If you want my candid opinion, Jacob Hartman has recovered from whatever ailed him, but Zoe is enjoying being back in New York too much to see the need to hurry back here. She's always been headstrong, but not often so selfish and inconsiderate. I find it upsetting, I'm afraid.'

Elsa's usually confident voice trembled a little, either with tiredness or displeasure. Sarah wasn't sure which, but she felt sorry for a woman who *was* being unfairly treated.

'Perhaps Giulio Leopardi is the one to hint that it's time Zoe came back?' she suggested.

'I've pointed that out,' Elsa said wearily. 'He seems to think she'll come when she's ready; like all men, he has no idea that a wedding doesn't just arrange itself. I shall soon lose patience with both of them!' But she tried to smile as she said it, and for the first time Sarah found herself liking Elsa Vandenburg.

'Zoe's lucky to have you,' she said impulsively. 'Right now I must go and collect Beatrice, but please let me know if there is

293

anything I can do to help.'

She walked away, thinking that it was more likely to be Zoe herself that she heard from, blithely announcing that she was back in Venice. But a week later, Elsa Vandenburg did ring, speaking in a voice that Sarah scarcely recognized; anger and despair seemed to be competing for the upper hand.

'You were kind enough to offer help. No help is needed – Zoe has changed her mind about marrying Giulio Leopardi.'

Sarah found herself clutching the telephone so tightly that her hand was numb. She transferred it to the other hand and tried to think of something to say.

'You're sure, of course ... I mean, *she*'s sure ... but it's so hard to believe that I really don't know *what* I mean.'

'Perhaps you'll find it easier when I mention that she didn't go to New York alone. We now know that Lucchino Vittoria went with her – Giulio's closest friend. It's very pretty, isn't it?'

'Lucchino will have gone to help Zoe,' Sarah said steadily, 'not to betray Giulio. If he saw that she was distraught – which she probably was – he would have been too kind to let her go alone.'

'He may be Sir Galahad himself for all I know,' Elsa snapped. 'The fact remains that the Leopardis will be humiliated, and I'm to be mortified in front of everyone in Venice.

I'm disgraced by my own god-daughter.'

'It's very painful,' Sarah agreed hoarsely, 'but please try to think of Zoe's unhappiness too. I've known all along that much as she longed to marry Giulio, taking on Belmonte as well was going to be much harder for her. Causing all this distress will have been the last thing she wanted to do.' There was silence at the other end of the line. 'What will she do? Stay in New York?' Sarah finally had to ask.

'I suppose so. About Sir Galahad's movements I have no idea, nor do I care; presumably he'll go back to Rome. My own task is to start cancelling every arrangement I've made. I'll speak to Laura di Brazzano, but perhaps *you*'d better be the one to break the news to Beatrice.'

With that she rang off, leaving Sarah still blindly holding the telephone. Yes, she ought to deal with Beatrice first, before she allowed herself to imagine what the news had done to Giulio and the *padrone*. What was it Lucchino had said? Zoe would bring back gaiety to Belmonte. That seemed a cruel misjudgement to remember now, but it *had* seemed possible at the time.

She climbed the stairs to the school room, knowing that the children always waited expectantly for whatever news her summons to the telephone had brought. Unaware that her face was sheet-white, she wondered why they looked suddenly fearful. She put an arm round each one of them, and willed her voice not to break.

'Nothing dreadfully *bad*,' she said at once, 'but dreadfully disappointing. Zoe went home to New York because her father wasn't well ... She's staying there for a bit ... not marrying Cousin Giulio after all.'

'Not soon, you mean,' Beatrice insisted. 'The wedding has to wait ... while her father gets well.'

'Not ever, *tesoro*; Signora Vandenburg telephoned. Zoe has changed her mind about marrying.'

'She can't ... she *can't* change her mind. How can she do that when I'm going to be her bridesmaid?' Beatrice's huge brown eyes filled with tears as she stared at Sarah's face. The truth was written there, and she could see it even half-blinded as she was. 'My lovely dress with the fur collar, Sarah,' she whispered. 'There *would* have been snow – I know there would.'

'I expect so, sweetheart,' Sarah agreed, now inclined to weep herself. It seemed too much to ask of a bitterly disappointed ten-year-old to think of anyone's woe but her own, but nevertheless she tried.

'Everyone else is sad as well, darling. Zoe herself and Cousin Giulio most of all, of course, but also Zio Luigi, and their friends.'

Beatrice sniffed loudly, very loath to give any one of them a thought. But gradually her sobs gave way to hiccups as a glimmer of consolation occurred to her. 'I shall wear my dress *not* to a wedding then. I'll go to Mass in it on Jesus's birthday.'

Sarah cravenly refused to point out that fur-trimmed white silk might make her seem a little overdressed in the Basilica on Christmas Day, and said instead that she would undoubtedly look very festive. Beatrice nodded and went next door to acquaint Bianca with the change of plan. Left alone with Sarah, Emmanuele smeared her wet cheeks with gentle fingers – a service she had occasionally rendered him.

'Don't cry, Sarah; tears don't mend things. That's what you say to us.'

'So it is,' she agreed tremulously, 'and, as you know, the governess is always right!'

Later, Bianca reported that the count and countess were dining out, so at least she was spared a summons from Laura that she certainly didn't want.

There was time to think quietly at last about a girl who'd been too dazzled to think clearly and had simply got swept along. However much it hurt now, Zoe had been brave to admit that she must change her mind. Elsa would eventually get over the shock, and Venice would enjoy the sensation; but it left Giulio without a wife, and

Belmonte without the bride who'd been going to bring it back to happy life. Sarah returned finally to the thought of Lucchino. Elsa was wrong if she thought Giulio would blame him for taking care of Zoe. He'd know that his friend had simply done what he would do himself – accepted responsibility for someone who'd badly needed help.

Twenty-Two

Autumn, with its lovely golden days, was nearly over. The first mists and rain-showers began to creep over the lagoon, the last tourists straggled back to the mainland, and the flock of black, swan-necked gondolas tethered along the Riva degli Schiavoni were battened down to await the return of spring. Venice belonged to itself again.

Sarah knew that Steven Harding was often away, cramming in as many journeys as he could before the weather in the Aegean made travelling too unpleasant. But she agreed with what the children said: they all missed the visits they'd made with him to out of the way museums and curios that he seemed to know more about that most of the true-born Venetians did.

There was no news of Lucchino, and the invitation to return to Belmonte for the *vendemmia* hadn't come. Sarah hadn't now expected it. Giulio Leopardi was probably in no frame of mind to think of having small children hinder all the work of the grape harvest that had to be done. Her only contact was with the *padrone*, with whom she exchanged such news as there was. His reaction to the cancelled marriage had been kinder than Elsa's – he was saddened, but not spiteful about a girl he knew had intended them no harm.

With no wedding to arrange, Mrs Vandenburg reverted to her normal habit of abandoning Venice for the winter. But she informed Sarah before she left that she refused to return to New York and risk bumping into her god-daughter. Until she'd forgiven Zoe, she'd give Paris a try instead, even though she had grave doubts about the French.

As Christmas approached, Sarah consulted Beatrice as to how the festival was normally celebrated at the palazzo. They always went down to Rome, Beatrice said, to stay with their aunt and uncle.

'Exciting for you,' Sarah replied and went next to see the countess, confident that after nine months' work no employer could think her children's governess hadn't earned a break. Laura looked put out, but found it hard to refuse Sarah's suggestion that she should return to spend Christmas at Highfold.

'Go if you must, of course,' she said with her usual lack of grace, 'but I'd assumed you'd come to Rome with us.'

'Highfold, please,' Sarah insisted firmly. 'I need to see my family again.'

She booked her flight and began to count the days, pleasure only lessened by the discovery that Emmanuele was also counting the days to the moment when he and his dear *Inglese* went their separate ways. Then one morning, returning from their usual walk, she found an agitated Count Fabrizio obviously looking for them. He waited for the children to rush upstairs, and then unburdened himself to Sarah.

'My wife and I must leave for Rome this afternoon,' he said with the slightly petulant air of a man whose well-laid plans were being disrupted. 'We were to have left at the weekend with the children, as you know, but my sister reports a family crisis of some kind. She was so *distraite* on the telephone that she scarcely made any sense at all, but there's no question of refusing to go, I'm afraid.'

'But aren't the children still going with you?' Sarah asked.

'No, she says not. Franco must bring them down later, as arranged. Your own departure needn't change, of course.' He tried to smile despite his agitation. 'It will prove a storm in a teacup, I expect ... you know what we Italians are!'

It didn't seem polite to agree, so Sarah merely said instead that she'd warn the children of a small change of plan – nothing they need worry about.

'English calmness,' he said wryly. 'So much easier to live with!'

'But not nearly so exciting,' she pointed out and had the pleasure at least of seeing him laugh.

The children weren't perturbed to watch their parents leave, and Sarah scarcely speculated as to what the storm in a teacup might be. But the following morning, when the count telephoned from Rome, it seemed that the marchesa had good reason to be *distraite*.

'I don't know where to begin, Sarah, we're in such turmoil here. Lucchino seems to have taken leave of his senses, and my sister and brother-in-law are in complete despair.'

Still very little wiser, Sarah gently led him back to the beginning, and rather incoherently the story emerged. Three days previously, Lucchino had arrived back in Rome after many weeks away. Parental pleasure at seeing him hadn't survived the discovery that he'd brought back with him the very girl who'd just humiliated Giulio Leopardi – an unreliable American who, according to the marchese, his son should never have accompanied to New York. But, the even worse news was Lucchino's announcement that he was going to marry Zoe Hartman himself.

'It's ... it's very strange,' Sarah murmured inadequately, knowing, as she did so, that even the count would think this was carrying English phlegm too far. She swallowed a rising bubble of hysteria and tried again. 'At the moment I can't make any sense of it at all, but Lucchino is wise and kind ... There must *be* an explanation.'

'He's been bewitched by a wicked girl – that's my sister's explanation,' Fabrizio said sadly. 'Lucchino will eventually talk her round – he always can – but God knows what Giulio and Luigi will think, and they were always such friends. The cancellation of the wedding was bad enough but *this*...'

It seemed time to remind Fabrizio about his own children, and Sarah was about to do so when he came to the point himself.

'Laura is coping wonderfully with my poor sister, but Christmas is quite ruined for this year. We *can't* pretend, I'm afraid, that there's any peace or goodwill here at the moment.'

'What is the alternative to letting the

children come?' Sarah asked, fearing that she knew the answer.

'There isn't one,' the count said miserably. 'We could *not* ask Giulio to have them. In the circumstances, it would be impossible to approach him even.'

'I realize that, but I *could* take them with me to Highfold,' Sarah all but shouted suddenly into the telephone. 'May I do that? The children at home would love it; Beatrice and Emmanuele have been corresponding with them for months.'

'Well, well, yes, Sarah,' came the flustered answer. 'Indeed, why not? Much, much better for them than coming here.' He thought for a moment, then spoke in a firmer, more decisive voice. 'If you'll bring Michele to the telephone I can give him instructions – he knows how to reach my man of business.'

'You'll have a less happy Christmas than we shall have, I'm afraid,' Sarah said regretfully. 'I'm so sorry about that, but now I'd better find Michele for you.'

By mid-afternoon, it had all been arranged. Even the hurdle of getting two more seats on her flight to London had been surmounted in some way by the count's influential man. But Meg sounded anxious when she was telephoned.

'Sarah, if this is to say you can't come after all, the children will *never* forgive you – nor, as a matter of fact, will Matthew and I.'

'I can come ... *am* coming, Meg dear, but I need to bring Beatrice and Emmanuele with me. Is that all right?'

'Not just all right, it's perfect! Wait till the children know – they're half mad with excitement already.'

'The story, which is complicated, must wait till I get home. But same flight, tell Matthew. See you all very soon.'

Now it was safe to break the news in the school room, where strange Christmas cards were being made to leave for Claretta and Michele and the girls. But halfway up the staircase, Sarah stopped and turned round, remembering that there was someone else who hadn't been thought of. She went in search of Franco, and found him in the library, staring moodily out across the Grand Canal at the Salute, now veiled in rain. When he turned round she could see at once that he'd heard from Rome as well.

'You've spoken with your father, I'm sure,' she suggested, and saw him nod. 'He says I may take the children to England, and it's all arranged. But what about you? Can *you* still go to Rome?'

'I expect so, but I don't intend to. My aunt has enough to cope with.' His white face looked shocked, and Sarah was suddenly reminded that he was much younger than he liked to seem. The strange family events had thrown him off-balance, leaving him uncertain for once.

'My brother's children are much the same age as Beatrice and Emmanuele, and we shall have a very simple family Christmas; but you'd be welcome, Franco, if you cared to come,' she said impulsively.

His expression changed, almost seemed inclined to waver on the edge of tears as he stared at her.

'You're inviting *me* to your home?' he asked unsteadily.

'Of course, my brother and sister-in-law wouldn't expect me to leave you to spend Christmas alone.'

'It's kind of you ... very kind,' he said jerkily. 'But I think I shall go to Belmonte. Lucchino and Zoe have treated Giulio very badly; he and Zio Luigi will need company.'

They might equally, she feared, prefer to be left alone, but Franco's intention was to behave as a true friend should, and she smiled warmly at him. It was a lovely smile, he noticed, and wondered why he'd only just realized that for the first time. 'I can drive you and the children to the airport,' he said. 'I'll go on to Belmonte from there.'

'That would be really kind, Franco. Now I must go and break the news upstairs.'

Beatrice was admiring her own Nativity masterpiece – a flock of angels, in full evening dress, of course, hovering about the cradle; while Emmanuele's drawing, just as predictably, was full of animals, with one small donkey about to lick the baby's face. They both looked at Sarah as she walked into the room, sensing something unexpected that they might not like.

'A small change of plan,' she said at once. 'You're not going to Rome after all – your aunt is not well; and Mamma is having to look after her.'

'So *she* isn't coming home,' Beatrice pointed out, 'but *you* won't be here either.' Her lower lip began to tremble; this was something serious – a matter for grief, not just a display of ill-temper. 'We shall be left here alone?'

Emmanuele couldn't have brought himself to ask the dreadful question at all, but his brown eyes were fastened on Sarah's face, imploring her to make everything all right again. Then she smiled, and he knew he could stop worrying.

'*You* won't be here either, my treasures. I've spoken to your father and he says that you can come with me to England – to Highfold.'

'To stay with James and John and Harriet?' Beatrice liked to be sure of the facts before she rejoiced too soon.

'And the cows and sheep and horses?' Emmanuele put in anxiously.

'All of them,' she agreed. 'We're going to

fly to London tomorrow. Franco will drive us to Marco Polo airport, and then go on to Belmonte himself, in case Cousin Giulio and Zio Luigi are feeling lonely.'

Tears magically forgotten, Beatrice was beginning to smile; then a problem occurred. 'You don't have Mass in England. Can I not wear my Christmas dress?'

Sarah thought of the antiquated heating system in the village church and shook her head. 'Some people do have Mass in England, but we don't at Highfold.'

They both looked so disappointed that she cheerfully swept a few liturgical differences away. 'What we have is much the same thing, but the church will be rather chilly. Better keep your dress for dinner at home, I think.'

Beatrice agreed to this, and then danced out of the room. She could be heard a moment later explaining to Bianca, in the tone of a world-weary socialite changing her mind about a season on the Côte d'Azur, that this year they'd be spending Christmas in *Inghilterra* instead of Rome.

The journey to Highfold took up most of the next day. They said goodbye to Franco at the airport, and so pleasant had he been over a shared breakfast that both children were momentarily sad to see him go. But their beautiful, gleaming aeroplane was waiting on the tarmac, and sadness couldn't survive the excitement of it all.

By late afternoon they were touching down at Heathrow. It was already almost dark, so overcast was the day, and the London air felt bitterly cold and raw. The children were beginning to feel tired, and suddenly their white faces looked pinched and miserable. It was nearly Christmas, and they wanted to be at home, not in this strange, alien place filled with a heaving throng of people. With their luggage finally claimed and heaped on a trolley, Sarah led them out into the arrivals hall, praying that if she couldn't pick Matthew out in the crowd, he might at least be able to spot them. Then, suddenly he was there, broad and imperturbable, and kind. Nothing to worry about now; he would take charge and get them home.

A brief, hard hug for her and then he turned his attention to the children. In old corduroy trousers and a thick sweater of Meg's making, he was a large and unfamiliar figure. Having to look up a long way, Beatrice feared there was too much of him to be manageable, and for once she wasn't sure what to say. But Emmanuele had seen Matthew smile, and his smile was just like Sarah's. He put out his hand with all the aplomb of Count Fabrizio himself, and felt it gently enclosed in this giant's huge one.

'You've had a long day already, and we're still not home yet, I'm afraid. Let's get going, shall we?' Matthew suggested.

He led them outside, found the car, and installed them and their belongings in it with the minimum of fuss. Ten minutes later they were clear of the airport and on the westbound road. The children tried to stay awake but they were soon nodding in the back of the car. When the traffic had thinned a little Matthew could spare his sister a quick glance.

'Good to be home?'

'Oh, yes,' she answered simply, and saw him smile.

'Meg's been thinking that we'd lost you to Venice for good. We're promised a white Christmas, by the way...'

It was her turn to smile. 'Beatrice would expect no less!'

Content to be together again, they finished the journey with little more said, once it had been established that everyone was well at home; there'd be time enough to talk later on.

The old, ivy-clad farmhouse awaited them, lights shining a welcome through the first flakes of snow that were already beginning to fall. Looking at the sky, Matthew predicted a heavy fall, and congratulated himself on having moved his livestock into shelter.

The sleeping children were carried in-doors and put to bed almost without stirring. Harriet had lost *her* struggle to stay awake, Meg reported, but James and John were holding out for Sarah to go and kiss them goodnight. But at last, with the house peaceful, she could sit down to supper with her brother and sister-in-law.

'Delicious – I'd forgotten the taste of steak and kidney pie,' she said contentedly.

'You've forgotten to eat at all,' her sister-in-law said accusingly. '*I* get rounder every day and *you*'re as thin as a pikestaff. I thought a diet of pasta was what made Italian women so wonderfully voluptuous.'

'Rice or polenta in Venice,' Sarah pointed out, 'not pasta! But no cars, remember, so we take a lot of exercise.'

Watching her across the supper table, Meg thought her sister-in-law looked not only thin and tired, but haunted as well by some private sadness, even though she smiled easily enough. Whatever Sarah said about it, Meg wasn't going to believe that taking Mr Crabtree's job had been anything but a serious mistake, but it wasn't until coffee was on the table that she asked for them to be given the 'complicated' story.

'It's the people involved who make it com-plicated,' Sarah answered, 'and I probably shan't describe them very well.'

'We know the *dramatis personae*,' Meg said,

pleased with herself for remembering the phrase. 'Fill us in on the plot, please.'

Sarah did her best, and at the end of the recital had only kept back one thing – her own entirely unreciprocated love for the *padrone*'s son. She wouldn't talk about it, even to Meg and Matthew, and in any case it had nothing to do with the story. With the 'plot' finally explained, she smiled at them and pointed out that it was nearly midnight; their day had probably been even longer than hers and it was time they all went to bed.

But when she'd kissed them goodnight and gone upstairs, Meg still sat lost in thought.

'It's not Lucchino who's the problem,' she said decidedly. 'He's no more than a friend she's very fond of and for the moment can't understand. My guess is that Steven is upsetting her again. The damned man *would* have to open up all the old wounds by turning up just where she happens to be.'

'He seems to have improved,' Matthew tried to suggest. 'Even *she* said so.'

'Much better if he hadn't,' Meg complained, 'she could have gone on hating him.'

Matthew couldn't remember that Sarah had ever hated her then husband, though she'd certainly been diminished and hurt by him. But he knew better than to try to persuade Meg to change her mind, and merely said instead that Sarah was safely home and could *they* now please go to bed as well. Meg sweetly agreed and they climbed the stairs, only stopping at the wide landing window to watch the thickly-falling snow, which Matthew predicted would be at least six inches deep by morning.

Twenty-Three

The farmhouse kitchen at Highfold was a lovely place – warm and welcoming, Emmanuele decided the following morning. And the fair-haired lady who smiled at him when he bowed over her hand as his father had taught him, she was lovely, too.

Sarah introduced the children already sitting at the table, but he could have guessed who they were: James, the eldest, clearly in charge; John, smiling a friendly hello; and small Harriet, for once not sure what to make of newcomers. This grave, dark-haired boy was nothing like the brothers she was used to.

But by the time porridge was on the table, and Matthew had walked in, bringing with him the sharp taste of snow and freezing air, awkwardness was at an end.

'The white stuff outside is specially for you,' he told Beatrice, then looked at the rest of them. 'I shall want help this morning; the animals need feeding.'

James nodded, expecting this request. Emmanuele, watching carefully, copied James's nod. 'Shouldn't we go now?' he asked anxiously.

Matthew smiled over the sugar he was spooning on his porridge. 'We can have breakfast first.' But he'd registered Beatrice's look of doubt. 'Ladies needn't come if they don't want to.'

'Of course she wants to,' James said firmly. 'Don't you, Beatrice?'

She found herself unable to confess to this more manageable edition of her host that horses and cows and such weren't in fact *quite* her thing.

James looked satisfied with her doubtful smile. 'You're much prettier than Janey Marriott – I'm glad about that.'

It took Beatrice another day to discover that Janey was the supercilious daughter of the vicarage with whom he fought an ongoing war, but the pleasing tenor of his speech was unmistakable and she became his handmaiden from then on.

Recovered from her fit of shyness, Harriet was now prepared to wave at Emmanuele whenever he looked her way, while John explained the rest of the morning's duties. After the animals had been attended to would come the decoration of the Christmas tree, where the female touch would certainly be needed. Emmanuele smiled at his sister, and then at Sarah. Highfold seemed to offer even more joys than Belmonte, translated to a white, glittering world that entranced him with its beauty when they went outside after breakfast.

From then on it was a Christmas to remember for always – learning to skate on the frozen pond, building a snowman complete with pipe and old hat borrowed from Matthew, carols in a candle-lit village church, and dinner on Christmas night at which Beatrice finally got to wear her white silk dress. She'd have liked Janey Marriott – now met in church – to see it as well; but it would have to be left to James to hint to Miss Marriott that she might as well concede defeat.

Too tired to stay awake any longer, the children finally agreed to go to bed, and Matthew went as usual for a last check that all was well outside; Meg, left with her sister-in-law, heaved a sigh of contentment.

'What a lovely day it's been. I don't understand people who pretend to hate Christmas, do you?'

'Not really, except that sometimes they're short of the things that make it beautiful, like the peace and love we have here.'

Meg nodded, then followed the direction of Sarah's thoughts. 'How will things have gone in Rome, do you suppose – unhappily?'

Sarah hesitated over an answer. 'I'm afraid so. Even Lucchino, charming and persuasive though he is, will have a job getting his family to accept Zoe after what's happened. But it's hard on her, too. She *must* know what distress has been caused, and her worst sadness will be if Lucchino's friendship with Giulio doesn't survive.'

Meg was more concerned with an anxiety nearer home. 'What about you, love? You forget to smile sometimes and then your face looks sad. I shall feel like throttling Steven Harding if he's upsetting you again. It was a cruel stroke of fate to send *him* back to Venice just now.'

Sarah was able to shake her head convincingly. 'No need to worry, Meg dear. There's nothing harder to revive than a fire that's gone out! But we *are* friends again, which is very pleasant.' It didn't answer Meg's concern though and she still had to find some adequate explanation. 'I know I'm only responsible – and temporarily at that! – for the count's children, but it's hard not to get involved. I'd like them *all* to settle down happily together, but I can't even feel sure that Fabrizio and Laura will lastingly sort themselves out – the truth is that they're a very dysfunctional family!'

'Which must surely include Franco as well.'

Sarah nodded, thinking back painfully to her first conversation about him with Giulio Leopardi. 'I was told right at the beginning that he hadn't recovered from his mother's death and the count's remarriage; then, I thought it was a poor excuse, but I understand him a little better now.'

'I hope you understand his stepmother, too. She sounds a thorough-going bitch to me.'

'Well, at least she remembered to telephone from Rome this morning, to speak to the children. I can forgive her quite a lot for that.' Sarah thought for a moment, then added something else. 'She isn't a bitch *naturally*, if you see what I mean. Her marriage was a mistake at the time and she hasn't been very successful since at learning to live with it. But ten years from now she may be thankful to be the Countess di Brazzano, instead of a superannuated opera star whose tantrums everyone is tired of.'

'Provided the marriage survives.'

'It will,' Sarah said definitely. 'I was wrong about Fabrizio too; he won't ever give up on her. For an Italian husband he's amazingly faithful.'

'Involved, you certainly are,' Meg commented. 'And you speak about the *padrone*, at least, as if he means a great deal to you.'

'He reminds me of my father, that's why – scholarly and shy and gentle. The tragedy of his wife's death was all the more terrible because he felt to blame for it. But the children managed to bring him out of his shell, especially Emmanuele who loves him dearly.'

'All the same, I hate your going back to Venice. It will be months before we see you again,' Meg complained.

'Not if the plot I'm hatching comes off! I want Matthew to bring you and the children to visit *me* – in the late spring, before the city gets too crowded. You can't *not* see Venice, Meg. Matthew might echo Robert Brenchley's panic-stricken cable back to New York when he arrived: "streets full of water; please advise!", but I guarantee that *you'll* be bowled over.'

Then, as the door opened and Matthew walked in, snowflakes melting in his hair, his wife smiled at him. 'We're going to Venice,' she said.

'I know. Quite soon, apparently. John says it's sinking into its lagoon.'

'Not noticeably for another hundred years,' Sarah reassured him. 'You'll be all right.'

Mindful of what Meg had said, she took care for the rest of her visit not to be caught looking mournful. Her family were not to imagine for a moment that, much as she loved Highfold, she was reluctant to leave it and go back to Venice.

There wasn't much chance that she would ever face Lucchino and Zoe again, but still she had to come to terms with what she thought about them. Zoe, seemingly, had weighed her future and decided that it looked better with a Rome banker's son and heir who would eventually inherit his father's title, than with Giulio and the life *he* had to offer. Lucchino presented more of a problem: this was the man she could have accepted herself only a month or two ago. Was he a liar, the thief of his friend's fiancée, or a cynical poseur looking for an advantageous marriage? The trouble was that none of these things matched with the Lucchino she thought she knew.

About Giulio she tried not to think at all. On top of losing the girl he'd chosen as a wife, he'd been betrayed by a man who'd been encouraged to look on Belmonte as a second home. It was enough to embitter the most easy-going optimist in the world, and Giulio, complex, reserved and fastidious, was far from being that.

But, however reluctantly, she had to persuade the children that it was time to leave their friends and go home. Emmanuele grieved in silence as usual, but Beatrice wept when the moment of parting came. Only Sarah's promise that the family would come to Venice in the spring enabled her to smile at James through her tears and promise him undying friendship. It was a silent car-load of passengers that Matthew eventually deposited back at Heathrow and his goodbye hugs were painful; but once on board the aeroplane, with their faces turned towards home, the children began to recover.

At Marco Polo airport Michele was waiting for them and they discovered that they were pleased to see him again. There was also a great deal that had to be told and they were ready to start at once while he was still turning the boat's nose towards home. Sarah, instead, could think back to her previous arrival, almost a year ago. Venice had materialized out of the steel-grey lagoon then, looking just as drab and winter-dead as it did now. Hunched inside her overcoat against the rawness of the afternoon, she shivered at the mournful hoot of a foghorn further out. It would become a familiar sound for the next month or two – that and the endless drip-drip of water; wetter, so the Venetians liked to claim, then anyone else's rain!

She smiled suddenly at the thought and, because he turned to look at her just then, Emmanuele smiled back. His small, loving

319

grin shamed her into cheerfulness again. The spring would return, with its miraculous message of hope and life renewed, however bleak the world looked now.

The di Brazzanos hadn't got back from Rome, Claretta reported at the palazzo. They'd stayed to attend Signor Lucchino's hastily arranged marriage. But two days later, when they did return, Laura seemed pleased to see the children and genuinely grateful that they'd been given a memorable Christmas.

'You could say that ours was, too,' she commented wryly afterwards to Sarah. 'No mention of a child born in a stable, of course – it was a full-blown domestic drama, with even the servants playing their bit parts for all they were worth! But the more Italian everyone else became, the more necessary it seemed to behave in a maddeningly calm, Anglo-Saxon way myself. Fabrizio was rather impressed!'

Laura in this mood was amusing and likeable, but Sarah asked for details about the actual wedding.

'Well, by Elsa's standards it was sadly low-key,' said Laura, 'and only the knowledge that her god-daughter will be the Marchesa Vittoria one day pushed her into coming at all! Jacob Hartman turned up as well, probably for the same good reason; but at least he did a splendid job of storming my sister-in-law's defences. He's not a clever, charming Jew for nothing.'

'But what about Zoe and Lucchino,' Sarah insisted. 'Did *they* look happy?'

Laura considered the question and finally answered it. 'I think so. You probably thought I was a jealous cow, hating Giulio to be taken up with another woman. That came into it, of course, but I hated most of all the idea of *Zoe* being the other woman – I *knew* that would never do. She and Lucchino haven't got off to a very good start, but that in itself will make them work harder at their marriage.'

Sarah nodded, not surprised that when Laura actually put her mind to thinking about other people she could do it rather sensibly. There remained the crucial question of what her attitude to Giulio would be, now that he was a free man again, but it seemed an impossible one to ask. Then Laura chose to answer it anyway.

'You're thinking that I'm going to get in a state again about Giulio. Well, I shan't – that's over now. I love the work I'm doing for Stefan – couldn't give it up even if Fabrizio asked me to. But he won't; he understands.'

It was quite a long way for her to have travelled, Sarah thought, from the time when she'd railed against a stupid husband.

The di Brazzanos seemed to be on an even keel for once, and Lucchino, with Zoe's help, *would* re-establish himself in society as everybody's friend and favourite. It only left Giulio to be concerned about, but at least he was away on the mainland, immune to the speculation that would keep Venetian gossips busy still for weeks to come.

Sarah did the only thing she could do, remembered him and the *padrone* in her prayers; and struggled to come to the sensible conclusion that it was pointless to worry at all about anyone else. It didn't matter if she never understood why Zoe, besotted with one man, should have married another. She needn't even know the reason for Lucchino's extraordinary volte-face. Let it be a useful reminder that she wasn't among her own kind and would never be able to guess what made them behave as they did.

Steven Harding's telephone call a few days later came as an unexpected pleasure; at least *they* sprang no surprises on each other. She even found herself looking forward to seeing him, and dressed carefully for it, remembering that Steven expected no less of any woman he took out to dinner. She went to the school room to say goodnight to the children, and Beatrice switched off the programme they'd been watching, to examine Sarah's jacket and skirt of black velvet.

'*Si ... ottimo*,' she said approvingly. 'The *professore* will be pleased, I think.'

Sarah was smiling at this verdict when the school-room door opened and Giulio Leopardi walked in. She moved blindly to a chair because she needed something to hold on to. It was the unexpectedness of seeing him ... The shock, she told herself crossly; that was the reason for the weakness that invaded her entire body at the sight of him. But, safely anchored to the chair, she could even manage to lean on the back of it, apparently calm and unconcerned.

Beatrice, of course, flung herself at the visitor, while Emmanuele's questions poured out about Bella and the donkeys and Zio Luigi. There was a moment when Giulio's attention was fully engaged with the children and Sarah could cast round for something suitably banal to say.

'You've come over with Franco, I expect; Donna Laura said he was due back today.'

'Yes – he was kind enough to spend Christmas with us.' Giulio's tired, gaunt face smiled at Emmanuele. 'Mamma says that you had a splendid time in England.'

'It was ... oh, it was...' But he couldn't find a word to do it justice, and simply opened his arms wide in a gesture that had to describe the full wonder of it.

Beatrice was all ready now to offer more precise information, but Agnese, on duty this evening instead of Bianca, had come to summon the children to bed.

'I must hear about it when we have more time,' Giulio suggested tactfully. 'When you come to Belmonte. Then Zio Luigi will be able to listen too.'

They reluctantly agreed and trailed out of the room, leaving silence behind. It was an uncomfortable silence, Sarah thought. Something needed to be said about Zoe and Lucchino, but what could she say that would do no more hurt than Giulio had already been offered?

'Franco wanted to be of help to you and your father,' she finally suggested. 'I hope he was.'

Giulio nodded, but didn't answer the question otherwise. 'He told me that you'd invited him to go to England. He was all the more grateful because he knew he hadn't always behaved very well towards you.'

'It doesn't matter,' Sarah said. 'We understand each other a little better now.' She hesitated a moment, then soldiered on. 'I'm sorry about everything that's happened, but you're probably tired of hearing people say that.'

'Only because some of them don't mean it,' he answered briefly. His eyes inspected her, registering changes. She was thinner than he remembered and, without its summer tan, her skin against the soft black stuff of her jacket was translucent and pale. She looked beautiful but fragile, and the discovery made him suddenly angry. Beatrice and Emmanuele were nice children, but she shouldn't be their surrogate mother, and Laura's paid employee; it was all wrong.

'Are you dressed for dinner downstairs?' he asked with a sharpness she didn't understand.

'You've forgotten,' she reproved him gently. 'I told you once before that I don't normally dine with Count Fabrizio and Donna Laura.' Amusement lit her grey eyes for a moment. 'Nor do I eat supper by myself up here dressed like this!' She glanced at her watch as she spoke. 'I must go, Professor Harding will be waiting for me downstairs.'

It wasn't fevered imagination at work, she knew that the atmosphere in the room had changed. From being uneasy, it had become charged with a current of electricity as dangerous as a high-voltage wire.

'You said once to my father that the failure of your marriage to Harding was complete and final. Have you changed your mind about that?'

The angry question goaded her into leaving the safety of her chair and moving towards the door. 'I might have done,' she said untruthfully, 'but it isn't something that need concern you.'

She was aware at once of having made a

mistake; she should have stayed where she was. There was a perilous moment when self-control all but deserted him. She could feel in her own bones his struggle not to catch hold of her, shake her, kiss her – all those things, perhaps. Then she saw him shake his head, like a dog emerging from a plunge in a river, and the danger was over.

'You're quite right, of course,' he agreed in a cold, impersonal voice. 'It doesn't concern me at all. Give my apologies to Steven Harding if I've made you keep him waiting.'

He stood aside for her to leave, and she went past him knowing there was no longer anything to fear; he wouldn't touch her now. All she need do was walk downstairs, and smile at Steven, and pay no heed at all to the tears that seemed to be trickling into some hidden corner of her heart.

Twenty-Four

As Sarah remembered it afterwards, the beginning of the new year was a bitter-sweet mixture – hope and sadness all muddled together. There was the pleasure of her renewed friendship with Steven, and the satisfaction of seeing the di Brazzanos getting to know their children. There was Emmanuele's love affair with his flute, developing nicely, and the signs of musical talent that Beatrice seemed to be showing as well. Even Laura, hard to please, was inclined to think that her step-daughter's singing voice showed promise.

But enjoyment was tinged with a melancholy that Sarah tried to blame on the winter awfulness of the lagoon. The licentious revelry of carnival time in the past made sense now. It wasn't just a self-indulgent prelude to the austerity of Lent; the Venetians had been cocking a defiant snook at their desolate, watery habitat. But the root of her own sadness lay further to the west.

Giulio paid no more visits to the palazzo, if he came to Venice at all, and the *padrone*'s occasional letters said so little that she felt excluded and ignored. She had no hope of anything for herself from Belmonte, but her heart craved the reassurance that its inmates were safe and well.

The grey days followed one another, monotonous but peaceful, until suddenly there was a surprising interruption to the routine when Zoe telephoned, asking Sarah to meet her. Not Harry's Bar this time; she and Lucchino were staying at the Gritti Palace for a day or two.

Half-disinclined to go, but half-curious as well, Sarah set off for the hotel expecting that the reunion ahead would be more awkward than enjoyable. But she found Zoe waiting alone in the lobby, and one glance was enough to show that Lucchino's wife was not quite the Zoe Hartman of old. This self-assured young woman, in a suit that shouted Parisian haute-couture, had left uncertainties behind; she was 'placed' now, settled and secure.

'I thought you weren't going to agree to come,' she said by way of greeting. 'You sounded very frosty on the telephone!'

'I wasn't sure I'd know what to say,' Sarah admitted. 'But half the problem has disappeared because Lucchino doesn't seem to be here.'

'He's gone to Belmonte. That seemed the best arrangement: for him to see Giulio, and for me to see you.'

'You needn't have bothered with me at all,' Sarah pointed out. 'Giulio obviously did deserve a visit, from one or other of you.'

The comment brought a flush to Zoe's cheeks, making her look familiar again. 'At least you're inclined to blame us both. Most people put it all on me, and no one gives me any credit for sparing Giulio a marriage that wouldn't have worked at all.'

'Laura does – at least, she believes you wouldn't have made each other happy, and I don't think that's said out of spite.'

'Spiteful or not, she's right.' Zoe stopped for a moment, looking back at the past. 'You know how I was, completely dazzled by Giulio, and not just because of the way he looks; the man he *is* mattered even more. It seemed a miracle that he seemed to want *me*.'

'So why didn't it work out?' Sarah asked slowly.

'I and Belmonte didn't work out,' Zoe admitted, 'but that wasn't the worst part. Giulio and I as a couple were even more wrong. I knew it every time he touched me. Instead of the chemistry I'd imagined between us, I could *feel* the effort he had to make. I told myself it was because we were new to each other, but in the end I couldn't

329

understand why he was working so hard to love me. That's when I got in a panic and decided to make a run for it back to New York.'

There was a little silence that Sarah found hard to break. At last she managed it. 'What about Lucchino? Is marriage to *him* going to work out?'

'It has to,' Zoe said soberly. 'He went with me to America out of kindness more than anything. He could see what a state I was in, but we *shall* be all right. It's a different thing altogether but we're two of a kind – we like the same things, laugh at the same things. That's important, I think.'

Sarah's nod agreed. This time it wasn't imagination at work. She could remember clearly enough how easily Zoe and Lucchino got on together during the summer weeks at Belmonte.

'Where will you live?' she asked. 'Up here in the north? Lucchino seemed to want a home in the Veneto.'

'No, that's not how I see it. We've got to settle down in Rome. That's where Lucchino belongs – where we must bring up our children.'

Sarah registered the change that a few weeks of matrimony had already made. In this slightly plumper, more confident Zoe she could see the elegant Roman matron of the future. She knew a moment's sadness for Lucchino. Was the charming, kindly, footloose wanderer of the past going to have to change as well ... and start by coming to terms with the society into which he'd been born? On the other hand, who was she to say that Zoe wasn't right? Perhaps he *was* content now, to have his life redefined for him by a young, delightful wife.

'I'm glad I didn't refuse to come this evening,' Sarah said suddenly. 'Now I can wish you both a long and happy marriage and mean it. *Tanti felici auguri*, Zoe!'

'I can understand that, I'm learning fast,' she answered proudly. 'My mamma-in-law says I must!' Her hand touched Sarah's for a moment in a little friendly gesture. 'Now, what about you? I know you went back to England for Christmas. Did that make you homesick?'

'Yes, but Highfold's always there for me to go back to.'

'If Steven Harding will let you! The two of you look so well-matched together that it's hard to see what went wrong the first time.' She hesitated for a moment, then went on, already anxious to join the married woman conspiracy to lure the rest of the single sisterhood into matrimony. 'Sarah, you *mustn't* stay a governess much longer or you'll never do anything else. God knows the di Brazzanos aren't the best of employers but you might get some that are

331

much worse.'

'Easily,' Sarah agreed. 'Laura is at least interesting, and I like Fabrizio very much. When it's time to say goodbye I shall probably go back to school teaching. I'm sorry to disappoint you, but I shan't re-marry Steven; nor does he even show any signs of asking me to!'

'Well, *we* must keep in touch in any case. We shall expect you to come and stay with us in Rome.'

The past was over, she seemed to be saying; nothing but the future mattered now, and to Zoe Vittoria, embarking on an exciting new life, the future looked all right. It prompted a question that Sarah hadn't known she was going to ask.

'Zoe, do you love Lucchino?'

The silence went on too long, and she was on the point of withdrawing what she'd said when an answer finally came.

'In the way you mean, not yet.' A sad little smile touched Zoe's mouth. 'And it will take him a little longer to love *me* – *your* fault, I'm afraid. But we shall get there in the end!'

Not very well hidden behind the lightly-spoken words was an adult acceptance of pain that took Sarah by surprise. It should not have done, she realized, as she walked back to the palazzo. Zoe's whole life had been an unsettling mixture of indulgence and hardship, comfort and dislocation. She'd had plenty of practice in understanding why human relations worked or went awry. If she was right about Giulio, he'd made a grievous mistake in asking her to marry him. The mistake had led to Lucchino taking on responsibility for her instead. It wasn't the ideal solution for either of them perhaps, but Sarah felt more optimistic about them now. Laura had been right: they would refuse to let the marriage fail.

As usual, one surprise was quickly followed by another. In the course of her next evening with Steven came the very suggestion she'd assured Zoe that he hadn't any idea of making. But to begin with, they talked of Venice itself. With the Piazzetta yet again under water, it was difficult, in fact, *not* to talk about the threatened city.

'I don't know where I stand in the battle,' Sarah had to admit. '*Will* a barrage beyond the Lido keep Venice safe from the sea or so upset the ecology of the lagoon that it perishes in a different way? I could argue just as easily for either point of view, and end up no more convinced of being right than when I began!'

'It *has* to be the barrage, I think,' Steven insisted; 'otherwise there'll be a conjunction of wind and tide one of these days that finally proves catastrophic. The environmental problems are also real enough but they must be dealt with, scientifically.'

Sarah smiled at him across the table. 'Argument settled by Professor Harding's cool, impartial logic! Now sort out my next dilemma for me: do we keep Venice alive by allowing it to be brutally modernized: canals filled in, cars parked in the Piazza, and even an underwater railway from San Marco all the way to Mestre? Or do we preserve a beautiful but decaying museum piece, whose only function is to relieve befuddled tourists of their money?'

'Put like that it's an altogether harder question to answer, but I persist in believing that it doesn't have to be one thing or the other. If the Venetians themselves can be persuaded to go on living here, instead of drifting off to the mainland, as they've been doing for decades, then the city can remain alive but substantially the same.'

'That's what Count Fabrizio thinks too,' Sarah agreed, 'and he's prepared to *do* something about it as well, by improving property that he owns without spoiling its outward appearance, so that people *can* go on living here in the decent comfort they have a right to expect.'

Sarah pushed her plate away so that she could rest her arms on the table. 'Confession time – I couldn't have been more wrong in my first estimate of Fabrizio di Brazzano; let that be a lesson to me! There may be people who get involved in Venice's preservation merely because it's the fashionable thing to do at a certain level of society; but *he* cares deeply what becomes of this place.'

Steven nodded, not uninterested in the subject but waiting for a chance to move the conversation into more personal channels. Then Sarah herself made it easy for him.

'By the way, Zoe and Lucchino have been here recently. I had supper with her. Elsa Vandenburg relented sufficiently to attend their wedding in Rome, but perhaps you already know that.'

'Yes, I've been in touch with Elsa. She's been a good friend, and I needed to let her know that I shall have left Venice before she comes back.'

'That sounds rather definite – as if you know when you're leaving,' Sarah suggested.

'I do – I shall be back in Oxford in a week's time. My research is done; now I've got five months in which to knock the very rough draft of a book into final shape.'

'Before the start of a new university term? I imagined that you'd turned your back on Academe for good.'

'Not Oxford's Michaelmas term. I've accepted an exchange: two years' lecturing at Yale.' He smiled at the astonishment in her face, but she had the strange impression that his nearly impregnable self-confidence was missing; for once he seemed uncertain of what to say next. While he debated with himself she could look at him and estimate the effect he would have on American students. The pleasant English voice, the authority, and handsome presence, were quite enough to wreak havoc on the female undergraduates, even if the young men struggled not to be impressed.

'I'm glad you're going back to university teaching,' she said. 'It's a waste, otherwise, of what you do best of all.'

'And you deeply disapprove of the media circus I got caught up in!' She only answered with a little shrug – it was an old and painful argument between them, no longer relevant now. But Steven was intent on clearing the air. 'I know there were other problems as well, but you *hated* all the television celebrity nonsense. I told myself it didn't matter, but I was flattered ... hooked, I suppose. You were right, of course, but it took me too long to recognize the fact.'

'At least it doesn't matter now,' Sarah insisted gently. 'I think you'll do wonderfully well at Yale. Lucky American students to have you!'

Steven stretched out a hand to cover Sarah's where it rested on the table. 'I want *you* to come, too. Will you marry me again? Will you forgive me for past mistakes and let me convince you that we'd do better next time round? I never stopped loving you, even when I was high on flattery and public applause. All the time a little voice kept whispering that I was an insensate fool, squandering treasure for pinchbeck that was worth nothing at all. My darling, could you live with me at Yale?'

He saw her hesitate, and hurried on himself. 'I should have asked you before I committed myself to going there, but the decision was all but taken before I even came to Venice. Perhaps you'd hate America, but I think we could have an interesting life there.'

He sounded unlike the Steven she remembered, but illogically she found herself regretting his new humility. Without the certainty and arrogance of old he became more ordinary, and she didn't want him to be that.

'The mistakes weren't all yours,' she answered finally, 'though at the time I thought they were. Now, I can see where I certainly *was* to blame: I didn't want anything to change – stupid, of course, because things that don't change eventually die anyway.'

'All right – let's agree to share the blame and then forget the past. It's the future we

337

have to think about.'

'My future is here, for another year or so,' she said. 'Thank you, Steven, for asking me to go with you, but I can't – I'm committed here.'

'To the di Brazzanos?' He sounded like the old Steven now, impatient with any sign of stupidity. 'My dear girl, the children are delightful, I grant you, but you can't put them before your own life. They're not orphans, dependent on *you* for love and care.'

'It's how they *were*,' she pointed out. 'Things are much better now, but they're still not central to their parents' lives, and I doubt if they ever will be.' It was tempting to make them her sole reason for refusing him but she knew it would be dishonest. 'The children are only part of my problem, though.'

'Because you don't like the idea of America, or because you won't take me as a husband again?'

'A mixture of reasons, the chief of them being that I'm not the girl I was ten years ago.'

She couldn't bear to have him ask why not, but thought she was probably safe from probing. Rejection had always hurt his pride and, although he'd changed, he still wouldn't persist in asking the reason for it.

'Think about it, Sarah,' he suggested

quietly. 'You know where to find me if you change your mind. And now, bloody but reasonably unbowed, I'll walk you back to your palazzo! When shall I be able to say that again, I wonder, to the girl I've been dining with!'

She smiled at him, grateful for the touch of unexpected, wry humour, but unable to match it herself. Beneath the lightness he was puzzled and hurt, and she hated being the cause of it. She knew she'd been meant to understand from his behaviour to Beatrice and Emmanuele that he wouldn't refuse her a child now if she asked for one; even that wasn't enough, but she couldn't tell him why not.

Nothing more was said until they reached the garden entrance. Then, she swallowed the lump in her throat and tried to smile at him. Lamplight shining through the misty darkness made an aureole round her head and showed him her up-turned face. It was the image of her that he would have to take away with him. He bent his head to kiss her mouth, and felt her lips tremble under his.

'I could persuade you, I think,' he said unevenly. '*Let* me persuade you to love me again.'

'That was only what Zoe would call a male-female thing!' she tried to explain. 'Not proof of anything very much except that you are probably lonely and so am I.

I'm sorry, Steven. I wish you all good fortune with the book, and much happiness at Yale.'

He touched her cheek in a little farewell gesture, and then quickly walked away. She could watch him only as far as the little humpbacked bridge over the canal before she lost sight of him. She could think of no reason why she would ever see him again. There was sadness in that, but certain relief as well. The past had finally been laid to rest.

Twenty-Five

The third surprise took a little longer to arrive. Then, returning from a visit to Beatrice's nuns one morning at the beginning of February, Sarah found the housekeeper waiting for her with an urgent message. She was to telephone Domenica at Belmonte.

'The poor woman sounded distraught,' Claretta said disapprovingly. It was a matter of pride to remain always calm herself, and she failed to understand why other people found it so difficult. 'I had to ask three times before she could remember the number.'

'It's because she doesn't like the tele-phone,' Sarah explained. 'Domenica is flus-tered by it because she can't understand how it works.' All the same, the message was unexpected, and she dialled the Belmonte number with a small prickle of apprehen-sion.

'*Signorina, scusami*,' came an agitated voice at the other end of the line. '*Sono Domenica ... Lei mi recorda?*'

'*Si, si, ti recordo ... dimmi il problema, Domenica.*'

The story came tumbling out in broken Italian phrases for Sarah to reassemble. The *padrone* was very ill, in a high fever, not eating anything, but he refused to have the doctor called.

'I don't understand ... why hasn't Signor Giulio—' She got no further before she was interrupted.

'He's away, signorina; I don't know where, but the *padrone* made me *promise* that I wouldn't try to find him; he said Signor Giulio needed a holiday very badly. But the *padrone* ... how do you say ... wanders in his mind now, and sometimes mentions your name. That's why I telephone – I didn't know what else to do.'

'Domenica, listen. Do you know the doc-tor? Do you have a number to ring?'

'*Si, si, signorina.*'

341

'Then telephone him *now* and say that he *must* visit the *padrone* urgently. It will take me several hours to get to you, but I'll come as soon as I can.'

It was one of Laura's teaching days at the Cini Foundation but Count Fabrizio, at least, was reachable in his study. He didn't question her request for permission to go to Belmonte, simply considered the best way of getting her there.

'The train to Padua will be quickest, I'm sure, and a taxi from there. Get ready to leave, Sarah, while I telephone the station.'

With his usual competence it was all arranged while she packed a bag and explained to the children that she must go to look after Zio Luigi, who was ill. An hour later she was on a train chugging out of Santa Lucia station, with the wad of notes the count had insisted she take stuffed in her handbag, and puzzled anxiety as her travelling companion. If Giulio wasn't at Belmonte, why at the very least didn't Domenica know where he was?

It was mid-afternoon when she got to the house. No Pan piped his music now; the fountain in the middle of the little lake wasn't playing, and most of the surrounding trees were winter-bare. But Belmonte was still beautiful; she thought it always would be at any season of the year.

A car was parked at the front steps; but

there was only a moment in which to hope that it belonged to the doctor before the door opened and Domenica rushed down to greet her. Yes, the doctor was with the *padrone* still; better, perhaps, for the signorina to wait for him to emerge.

'Tell me how all this happened,' Sarah asked as they went indoors and Domenica mopped her tears.

'There was a funeral – an old friend of the *padrone*'s, so he said he must go even though he wasn't feeling very well. It was a dreadful day, cold and wet, and I could see that he was shivering when he came home. The next day he wouldn't eat, and he had fever. But still he refused to call the doctor. Yesterday he was worse, and this morning I telephoned you.'

'Where is Signor Giulio?'

'Up in some mountain – Greek, I think.' Domenica said it in a tone of despair, since Greece seemed to her no nearer than the far side of the moon. 'After Signor Lucchino left he agreed that he would take a holiday at last. He said I was to telephone Franco if I needed anything, but the number wasn't right. I kept trying but no one knew Franco di Brazzano at all.'

Domenica showed signs of weeping again and Sarah gave her a little hug. 'Don't cry ... The doctor's here now.'

But at that moment he walked down the

343

stairs – a small, tired man who looked puzzled as well as anxious. Introduced to Sarah, his expression relaxed slightly.

'Thank God you speak Italian; otherwise we'd not understand one another at all. Are you a nurse by any miraculous chance?'

'No, but I looked after my father when he was very ill. I'll try to manage if the *padrone* refuses to go to hospital.'

'He *does* – he says he'd rather die in his own home.'

'*Is* he going to die?' The quiet question made Domenica sob again, but the doctor shook his head.

'He shouldn't do so. We ought to be able to keep him alive, but he seems to have made up his mind that he doesn't want to go on living. That makes it much harder.'

'Tell me what I must do,' Sarah suggested. 'If I'm not competent enough then surely we can't allow him to stay here.'

The doctor nodded approvingly. The *Inglese*, unlike Domenica, would keep her head and waste no time in weeping. 'I can give you the drugs he needs, but *you'll* have to get him to take them, and also the nourishment he's been refusing. Can you do that?'

'I can try,' Sarah answered steadily. 'If I fail, we shall have to trouble you again, I'm afraid.'

'I can manage *one* more night without

sleep. If a nurse is available I'll send her, but there's a flu epidemic raging. Now, I'll show you the drugs he must have. This ... and this every four hours, even during the night, I'm afraid. The fever may get worse before it gets better, and it will seem more frightening at night. Call me if you lose heart, signorina; otherwise I'll be back tomorrow morning.' Then he shook her hand again, nodded at Domenica, and walked out.

Sarah looked at the housekeeper's frightened face, thinking that her own probably looked just as fearful. It wouldn't do, of course; somehow she must pretend that they would get through the next day or two without losing the *padrone*.

'Domenica. I'm going up to see Signor Luigi. If he won't eat, he must have liquid food at least – chicken broth, beef tea ... that sort of thing.'

'I have it made,' the housekeeper said quickly. 'I'll bring it up to you, signorina.'

A moment later she let herself into the *padrone*'s room. He lay so still and made so little of a mound in the bedclothes that for a dreadful moment she thought he might have died while she talked to the doctor downstairs. No, she could see the faint rise and fall of his breathing; but his face was colourless, and skeletally thin. Then, he opened his eyes and one of her anxieties was removed. Domenica had said his mind wandered, but she knew that he recognized her because he tried to smile and whisper her name. If she could still reach him, she needn't lose hope.

'Domenica said you were unwell,' she said in a voice she tried to keep level. 'I've come to help look after you, but you must help us, please, otherwise the doctor will say we aren't trying hard enough.'

His head moved on the pillow, signifying that whatever she did would make no difference. She knelt down by the bed and took his thin hands in her own warm ones.

'*Caro padrone*, you have pneumonia which is causing the fever and the pain in your chest. The doctor's pills, if you agree to take them, will cure the infection, but you must also accept nourishment as well.' Instead of looking at her he closed his eyes, and she had to resist the temptation to shout at him. 'I promised the children I could manage without their help. If you won't try to get better I shall have to tell them that I failed.'

He still didn't reply and she felt very close to defeat. Then, he suddenly did look at her, and he saw the tears that had begun to trickle silently down her cheeks. Without saying anything he pulled his hand away from hers but held it out open on the counterpane, mutely agreeing to accept the pills he must take. The exertion of being propped up made him cough but when the spasm was over he managed to swallow the pills. A moment later Domenica came in with a cup of chicken broth, and Sarah persuaded him to swallow it, sip by sip. It was the beginning of a vigil that lasted throughout the night – an anxious routine of pills, small offerings of soup, spells of painful coughing, and brief snatches of exhausted sleep that never lasted long enough to give him any real rest.

As the long night wore on, it seemed to her that his fever mounted; the thermometer climbed a degree or two higher and his muttered words grew incoherent. But the fever *would* get worse the doctor had said, before it got better. Keeping terror just in check, she clung doggedly to her instructions – the antibiotics every four hours, hot soup from the thermos Domenica had brought up whenever the *padrone* could be persuaded to sip some, and the agonized hours in between spent sitting by the bed, holding his hand. She told herself that he wouldn't slip away as long as she held on to him and willed some of her own strength into his frail body. He couldn't be lost while she prayed for him, and for Giulio, who *must* come home and find his father still there.

The late winter daylight crept slowly into the room, and that in itself was a relief. But she felt fractionally more confident now that some moment of crisis had also been reached and survived during the night. Surely the *padrone* breathed a little more easily now, and when he coughed there was less blood-flecked sputum than before. She could smile at Domenica with a finger to her lips when the housekeeper, already dressed, came into the room.

'*Poverina*, you look so tired,' she murmured distractedly. 'No sleep, and no supper last night. How could I have forgotten that?' She tiptoed over to the bed and a transfiguring smile touched her anxious face. 'Blessed Mary, Mother of God, has heard our prayers, I think. The *caro padrone* is still with us after all. Now *you* must rest while I watch. Just tell me what I have to do.'

'Nothing for the moment, Domenica, except stay with him while I take a shower. Then we must make the *padrone* comfortable, but I think he would prefer one of the men to do that. Afterwards he must have some breakfast – hot, sweet milk with bread broken up in it would be good.' She examined the sleeping face on the pillow and gave a thankful little nod. 'He *is* better; I'm sure of it. But I'll try to reach Franco later on, just in case we might need him.'

Tired, but refreshed by the shower and a change of clothes, she ate some breakfast and then asked to be connected with Bologna University. It took a little while to trace Franco's whereabouts – a number that Domenica must simply have misdialled in her agitation – but at last his voice, still rather sleepy-sounding, answered her. She apologized for so early a call, not mentioning that it didn't seem early at all to someone who hadn't been to bed.

'Do you need me to come, Sarah?' Franco asked hesitantly when she'd explained about Luigi Leopardi's illness. 'I would come at once, but we're in the middle of exams. I can ask if they'll excuse me.'

'No, there's no need,' she said firmly. 'I just wanted to be sure I could get hold of you if the *padrone* suddenly got worse. You seem to be the only person who knows where Giulio is.'

'I don't know that exactly either, but I do have a number where he can be contacted.' He called it out to her, and promised to leave for Belmonte as soon as the exams finished. She went back upstairs feeling relieved, to find the *padrone* staring doubtfully at the bowl of bread and milk Domenica had brought him.

'This is a very strange breakfast,' he pointed out in a frail voice but with a glimmer of his old humour.

'A nursery remedy that has put heart into countless English invalids,' she explained solemnly.

'Then who am I to refuse it?'

349

He was asleep again when the doctor returned, but woke at the sound of a male voice in the room.

'I was expecting you to telephone during the night,' the doctor said to Sarah. 'By the look of *you* perhaps you should have done, but my old friend here seems a little better. Well done, signorina.'

She smiled at him, shaking her head. 'Your powerful pills and Domenica's chicken broth must take the credit, I think. The *padrone*'s temperature did go up during the night, but I kept telling myself that you thought it might happen.'

The doctor stared at his patient, lying half-propped up, still drowsy but not missing any of the conversation. 'You make more of an effort for the signorina than you do for me – understandably perhaps. Now, let me take a proper look at you.'

Sarah left them and went downstairs. She was filled with the pleasant lassitude that follows a time of great stress, but knew that she wouldn't sleep even if she left the *padrone* in Domenica's hands and went to bed. The day was cold, but sparklingly bright, and she suddenly wanted to be out in the freshness of it. With a borrowed coat round her shoulders, one of Giulio's hanging in the lobby, she suspected, she let herself out into the brilliant morning. It was easy to remember now how close Belmonte was to the Alps, and very hard not to wonder about the mountains where Giulio was. She could imagine him enjoying Greece – somewhere softer and more luxurious would make no appeal to him.

The doctor emerged out of the house and she walked back to his car to say goodbye to him. 'Use up all the drugs I've left you,' he said, 'but he'll do now. A visit to some warm, sheltered spot would be good for him – Ajaccio, say, or Amalfi – when he's got a bit stronger.' The doctor bowed over Sarah's hand in an unexpectedly formal gesture.

'Perhaps you'll have left by the time I call again. I'm glad to have met you, signorina.' Then he got into his car and drove away.

She smiled at the abrupt departure – typical of an overworked man with no time to waste; but she thought that it was probably how he always behaved. He was an unusual Italian.

Indoors again, she went to release Domenica from the sickroom, and the pattern of the previous day repeated itself, except that she now had the doctor's reassurance that her patient was mending. In between giving him pills and food, she could catnap herself while he was sleeping, and go downstairs to eat the evening meal she'd missed the night before. The *padrone* was awake when she got back, and now feeling anxious about *her*.

'Sarah, my dear, I can't allow you to watch

over me again as I'm sure you did last night. You must go to bed yourself.'

'I slept this afternoon,' she said calmly, 'and I can nod off in this very comfortable armchair whenever I want to. Tomorrow night you'll not have to be woken; I can go to bed then as a good Christian should!'

He could smile at her again now as she handed him yet another pill. 'A stubborn race, the English – it's something the rest of us have often noticed about you!' But his fingers touched her hand in a little silent thank you.

She expected him to slip into another doze, as he'd done throughout the day, but his inclination now seemed to be to stay awake and have her talk to him.

'I spoke to Franco this morning,' she remembered to say. 'He's in the middle of exams, but they'll be finished by the weekend and then he wants to come and stay until Giulio gets back.' She hesitated a moment, then broached the matter that had been worrying her ever since she got there. 'If I'd known where to reach Giulio last night I should have begged him to come home, because you seemed not to want to get better, and that worried me very much.' In the way that had become habitual now, she sat by the bed and held his hand. 'What was the matter? Had you given up hope of seeing him again?'

'He only went because I talked him into taking the first holiday he's had in years. He needed it so badly that I *couldn't* have him brought back just because I was feeling unwell.' The *padrone*'s murmur halted for a moment, but went on again with difficulty. 'Then I got to thinking that perhaps the best thing I could do for him was to just ... slip away. At least I wouldn't be here to spoil things for him any longer. That's why Zoe ran off, you know. She didn't like Belmonte very much, but I was the last straw – a tiresome old man who knew nothing about the things she was interested in and might for years to come be very much in the way.'

Sarah let out a little sigh of relief. It was such a simple explanation after all, and it was something she *could* deal with.

'She's a town girl, admittedly, and it would have been hard for her to settle down here. But that had little to do with her running away, and *you* had nothing to do with it at all.' What had to come next was a confidence that she wouldn't normally have broken, but it seemed more important now for the *padrone* to be reassured. 'I saw Zoe in Venice a few days before I came here – Lucchino visited Belmonte at the same time, I think. She left because she was convinced that marriage with Giulio would be a mistake for both of them.'

'Because she didn't love him enough?'

Luigi asked slowly.

'No; because she'd come to realize that he didn't love her. Having asked her to marry him, *he* couldn't back out, but Zoe could, and did, with Lucchino's help. *Their* marriage puzzled me because it didn't seem to be what either of them would have chosen; but it's going to work out very well. I think Zoe is sure of that already.'

It left the painful subject of Giulio himself untouched, but about that there was nothing she could say, and nor did his father seem inclined to comment either. Instead, he nodded gently.

'Good, Zoe is a nice child; I should like her to be happy. I didn't see Lucchino, but Giulio told me of his visit, and their friendship hasn't been spoiled. That was hard to believe at the time, but perhaps it does make sense after all.' His thin face creased into a lovely smile. 'Now, I don't know whether to get better or not; if I do, my *cara* Sarah will go back to Venice!'

'She must go soon, anyway. It's nearly Beatrice's birthday. But Franco will be here. You'll be able to do without what he calls "Britannia on the warpath"!'

'Does he? It wasn't how he spoke of you at Christmas time. I used to think my cousin didn't treat him very wisely – too much money lavished on him to make up for what he *wasn't* given once Fabrizio had remarried; but he's growing up now, largely thanks to Giulio.' The *padrone* was silent for a moment, looking back into the past, Sarah thought. She didn't disturb him and didn't know whether to be glad or sorry when he went on at last to speak about his son.

'Happiness for Giulio is the only thing I pray for now; he deserves it more than most men do. His youth was spent in saving Belmonte from collapse, and Laura di Brazzano from self-destruction. You know about that, I think, or I wouldn't mention it.'

'I know how the relationship ended,' Sarah admitted; 'not how it began.'

'She was singing at La Scala, Milan, when Giulio met her for the first time. He was a very young man, in love with beauty and, as his mother had been, passionately fond of opera. Laura then was something very remarkable, to see and to hear.'

'She still is,' Sarah put in fairly.

'Well, yes, but imagine her as she was twenty years ago! I think Giulio knew it was hopeless – he had nothing but a remote, broken-down estate to offer her and she was a star of the first magnitude. Ten years later it was a different story; her tantrums and unreliability had become a by-word and managements were very wary of her. She met my cousin while she was appearing at the Fenice, and quickly accepted him. The marriage wasn't a success, but it brought her into contact with Giulio again. I regretted that very much, because she made him feel that she depended on him. He revered her for what she'd been, and got trapped into propping up a neurotic, unbalanced woman. The rest of the story you perhaps know better than I do.'

'Yes, I expect I do,' Sarah agreed slowly. 'But things are better than they were. Laura is content again, giving her masterclasses for Stefan Demetrios, but she's also learning to value the treasure she's got in her husband and the children. It's taken far too long, of course, but you can't judge her by normal standards – they simply don't apply to someone like her.'

She put the thought of Laura aside and asked one last question. 'What made Giulio choose Greece in the middle of winter for a holiday?'

'A liking for the Greek Orthodox Church!' the *padrone* said surprisingly. 'He goes to San Lazzaro quite often because the Armenian monks like Belmonte wine! When he was there one day he met the visiting Abbot of the Order and they became friends. This was a long-standing invitation to visit the monastery – on top of a mountain in a remote part of Greece. Of course, that appealed to my son, but I think he especially wanted peace and solitude just now ... Refreshment of the spirit, perhaps.'

That made sense, too. Sarah could see him vividly in her mind's eye, content in his austerely beautiful refuge on top of the world. He was a man whose deepest instinct was to remain solitary, even though he was constantly needed by other people. No wonder Zoe, a social animal if there ever was one, had panicked; Giulio Leopardi wouldn't have made her an easy husband.

But there'd been too long a conversation and the *padrone* was looking tired. 'Time for you to rest,' she said. 'I'm sorry that I shall have to wake you again presently.'

'I'm better already for what you've told me about Zoe and Giulio,' Luigi said definitely. 'That was very important for me, Sarah ... knowing that I wasn't to blame.'

By the following morning his improvement was even more noticeable – less chest pain, and fewer spasms of coughing. In the afternoon, when he asked to sit up in an armchair, she knew that the crisis was safely past. With Franco due to arrive the following day, she could telephone the palazzo and promise to be back on a late-afternoon train.

Franco reached Belmonte so early that he must have set out at dawn. 'I was anxious,' he admitted when Sarah remarked on this. 'I'd have come yesterday if I could. Was Zio Luigi very ill?'

'Yes, he was, for a little while, but he's

doing well now. The drugs can be tailed off, but he still needs building up. You'll have to bully him a little to make sure he eats.'

Franco stared at her pale, fine-drawn face. 'You look very tired – I should have been here in Giulio's place.'

What had happened, she wondered, to the arrogant youth she'd so disliked at the beginning of their acquaintance? 'Exams can't be ignored that easily! But Signor Luigi will be very glad to see you. I'm sure he's getting tired of female company!'

She got ready to leave for Venice, and then went to say goodbye to her patient. For the first time he sounded cross with her; it was a sure sign, she told him cheerfully, that he was feeling better.

'Of course I am,' he agreed, 'but I shall miss you.'

'Franco can stay with you until Giulio gets back. You'll be most carefully looked after.'

He nodded, then spoke in a different tone of voice. 'There aren't any words, though, to thank *you*. I'm ashamed of the stupid muddle I got into, Sarah.'

'You had a high fever – not the best time for thinking clearly!' she pointed out. 'Be prepared for Franco to bully you a little – I've told him he must.'

He smiled at her as she bent down to kiss his cheek, then caught her hand and carried it to his own lips. *'Grazie tanto, cara.'*

Downstairs, Domenica waited to say a tearful goodbye. *She* had to be hugged and kissed, and Sarah was finally driven away thinking that, as usual, Shakespeare's words had been exact: parting was 'sweet sorrow' all right.

But at least she felt confident that Franco would manage very well; he'd only needed to grow up a little. Giulio's handling of *him* had been so successful that his failure with Zoe seemed all the more extraordinary. She'd given up too soon, but so might any girl not offered the proper encouragement. It wasn't that he didn't love her – Sarah felt sadly sure of that. But either he'd simply not understood her or ingrained reticence had prevented him from showing his feelings clearly enough. The result was that *he* was alone in Greece, while Zoe was teaching herself to fall in love with Lucchino instead.

Twenty-Six

Pietro, instead of Michele, was waiting for her at Santa Lucia station. Unlike Claretta's husband, he was a shy, awkward man whose thick Venetian accent she still found hard to penetrate. But she at least understood him to say that there'd been nothing but rain since she left the city, and at this very moment there was yet another *inondazione* in the Piazza.

He was careful not to say – having been sworn to silence on the matter – that she would find the children waiting in the motor boat moored outside the station. They couldn't wait for Pietro to bring her home, Beatrice explained when she'd been hugged and kissed – she'd been gone so many days.

'Four, to be precise,' Sarah pointed out; 'not so many really. Now Zio Luigi is looking forward to a visit from *you*.'

'Is he better?' Emmanuele wanted to know. 'We prayed as hard as we could but Agnese said God doesn't always listen.'

'He's much, much better, *tesoro.*'

'Then I shall tell Agnese she's wrong.' That happily settled, Emmanuele tucked his hand in Sarah's and smiled at her. 'We missed you.'

'But we've been very busy,' Beatrice thought it time to make clear. 'Mamma took us with her one day to San Giorgio Maggiore. We listened while she gave a lesson to a German student. I mean to do better than the poor *fraülein*; Mamma lost patience with *her* in the end.'

'Then we went with Papa to ... to inspect' – Emmanuele remembered the word his father had used and brought it out with pride – 'a church that is being repaired; we saw some of his houses, too, that are being made nice for people to live in, then we had lunch with him at a *ristorante.*'

Sarah smilingly agreed that they had indeed been busy. But her thought was that perhaps she should leave the children more often; it seemed to be exactly what would make their parents responsible for them at last.

The count was at home when they got back, waiting to hear about his cousin. He seemed pleased to know that Franco was making himself so useful in Giulio's absence, and he thanked Sarah very kindly for what she had done. It was left to Laura, when she appeared later in the evening, to

361

point out that her children's governess looked exhausted as a result.

'No surprise, of course,' she added tartly. 'Even when he's well, Giulio's father is hard enough to deal with.'

'He was a good patient,' Sarah insisted. 'I just need to catch up on a little missed sleep.'

Laura nodded but now seemed to be concerned with something else. 'I've never known Giulio go away before in the middle of winter – it's most unlike him. He can't be as upset as all that about Zoe, surely?'

Having no view to offer on the matter, Sarah said nothing at all. The countess gave a little shrug, and then came to the point of her visit to Sarah's sitting room: Beatrice's approaching birthday.

'She won't want a children's party – at eleven going on twelve she reckons she's almost grown-up. Would she like a formal dinner with us downstairs? A chance to dress up, and perhaps some music afterwards? I could ask Stefan and Angelina, and Lucchino and Zoe are still in Venice as well. Franco must come too, of course, if Giulio is back at Belmonte in time.'

Sarah agreed at once. 'I think it's just what she'd love. Children of her own age group are "boring" – her favourite word – and she won't ever become the sort of sloppy teenager you see in England now; *far bella figura* at all times is her motto.'

'Of course – she's an Italian in the making,' Laura agreed. 'In any case, there's no excuse for slovenliness.'

'Shall I mention the dinner party to Franco? I ought to ring and check that everything is still well at Belmonte.'

'Then tell him to come whether Giulio is back or not. They've got enough servants there to look after one old man, and Beatrice *is* his sister after all.'

'I'll remind him of the fact,' Sarah said coolly.

Laura raised one dark eyebrow. 'The frosty tone of voice means, I suppose, that you dislike having Luigi called an old man. May I point out something you quite often forget? *I'm* the boss around here!'

But she said it without malice, and went away smiling at having scored a point. Sarah realized that what the *padrone* had said of her was true – she would have been irresistibly beautiful to an impressionable young man twenty years earlier. Had Giulio continued to see her as she'd been then? It *was* what happened; if an image had been implanted deeply enough at a vulnerable age it stayed unchanged. She forced herself to put the thought aside, and telephoned Franco instead. There were no fresh alarms at Belmonte, and he would do his best to return to Venice in time for the party.

With inspired timing or a large slice of luck, a parcel arrived from Highfold on the very morning of Beatrice's birthday. As well as cards from all three children, and photographs that Matthew had taken of them skating on the frozen lake, there was also a small wooden figure carved by James's own hand. Only the eye of love could discern in it the shape of Tabitha – Highfold's beautiful marmalade cat – but Beatrice had no difficulty at all in recognizing her. She was given pride of place on the table beside Beatrice's bed, and visited and wept over at intervals throughout the day.

Franco did arrive back in time, bringing with him an envelope for Sarah with her name written on it in a 'fine Italian hand' that she'd never seen before but knew instantly. She opened the envelope, the message inside was brief, courteous, and chilling. Giulio wrote to thank her, he said, for her exceptional kindness to his father, who was now almost restored to health. They both hoped that she was well herself and happy to be back among the friends who would have been missing her in Venice. He remained gratefully hers, Giulio Leopardi.

She read the note a second time, desperate to find in it some hint of warmth she might have missed; but only the merest courtesy was there. A simple 'Dear Sarah, thank you!

Giulio' would have been enough. That she *wouldn't* have torn into the small pieces that, even thrown away still felt like fragments of ice embedded in her heart, but she told herself that a too vivid imagination was at work. She *wasn't*, in reality, slowly bleeding to death, and instead of dying, her next task was undoubtedly to change for Beatrice's birthday dinner.

Dressed in the bridesmaid's outfit that wasn't, the heroine of the evening helped her parents to receive the guests. If, as Sarah feared, there might have been some embarrassment to begin with, no party that included Lucchino and Stefan Demetrios *could* remain ill at ease. By the time dinner was over and they were reassembled in the salon, Beatrice was flushed with happiness and Fabrizio's smile for Laura told her that she'd got his daughter's celebration exactly right.

Accompanied by Sarah, Emmanuele performed a small flute piece with great aplomb; Laura and Beatrice sang two charming duets; and Sarah played Debussy's 'Arabesques', then – to everyone's astonished enjoyment – Fabrizio himself concluded the concert and brought the house down with a Neapolitan tenor's agonized rendition of 'Come back to Sorrento'. Struggling to play the piano part, Sarah could no longer be sure whether the tears streaming down her face were for the count's bravura performance or for the sadness at her heart's core; but it scarcely mattered. Beatrice had had a birthday to match Emmanuele's at Belmonte, and Laura had surely seen her staid husband in an entirely new and happy light.

The evening was almost over when, Emmanuele having moved from her side, Lucchino took his place. Sarah spoke first.

'Matrimony suits Zoe – she looks beautiful; and you, my dear sir, look pretty good yourself!'

Lucchino acknowledged the compliment with a graceful bow. Then he spoke in a voice that only she could hear. 'We *shall* be happy together, Sarah – we both insist on that now. This may seem hard to believe, but the fact that Zoe will probably never quite forget Giulio, and I shall certainly never forget you, won't prevent us from making a successful marriage. Say that you understand that, please,' His usually smiling face was grave now, and his eyes seemed to be saying that she must also be aware of all that he hadn't said.

'Yes, I understand,' she answered quietly. 'Zoe was right and brave to change her mind about Giulio; you and she are right to make each other happy. I'm truly glad for you both, Lucchino.'

'What about you, Sarah? I expected to see

the professor here tonight; he must have been invited, surely?'

'The professor is back in England, writing his history of the Venetian Empire! In the autumn he'll move to America for two years. I think he'll be a great success at Yale.'

'But you ... you aren't going with him?'

She shook her head in answer to the insistent note in Lucchino's voice. 'I could have done, but I can't marry Steven. When Emmanuele goes away, I'll return to England – but not to be a governess again; I might not be so lucky next time! I think I'll find a village school to run instead.'

Lucchino was silent for a moment. Then he asked the question she least expected.

'Just now, when Fabrizio was singing, there were tears on your cheeks – from laughter or were they tears of sadness?'

'I don't know,' she answered simply, 'a bit of both, I expect, but you don't have to worry about me. At my advanced age I no longer expect life to deliver my heart's desire!'

She smiled as she said it, to convince him that she wasn't on the brink of some terminal decline. But his affection for her was true, and his understanding very acute. He thought he could identify clearly at last the cause of her sadness, and the extent to which he'd been mistaken about her in the past.

He might have said something more, but his wife chose that moment to come and stand beside him.

'You're both looking too serious,' she announced gaily. 'Now don't forget, Sarah, we shall expect you to come and stay with us in Rome before you go back to England. We'll be ready for guests by then.'

'It's a promise,' Sarah agreed. 'But now I'd better remove Emmanuele before he needs carrying up to bed.'

Lucchino watched her lead the sleepy small boy to his parents to say goodnight, and then out of the room. After a moment, with the past put aside, he could smile at his wife. 'Time *we* left as well, *amore*, I think.'

Twenty-Seven

Two days later, with struggling flautist and would-be ballet dancer delivered to their appointed teachers, Sarah sat in her favourite spot under the arcade on the Piazza. Sheltered from the cold wind, she could look out across the Bacino to the island where Laura at this moment was probably giving hell to some unfortunate *fraülein* whose *coloratura* wasn't quite right. She smiled at the thought and was taken completely unawares when a man's voice spoke beside her.

'May I join you, Sarah?'

She glanced at him, not needing to be sure who it was; the voice was enough. A moment for her heart to resume some sort of chaotic beating and then she could manage an answer.

'For the price of a cup of coffee, you can sit anywhere you like. It doesn't have to be at my table.'

'I'm afraid it does because I need to talk to you, not shout across the Piazza.'

Staring fixedly now at San Giorgio's famous campanile, she went on in a voice she didn't recognize as her own. 'There's no need at all. Your note thanked me – very adequately – for looking after your father.' She glanced at her watch, about to say that it was time she left, but he forestalled her. 'You haven't ordered your coffee yet, much less drunk it. Stay and listen to me, please.'

'I must collect the children soon.' She thought it was all she meant to say, but more words forced themselves out. 'I hope you didn't blame Domenica for getting in touch with me. She couldn't reach Franco and she was getting very worried about your father.'

'I know – she told me.'

'Franco came as soon as he could. You were right to persevere with him; I was quite wrong.'

'Handsomely said! Now, will you please stop staring at that damned bell tower, pure Palladian though it may be, and look at *me*?'

She did what he asked, struggling to hold on to anger and resentment despite the heart-tugging expression on his face – rueful humour on the surface, strain and sadness underneath.

'I came back early from Greece,' he explained quietly, 'because when I rang Franco to check that all was well, I was told that he'd left for Belmonte at the crack of dawn that morning; so I knew something was wrong. The doctor confirmed Domenica's view that without you there my father would have died. There are no words to thank you for that. But the ones I chose couldn't have been worse, because having made a mess of my own life, I was mortally afraid of having screwed up yours as well. I know that Steven Harding has gone back to England – you should have gone back with him instead of having to nurse my father.'

'My life is fine – not screwed up at all,' she said as firmly as she could. 'Steven has changed a great deal, but I still don't want to remarry him, now or in the future. He understands that.' She hesitated for a moment, then went on. 'Your father spoke to me about Laura. If that's the "mess" you meant, it wasn't of your making.'

'The way I went about sorting it out certainly *was*,' Giulio insisted. 'To convince Laura that our old relationship was over I had too confront her with the actuality of a flesh and blood woman. That was when Zoe was good enough to appear on the scene: charming, lovable, and obligingly eager to seem drawn to *me*. I suppose the ugly truth is that I made use of her, but I was convinced that she saw it as a game, enjoyable while it lasted. I'm nearly twice her age and irrevocably bound up with Belmonte – not remotely the sort of long-term prospect I imagined she'd be looking for.'

'But she took the game seriously after all, and then you were committed to *her*,' Sarah said slowly.

Giulio nodded, looking sombre and sad. 'I made sure that she realized what life at Belmonte is like, but even then I couldn't get her to admit that she wouldn't be happy there. So I did my best, and tried to be the lover she deserved, but in the end she understood the effort I was making, and rightly fled to New York.'

'You *weren't* hurt ... angry even ... when Lucchino went with her?'

'How could I be? She badly needed someone to help her, and I'd given too much

371

away to Lucchino, so that he knew the mess I was in. But, loving you, he still went to her rescue. It was an heroic act of friendship.'

'And you're whipping yourself now for having spoiled *his* life, I expect. Well, all I can say is that you've not seen the two of them together,' Sarah pointed out steadily. 'I promise you that they're very content with each other already, and they'll be still happier as time goes on.'

'Lucchino was in love with *you*; I know that, Sarah.'

'Another game of make-believe perhaps,' she managed to suggest, hoping that it might be true. 'I was different from the gorgeous women he'd always been accustomed to. He'll take perfect care of Zoe, and she'll persuade *him* to enjoy the life he was born into in Rome.'

A sweet, rueful smile lit Giulio's face for a moment wiping away regret. 'Put your mind to it and you could convince me that black is white! I feel responsible, all the same, for the mistakes of the past year.'

'What mistakes? Steven's disappointment – which is nothing to do with you – won't last.' That was less than true, of course, but she was on safer ground with what was coming next. 'Laura is happier than she's been for years and so, probably, is her husband; and Zoe and Lucchino *will* do well together. It isn't a bad outcome, surely?'

The question was serious but her eyes suddenly smiled. 'Dear me, I sound like an accountant drawing up a balance sheet – emotional profit and loss!'

'In fact everyone is dealt with except us,' Giulio suggested. 'May I ask where you and I figure in this picture of hard-won contentment?'

It was the home-thrust she hadn't anticipated. She struggled not to let her voice tremble, but she had to look away in case he detected her lie. '*I'm* where I've been for some time – very happy with the children. *You're* free of attachments at last; not lonely, as I was afraid you would be without Zoe, until I realized that you don't *need* anyone else.' Then, before he could answer, she sprang to her feet. 'I *must* go – the children will be waiting.'

Giulio got up too, apparently seeing no need to argue with what she'd said. 'I'll walk with you – I have to apologize to Beatrice for missing her birthday.'

He sounded calm again, concerned only to make his peace with a child he was fond of. The difficult part of the conversation was over and she need fear nothing more as they walked together out of the square.

'I haven't asked after the *padrone*,' she remembered, 'but Franco said that he was doing well.'

'Almost himself again. He loves you very

much, but I expect you know that.'

'We have a mutual admiration society of two!' she explained solemnly. 'It gives us both huge pleasure.'

'But I – how did it go: "needing no one else"? – am excluded. It doesn't seem quite fair when I need you so very badly.'

Nothing more to fear, she'd thought a moment ago, but now her danger was very great. Somehow she must keep her head, take deep breaths, and smile as if to acknowledge the joke he'd intended. But he halted her in mid-stride, suddenly gripping her shoulders.

'Admit *me* to your society, please, Sarah.'

Dear God, it wasn't a joke at all. How could it be when his face looked so grave? She understood now that she must have given herself away and he knew exactly what her trouble was. She grasped at anger again and answered with sudden fierceness.

'There you go again – imagining that you must feel responsible for any poor fool who needs a helping hand. Well, I won't have it. I'm not Laura or Zoe; I'm used to managing on my own.'

'I'm afraid that's probably true,' he agreed wryly. 'The trouble is that I don't manage very well without you.'

Tears of anger or grief – he couldn't be sure which – sparkled in her eyes, but she tried to speak more calmly now. 'This is a ridiculous conversation to have in the street, but what I suppose you mean is that you need help at Belmonte, help with caring for the *padrone*, perhaps ... Well, thank you but I already have a job.'

His grip on her tightened painfully. 'God dammit, Sarah, I'm not offering you one. I already have an excellent housekeeper, and my father isn't an invalid.' Aware of shouting at her, he tried to speak more quietly. 'What I'm trying to tell you is that I love you more than life itself, and if you can't love me at least a little in return I shall go lonely for the rest of my days.'

Her grey eyes – the most honest eyes he'd ever seen in a woman – searched his face. 'We've done nothing but snap at each other from the moment we met; how can I not think that you're just being quixotic again – insanely so this time, as it happens, because I *might* be tempted to grab the chance of always living at Belmonte!'

'I dearly hope you will – it's where you belong. I knew that the moment you first arrived, but there was nothing I could do about it. As things stood then, Zoe's game had to be as real for me as it seemed to be for her. But I was so intolerably frustrated whenever I looked at you that I *could* only snap at you; you quite rightly snapped back.'

Still she stared at him, afraid to be

persuaded. 'I realize that you no longer have to worry about Laura or Zoe, but I was right about your self-containment. You went off to Greece to find the solitude or peace you were looking for. There's no need to pretend that you need me as well.'

His mouth twisted in a wry smile. 'Zoe could tell you what my efforts at pretence add up to. I went to Greece believing that your future would be back in England. Since then Lucchino has been generous enough to tell me that you'd refused not only him but also Steven Harding. Perhaps those refusals had nothing to do with me, but you'll have to tell me so before I give up hope that you'll marry me instead.'

She'd set out, she vaguely remembered, on a morning that Emmanuele would have said was coloured a sodden, dismal grey. All wrong of course, because the day was suddenly as golden as the spring king-cups in the stream at Highfold, as gloriously bright as the sound of trumpets or the sweep of angel wings!

'The refusals had everything to do with you,' she confessed simply. 'I couldn't marry Lucchino or Steven – not when I loved you, and the *padrone*, and Belmonte so entirely.'

She was pulled against him, held close, and kissed, both of them oblivious of a gathering audience of passers-by until their enthusiastic applause finally awoke Giulio to the fact that they were in the middle of a busy square. A transfiguring smile lit his face as he looked down at Sarah.

'All your fault, my love. Venetians are renowned for being discreet and well-behaved in public; the disastrous influence must be entirely yours!'

'And it must now extend to having us run like hares to Beatrice's dancing school, otherwise we're going to be late.'

'All right, but before we do, there's one more thing to say. I know what the children mean to you, and if I *must* wait for the next year to run its course, I'll try to be as patient as I can. But we've lost precious time already, and Laura should find another governess or look after the children herself.'

'She'd do better to find them a good school in Venice,' Sarah said slowly. 'They need the company of other children. Beatrice is too old for her age, and Emmanuele knows nothing about the way small boys behave. He *must* learn before he goes away to school. I was going to have to tell Laura soon in any case; but now I have an even more compelling reason to do so!'

Giulio rewarded such excellent common sense with a brief, sweet kiss, but allowed himself afterwards to be hurried away. Nevertheless, they *were* late, and Beatrice was looking cross until she caught sight of Giulio. 'You didn't come to my party,' she pointed out.

'I'll do better next year; in the meanwhile you can attend my wedding after all. Is that a good enough peace offering?'

She stared doubtfully at him, not sure what to make of the shimmer of amusement in his face. He looked different as well, carefree, and lit up inside in some way, but before she could enquire why, Sarah tugged at her hand, and set off again at such a gallop that even Beatrice was too breathless to continue the conversation.

Emmanuele was waiting at the door with Signora Artom, but at the sight of them he shook her hand politely and then hurled himself at his cousin.

'Giulio says he's getting married after all,' Beatrice couldn't wait to announce. 'Do you think he means it this time?' Then the obvious snag occurred to her. 'How can he when Zoe's already married to Lucchino?'

Giulio smiled at the two upturned faces. 'I know, but Sarah is going to take pity on me instead.'

This time it was Emmanuele who got in first. 'She can't, *she* lives with us. You live in Belmonte with Zio Luigi.'

'That *is* a problem,' Giulio admitted. 'You or I must do without her, but the trouble is that I don't think I can.'

Emmanuele's troubled eyes were fixed on Sarah now. 'Don't you *want* to stay with us?'

She saw the hurt in his face, and wondered why joy and pain had to go together quite so inevitably as they always seemed to do. It was a lesson that had to be learned, but Emmanuele was too young to understand anything but the brutal fact that she was going to choose to leave them. He'd trusted her, and now she was betraying him. She wanted to offer the comfort of a hug, but it wouldn't be accepted – his closed little face said as much. All she could fall back on was the truth – no easy fib, no pretence, would do.

'*Tesoro*, listen please. Governesses like me aren't meant to be a fixture. One day I'd have gone back to England in any case when you and Beatrice no longer needed me. At Belmonte, with Giulio and Zio Luigi, I *shall* always be needed – that's why I'm going there instead. I'd love you both to come too, but that would leave Mamma and Papa very lonely.'

His lower lip trembled, but he tried to nod – yes, at least his parents' need of them was something he understood.

Then Giulio squatted down, the more easily to talk to him, man to man. 'This way, *caro*, instead of letting Sarah return to England when you go away to school, we can keep her here with us in Italy. Isn't that a good idea?'

'Yes, but it isn't the reason,' said Beatrice,

watching closely. 'I think you're in love with her.'

'There is that, too,' Giulio had to admit.

'I s'pose it's all right then,' Emmanuele was forced to agree. 'But we shall often come to Belmonte, won't we, Bea?'

She nodded, but was already more inclined than her brother to concentrate on events nearer at hand. 'James has already seen my bridesmaid's dress, of course, but this time I shall look complete – with a lovely posy, and flowers in my hair.'

'James?' enquired Giulio, bemused by this turn in the conversation.

'My eldest nephew and Beatrice's special friend,' Sarah hastily explained. 'Matthew is bringing the family for a visit at the beginning of May – much too soon, of course, for us to think of marrying by then.'

But Giulio was now gratefully kissing Beatrice's hand, and she, aware that the key role she knew fitted her best was now hers, smiled kindly at Sarah.

'There's no need to worry, *tesoro. We'll* see that it's all arranged in time, won't we, Emmanuele?'

Her brother's dark head gave its decisive little nod – of course, they'd do it if it was what Sarah wanted.

He walked home beside her, stiffly to begin with, but habit reasserted itself and he tucked his hand inside Sarah's. She smiled at him and he was comforted, because the smile said that she wouldn't ever stop loving them. He knew that life would be different now but perhaps it didn't matter after all. The gift she'd given him remained. He was Emmanuele di Brazzano, his father's son, and whatever happened he'd always be able to manage from now on.